Knocking On

'. . . sharing a joke or two with the locals . . .' (see p. 89)

Knocking On

CHRISTOPHER MATTHEW

JOHN MURRAY

Albemarle Street, London

Typeset in Monotype Garamond by
Servis Filmsetting Ltd, Manchester

Printed and bound in Great Britain by
St Edmundsbury Press Ltd, Bury St Edmunds, Suffolk

For Bob and Amanda and Benjamin

Knocking On

March

Thursday, March 23rd

An extraordinary thing happened. Was on the top deck of a bus in Mitcham Lane when who should come pounding up the stairs and sit down slap in front of me but Sir Alec Guinness! No one seemed to have noticed except me. But then, of course, anonymity is his middle name, hence his ability to transform himself into any character he takes on.

In normal circumstances would not have dreamed of addressing him. I am a firm believer in man's inalienable right to his privacy and once sat in a dentist's waiting room for half an hour with Norman St John Stevas without as much as catching his eye. On the other hand, it is not every day one gets the chance to tell a man how much one admires him and what pleasure he has given one over the years.

Choosing my moment carefully, I leaned forward and whistled a few notes of 'Colonel Bogey'.

It was unfortunate that my lips should have chosen that moment of all moments to dry up, with the result that it must have looked as if I was trying to blow into his right ear. By the time the sound actually came out I was already two and a half bars into the main theme. It wouldn't have mattered so much if I hadn't suddenly gone musically haywire and for no obvious reason found myself giving full vent to *'Deutschland über alles'*.

However, a man like Sir Alec does not take on some of the great comic roles in modern cinema without himself having a good sense of humour, and he gave me one of his famous enigmatic smiles.

'Tunes of Glory, eh?' I murmured.

'Ah,' he said.

The *on dit* in the profession is that he is a man of few words at the best of times, so was not altogether surprised that he made no attempt to force the conversation. However, felt it my duty to leave him in no doubt as to my intentions.

'May I say how very much I enjoyed your diaries?' I said.

'Ah,' he replied, modest as ever.

I said that, unfortunately, I had not yet had the opportunity to read his latest volume, but would certainly be adding my name to the waiting list at my local library at the earliest opportunity.

'Ah,' he said again.

I said, 'I gather there is an amusing anecdote about the Duke of Wellington.'

'Oh?' he said, as if this were news to him.

I smiled knowingly and said that, interestingly enough, I was something of a diarist myself.

'Really?' he said.

I added that, to my shame, I had let it lie fallow for far too long.

'Ah,' he said

I said, 'It goes without saying that although my previous volume was published, I cannot pretend my jottings and musings are in the same category as your own.'

He said, 'I believe this is my stop, but I hope you are going on.'

I can think of a lot of people who would have failed to spot the obvious subtext in an otherwise apparently casual remark, but there is a natural empathy between writers, however great their fame, and even in the brief time we spent together an intimacy had sprung up between us that would not have been the same had my travelling companion been the chairman of the Stock Exchange, say, or Sir Trevor Baylis, the inventor of the clockwork radio.

The hint was clear enough. My pen has lain dormant for far too long and it is high time I took it up again as I head into the foothills of the twenty-first century. I must go on, and I will. Sir Alec may never realize the debt I owe him for his kindness but, who knows, one day he may chance to pick up my latest volume and suddenly remember a moment on a sunny morning in March when the minds of two writers made contact on the top of a bus in SW16.

Stupidly mentioned to Priscilla that my encounter with the great man might make a good topic for my 'Up Your Way' column. Needless to say, she could not resist throwing cold water over the episode. Like mother, like daughter. She said perhaps it wasn't Sir Alec at all, merely someone who looked like him. After all, he has based his entire career on looking like lots of other people.

'Piggy,' I said, 'I have not reached the age I have by not being able to recognize Sir Alec Guinness.'

She said, 'I am not doubting your powers of recognition. I merely question what on earth a man like Sir Alec Guinness could possibly be doing on a bus in Mitcham Lane.'

I said, 'Travelling from A to B, presumably, like anyone else.'

She said, 'He must be a multimillionaire on the proceeds of *Star Wars* alone. He could afford a taxi, if not a luxury hire car.'

I said that perhaps he was visiting relatives in the area and didn't wish to embarrass them in front of the neighbours. It wouldn't surprise me, knowing Sir Alec.

She said, 'As, of course, you do now. Intimately.'

Could see no point in pursuing this line of conversation and did not do so. I may write about the incident or I may not. I still have until next Tuesday to decide.

Friday, March 24th

Am beginning to wonder if lodging with my sister in Mitcham is working out quite as well as I had hoped. It seemed such a good idea when first mooted, but, like the European Community, New Labour and the Dome, it has failed to live up to expectation.

Had the Colliers Wood house achieved anything like the price Loomis Chaffee led me to expect, I would have had enough left over from the divorce settlement to put down a deposit on a small flat somewhere. As it is, the personal trainer with whom Belinda now cohabits in Marble Hill has revealed hitherto hidden talents as a personal financial adviser, with the result that I find myself in middle age *sans* wife, *sans* roof over head, *sans* nest egg. Thank goodness I took Tim Pedalow's advice and stuck out for the limp golden handshake when I decided to take early retirement from TCP Public Relations. I am only sorry it didn't amount to anything like as much as I had anticipated.

It still sticks in my craw that the company would persist in substituting the word 'forcible' for 'early', but can console myself with the thought that, of all my friends, only Tim is privy to this semantic nuance, and that everyone else accepts my version of events without question.

Indeed, the fact that the whole wretched business happened only a few weeks after Belinda left me to live with her personal trainer, Guy (or Guy the Gorilla as I have dubbed him), has earned me a degree of sympathy that I would otherwise be denied.

Unfortunately, my credit in that department seems to be hovering on the overdraft boundaries as far as P is concerned. Personally I would have thought she would have welcomed any addition to her income, however modest, what with James's 'year-off' with the Australian Aborigines to fund, not to mention Katie's book budget at Mitcham High, the dog's ever more frequent visits to the vet, Nigel's persistent failure to come up with his monthly maintenance payments, and Chad's failure to pull his weight on their 'Serendipity' stall in the market. If he pulled his weight half as effectively as he pulls young women at the Bridge and Two Crowns in Clinton Road, he might deserve to call himself her partner, in and out of the bedroom.

Wrote my Alec Guinness piece after tea, quoting the great man verbatim and giving it the title 'The Face Escapes Me'. Hope the literary *jeu de mots* does not escape *him*.

Saturday, March 25th

Contributing a weekly column to the *Mitcham & Tooting Times* – or the *Mitch & Toot* as it is fondly known to all and sundry in this corner of south London – may not be everyone's idea of the cutting edge of opinion-forming journalism, especially when the editor, for no particular reason that I can see, fails to run it, as happened again this week. The £100 fee is hardly princely, but becomes even less attractive when paid only on publication – i.e. not very often. On the other hand, when one is a fifty-something ex-PR man who has taken early retirement and decided, like an increasing number of erstwhile high-fliers do in their middle years these days, to start a new career, one has to begin somewhere.

Doubtless there are some people who would pooh-pooh

the idea of a man of my age setting out to become a major media figure. Mother expressed her opinion in no uncertain terms the other day when she said, 'What are you up to these days, you silly old thing? Something daft, as usual, I daresay.'

Poor Mother. She's getting so absent-minded these days that there are times when I wonder if she knows who she is speaking to. Personally, I blame it on a lifetime's devotion to aluminium saucepans. That and metal tooth fillings. Which reminds me: I haven't had my usual reminder from the dentist re my six-monthly check-up. A sharp telephone call is in order.

In fact have been considering the possibility of some serious orthodontic work. Kirsty Young did not get where she is today by having crooked incisors, and Trevor McDonald's teeth are a shining tribute to British dentistry.

Apart from anything else, I can always put the cost down to expenses. Not in this financial year, perhaps, but if my face has not appeared on national television before April 5th 2001 I shall eat my old school straw boater. I shall certainly have the teeth for it!

Sunday March 26th

I give up. My British Art Lovers Diary for 2000 has let me down again. If they are going to jog the nation's memory re important events like the start of British Summer Time, why on earth don't they do so in letters that are big enough for people to read? As it was, I failed to notice that it began in the middle of last night – at two o'clock, if you please – and, as a result, turned up at the paper shop to find that I was an hour late and they had sold every last copy of the *Sunday Telegraph*.

When I pointed out to Mr Patel that the least I expected in return for months of loyal custom was that he should put a newspaper on one side for me, he said, 'I am running a business, Mr Crimp, not a friendly society.'

Ignoring the obvious discourtesy re my name, I said that in my humble opinion it is the duty of every citizen of this country, whatever his creed or colour, to be friendly, and reminded him of Jesus's classic saw on the subject of loving one's neighbour as oneself.

Mr Patel said, 'I am a Muslim and you are cluttering up my shop.'

Left without a newspaper, but with my dignity very much

intact. In future I shall take my custom elsewhere. It is unfortunate that the nearest alternative paper shop is a brisk ten-minute walk away, but then Christianity has always demanded a certain degree of self-sacrifice.

Monday, March 27th

An over-excited call from Vanessa Pedalow, as was, to say she has been on the London Eye and can thoroughly recommend it and why doesn't she get up a party and we'll all go together?

Have been having a bit of trouble with my hearing lately – especially in my right, or telephonic, ear – and, as has happened once or twice recently, slightly got hold of the wrong end of the stick. Could have sworn she said something about having been to the London Eye Clinic and, as a result, made an unnecessary fool of myself.

I said, 'It's my ear I'm having trouble with, not my eye.'

She said, 'Sounds as if your brain could do with looking at, too.'

Felt like saying that a few diction lessons would not come amiss, but did not press the point. However, I did take the opportunity to remind her – as I did a dozen times over the New Year to people who invited me to so-called Millennium parties – that it is not normal practice to celebrate birthdays at the beginning of the year. Our Lord, being flesh and blood like the rest of us (though obviously with one or two notable differences), celebrated his first birthday on December 25th 1 AD and you do not have to be Albert Einstein to work out that His two-thousandth falls on December 25th 2001, which is when I had been planning to bake symbolic cake, don paper hat, blow symbolic squeaker and sing 'Happy birthday, dear Jesus'.

Clearly, however, I am alone in my quaint grasp of elementary maths, if not in my understanding of the purpose of the Millennium.

Of course, if all the razzmatazz of New Year's Eve was merely to mark the passing of the twentieth century and the arrival of the twenty-first, that is something entirely different. Far be it from me to be a party-pooper, and just because I chose to spend the evening at home watching a video of *Reach for the Sky* it did not mean that everyone else had to do the same.

Frankly, am surprised that I have not been invited on one of the many special preview trips on the Eye that have been laid on by British Airways for journalists and VIPs over the last few weeks, and can only assume that, knowing modern press offices, someone has forgotten to add the *Mitch & Toot* to the list of invitees.

Unfortunately, am one of those people who, if they do not attend a new event straight away, be it a play, film or exhibition, would rather not attend it at all. Though not a professional critic per se (though I did once hold the fort as radio reviewer on Mother's local newspaper in Kent when the regular man went stone deaf for a week following an exceptionally large build-up of ear wax), I like to make up my own mind about each new artistic experience that presents itself. I do not wish to approach it having been bombarded with every imaginable comment, informed or otherwise.

Still haven't forgotten the day I stupidly mentioned to Mollie Marsh-Gibbon that I had booked to see Nicole Kidman in *The Blue Room* at the Donmar Warehouse. 'A nine-day wonder if ever I saw one,' she said. Not that she *had* seen it, as I later discovered, but by then it was too late as I stupidly gave the tickets away to Theresa and Philippe de Grand-Hauteville, who promptly sold them for three times their face value.

Were John Julius still a small boy, I might seriously have considered pulling rank and getting a couple of press tickets for the Dome, but at eighteen he is far too old for 'interactive games' and I doubt if the Body Zone can tell him much about the intimate workings of the female body that he does not know already.

Would have taken Mother – she has been pestering me for weeks – but fear that, unlike my son, she might learn things about human physiology that could tip her over the edge once and for all.

As for the Eye, I cannot see that there is anything to be gained from spotting familiar landmarks from 450 feet above the Thames that I can see any day of the week standing only a few yards away – and often do.

Said as much to Vanessa. There was a long pause, then she said, 'So that's a no, is it?' Said I'd think about it, but could have saved my breath as she had already put the phone down.

Tuesday, March 28th

An extraordinary coincidence. Hugh Bryant-Fenn rang out of the blue this morning to say that he was planning to celebrate his birthday on April 27th on the Eye with a few close friends and would I care to to join them? There will be one or two fellow journalists in the party who I might enjoy meeting, including Simon Hoggart, A. N. Wilson, Boris Johnson and Melvyn.

Not wishing him to think that his was my first Eye invitation, my immediate reaction was to refuse. On the other hand, the opportunity to meet fellow Grub Street regulars of this quality is not something that comes along every day. As it happens, have always thought of myself as a *Spectator* type and have long wanted to meet its famous editor. I think Boris and I have a lot to offer one other.

Networking is the sine qua non of a successful media career, and it is often the most casual encounters in the unlikeliest surroundings that result in the most enduring and rewarding professional partnerships.

Cannot put my hand on my heart and say that in the world of PR men Hugh could be mentioned in the same breath as Freud *fils* or Max Clifford, but he still handles one or two accounts that could be of use to me in the future, and it would be a foolish man indeed who cut off his nose to spite his face at this stage in a journalistic career.

Have therefore written to accept – with the proviso that if a story breaks at the *Mitch & Toot*, I may have to pull out at the last moment.

Wednesday, March 29th

Have never really got close to another dog since Vita died, but am gradually growing fond of Woodhouse – named after Barbara Woodhouse, who was P's favourite television personality. In fact I think P misses B even more than I miss V. Funnily enough, Barbara and Vita had a lot in common, though I do not imagine Barbara was in the habit, like Vita, of mounting any dog that presented itself, regardless of gender. Not on television, anyway.

On the other hand, cannot help feeling that Woodhouse underwent a definite character change after one of his rela-

tives won Best in Breed in Cruft's in February. It is the first time a West Dartmouth Sharp-Toothed Terrier has ever won at Cruft's and success has clearly gone to his head – or, to be more precise, his teeth, since he now lunges at everything that comes through the letterbox and tears it to shreds. Not least my free copies of the *Mitch & Toot*. Managed to rescue this morning's remnants only to find, to my astonishment, there was no sign of my Alec Guinness piece.

Not only is this a major editorial oversight, but it represents a real snub to Sir Alec. Needless to say, it is no reflection whatever on him or his glittering career.

Talking of which, have been reflecting on the recent Oscar ceremony in Hollywood and wondering if I am the only person in the world who thought *American Beauty* was wildly overrated.

Have decided to award a few Oscars of my own. Best Actress award goes to Alyson Pedalow for her performance as my apparently sympathetic, but in reality rather treacherous, mother-in-law. Hugh Bryant-Fenn gets the Best Actor award for managing to conceal his venality for so long under the guise of friendship.

Best Supporting award would undoubtedly have gone, *nem. con.*, to Mollie Marsh-Gibbon, who has been a tower of strength over the years, had she not blotted her copybook when I told her Belinda had left me by cackling with laughter and saying, 'I told you you were mad to marry her in the first place.' The award therefore goes instead to dear old Piggy, who, for all her failings, has at least taken my side throughout this difficult period of my life.

The award for Best Costume Design goes to Vanessa Pedalow for being the only example I know of mutton that can dress as lamb and get away with it. Best Foreign Language award goes to Philippe de Grande-Hauteville for the outrageous way he plays on his French accent in order to attract silly and susceptible Englishwomen.

A Special Award for Mother for her services to the local branch of the WI, local widowers over the age of seventy-five, and me.

April

Saturday, April 1st

Was on my way to buy the paper this morning when a road sweeper with Walkman earpieces protruding from his ears rounded the corner in front of me, pushing a mobile bin. He stopped, left the bin where it was, walked off up the street and began brushing the pavement in a typically desultory way. Could not help noticing when he turned the corner that he had missed a squashed cigarette packet, so decided to do my bit for the environment by picking it up for him.

For some reason I cannot explain, I was carrying my newspaper money in the same hand, and when I tossed the packet into the bin the coins flew in as well.

Am not the kind of man who loses sleep over a piffling amount like 45p. On the other hand, the newsagent I am now using, Mr Rathna, is quite a step away from the house, I do not know him well enough to ask for goods on credit, and I did not fancy walking all the way back home. And, as it happened, it was my last 45p anyway.

Had no alternative but to rummage around in the rubbish. Luckily, there are not too many dead leaves around at this time of year, but, even so, the coins seemed to have buried themselves carefully in the muck, dried dog mess, used lottery tickets etc. that occupy every sweeper's attention whatever the time of year.

Found the first 20p piece quite quickly, and the second lurking under a piece of used tissue paper. No sign, though, of the coppers. Finally ran the two 2p pieces to earth and was rooting around in search of the final 1p when I felt a sharp pain in my right forefinger. Must have cut it on a piece of glass.

Though not deep, there was quite a lot of blood.

Obviously could not suck it in order to staunch flow, and was unable to reach across with left hand into right-hand pocket to get handkerchief, but remembered the old Boy Scout adage about blood not travelling uphill and continued the search for the remaining coin with one hand raised above my head like a schoolboy asking permission to be excused.

Was almost at the bottom of the bin when I spotted it. Was on the point of picking it out when I heard a man's voice shouting. Straightened up to see sweeper marching down road towards me, brandishing his broom and calling out in what I think was an Estonian accent, but could have been Polish, 'You piss away, you piss away.'

Was about to explain situation when who should round the corner but our neighbour Mr Wisby with his snappy King Charles spaniel in tow. By an unfortunate coincidence, he and I have had words recently concerning dustbin rights, in the course of which he accused me of allowing our rubbish to spill over on to his front path – though how he could tell, given the muck that permanently litters the whole of what he laughingly refers to as his 'front garden', is a mystery that beggars belief.

'Looking for more rubbish to throw in people's gardens?' he called out.

Decided to leave last coin rather than add fuel to his fire and walked on up the street. The sweeper was still gibbering something at me in pidgin English, so I pretended to be deaf, gave him a blank stare and left him speechless.

Would have tried to explain situation to Rathna, but worried that dirt might have got into my cut and suddenly remembered it is several years since I last had a tetanus jab.

Did not wish to bump into Wisby again, or the sweeper, so obliged to take a tortuous route home, by which time finger was beginning to throb.

Rushed into kitchen and ran it under the cold tap for several minutes. Dabbed it with disinfectant, slapped on a large plaster and rang the doctor's surgery, only to be informed that I was not registered with the practice and advised that if I was worried, I should go to Casualty Department of Mitcham General.

Finally caught a bus to the hospital, minus tetanus certificate but with curiously tight feeling in jaw, only to find myself having to sit for two hours in Casualty waiting to be seen.

At one point could not resist suggesting to nurse in charge that the department might better be called Casually. Was it my imagination or did the builder's labourer, who got seen at least half an hour before me, arrive a good hour after I did? Cannot believe that getting one's fingers stuck together with superglue is more of an emergency than a possible case of lockjaw. Nor am I convinced that the tightening of my jaw muscles was entirely due to stress on my part, as per the nurse's snap diagnosis.

Sat there for an hour and a half reading the same *Hello!* article about Richard Branson's lovely Oxfordshire home until I was heartily sick of him, his home, and Oxfordshire. Finally went to desk and told nurse that if I developed lockjaw, someone would be feeling the rough side of my tongue.

She said, 'If you get lockjaw, you won't be feeling anything' and told me to go and sit down and wait my turn like everyone else.

Eventually another, much younger, nurse directed me to a curtained-off booth and told me to sit on the bed, someone would be with me shortly.

Was surprised when the young Indian doctor who finally examined me said airily, 'It looks like a straightforward cut to me. I'll get someone to dress it for you.' He was about to walk out when I said, 'Hang on a minute. Is that it? Aren't you going to run some tests, get a C-spine, head and chest CT, order a CBC and a haemo consult?'

He said, 'Perhaps you'd like a quick go with the paddles while you're about it? This is the Casualty Department of Mitcham General Hospital, not a Hollywood TV studio.'

'Ah well,' I said to the nurse as she was giving me my tetanus booster, 'if nothing else, it will make a good subject for my next column.'

'You a builder, then?' she said.

'I beg your pardon?' I said.

'Sorry,' she said. 'I thought you said something about a column, so I assumed you must be building one.'

I laughed and said, 'Do I look like a builder?'

She stepped back and looked at me. 'No,' she said. 'You look more like an accountant, actually. They do columns, don't they? Columns of figures. Are you an accountant?'

'No,' I said. 'I am a writer.'

'Get away!' she said. 'Should I know you?'

I said that depended whether or not she ever read me.

'Do you write under your own name?' she said.

'No,' I said. 'Graham Greene.'

'I've heard of him,' she said. 'Are you famous, then?'

'Some people might think so,' I said.

'What sort of things do you write?' she said.

'Oh, this and that,' I said. 'I'm probably best known as a journalist.'

When I told her I contributed a weekly piece to the *Mitch & Toot*, she said, 'Up Your Way?'

I said, 'So you do read me, then?'

'No,' she said. 'I just happened to spot it when I was changing the paper in the budgie's cage.'

Arrived back in the house hours later than I had anticipated – minus newspaper but plus throbbing pain in finger, aching jaw and strict instructions not to drink any alcohol for twelve hours – to hear P calling out from upstairs. She sounded so panic-stricken that I dropped the carton of semi-skimmed which I had remembered amid all the drama to pick up from the little shop next to the hospital. This promptly burst, covering the walls and floor of the hall with what looked like thin distemper. Rushed upstairs, fearing the worst, only to find her standing in the bathroom holding a medicine cupboard up against the wall.

'Hang on to this a minute, will you?' she said. 'Don't let it drop. I've just got to go downstairs and get something.'

I stood there holding the thing for fully ten minutes, by which time my arms were aching. Eventually she wandered in, followed by Katie, and casually said, 'Oh, you can let go of it now.'

I did and found it had been attached to the wall all the time. When I asked her what she had been playing at, she and Katie sniggered and then shouted in unison, 'April Fool!' and danced around like a couple of silly children.

I'm afraid I was unable to join in. P said, 'Oh, do lighten up, Simon, for goodness' sake. It's only a joke.'

Reminded her that since it was after midday the joke didn't count. She said that although I was right in saying that it was now twenty past, the joke had in fact been set in motion twenty-five minutes previously and therefore counted as much as a joke that was started and completed before noon.

Frankly, I have better things to do than bandy facts and figures with childish pranksters – even if they do happen to be my sister and niece. Said as much in language that left them in no doubt of my feelings.

P said, 'What sort of things? You mean like standing around in the bathroom holding up a medicine chest that's already attached to the wall, looking a complete prat?'

I maintained a dignified silence and left the room.

Sunday, April 2nd

Bryant-Fenn rang first thing to say that the London Eye was completely booked for the 27th, and that the earliest he could find a slot was May 18th. He hoped I hadn't got other plans.

Said that my diary was getting pretty chock-a-block around that time, but felt sure I could rearrange, if necessary. Unless he heard otherwise, I would be there. What time was our booking?

He said, 'We're on the midday flight.'

Said I hoped he hadn't chosen the moment when the pods finally shoot off into outer space.

He said, 'And I hope you're not going to make stupid jokes like that. If you are, I'll ask someone else.'

Would have pulled out there and then, had he not added, 'You'll be glad to know that Melvyn *is* coming. Wilson sounded decidedly iffy when I last spoke to him, but Hoggart and Johnson are looking good.'

This is excellent news. I have always been one of Melvyn's biggest fans. Funnily enough, he was at Oxford at the same time as my cousin Tony, though not, I think, in the same college. Have often wondered if they ever bumped into each other. I shouldn't be at all surprised, knowing Tony. Not that I do very well. In fact I haven't seen him since Mother's sixtieth birthday party when he walked off with Sally, who was my girlfriend at the time – or, rather, would have been if he hadn't walked off with her.

Tuesday, April 4th

Happened to be passing the *Mitch & Toot* this morning on way to chiropodist, so dropped piece off en route. It's all too easy for us freelances to get out of touch with our newspapers these days, and for those who work at the coal-face to become mere names.

One of the things I learned during a long career in public relations is the importance of personal contact. I do not hold with many of Hugh Bryant-Fenn's *soi-disant* words of wisdom, but I am sure there is some truth in his theory that editors give work to those they know personally and whose faces immediately spring to mind when a job needs doing.

Being able to visualize the expressions of disappointment on the faces of those with whom they have regular contact might also make them think twice about 'spiking' one's copy in quite such a cavalier fashion.

Have come to feel very much part of the *Mitch & Toot* family, and if a regular contributor cannot walk in off the street, unannounced, say 'Hi' to the gang, have a cup of coffee, chew the fat and pass cheerfully on his way, who can?

Am sorry sour-faced girl at Reception does not appear to share similar views. It was perhaps unfortunate that this is only her second week and that my last two columns were dropped in favour of advertising features on this new garden super-centre which has been the talk of SW16 in recent months. Even so, felt it was extremely high-handed of her to take it upon herself to decide who should see the editor and who should be left out in the cold among the mock leather furniture, the coffee machine and the back numbers.

Finally convinced her that, with the best will in the world, there's many a slip 'twixt Reception desk and editor's in-tray and she grudgingly agreed to ring through to the editor's secretary and tell her I was there.

She rang a number and said, 'I've got a Mr . . . what was your name again?' When I told her, she said, 'A Mr Simon. He's got something he wants to give you . . . One moment . . .' She turned to me and said, 'What is it exactly you want to give her?'

Felt strongly tempted to say a clip round the ear, but bit my lip and said quietly, 'It's the copy for this week's Up Your Way column, and actually it's Mr Crisp. Simon is my Christian name.'

Whether Miss Hollingsworth-Palfrey misheard the message I don't know, but when she finally appeared, with what Mother calls a sudden rush of teeth to the front, practically the first thing she said was, 'Do I gather you're a Christian?'

Was completely taken aback and said that, in the sense that

I was baptized into the Church of England, I supposed I was.

She said, 'I had a feeling you were.'

When I asked her why, she said, 'It takes one to know one,' seized my copy and rushed off towards the lift.

Am not sure whether to be pleased or not.

Wednesday, April 5th

My latent religiosity has paid dividends in no uncertain terms. However, my pleasure at seeing my byline in the *Mitch & Toot* for the first time in three weeks somewhat diminished on discovering that the spotty Herbert of a sub-editor had managed to get his fingers on my copy, yet again.

To cut my witty aperçu on the similarity of dogs to their owners and vice versa, thereby making complete nonsense of the paragraph beginning 'My aunt Ingrid who was half Alsatian . . . ', is annoying enough, but to play fast and loose with my carefully researched statistics is more than flesh and blood can stand. When I wrote that 'on average sixty-five tons of dogs' doings are deposited in the capital every day', I meant exactly that – i.e. 145,600 lb avoirdupois. If I had meant to say sixty-five *tonnes* – i.e. 65,000 kilograms – I would have said so.

'. . . *something to do with Venice*'

P tried to argue that it comes to much the same thing, and when I stood my corner she said she couldn't imagine how anybody could possibly arrive at such a calculation in the first place.

Like most women, she has an unerring eye for the irrelevant.

On reading piece through again, noticed they had managed to spell the word 'dog' with an 'e' on the end. Now people will think the piece is something to do with Venice.

Thursday, April 6th

A rare visit from John Julius and, unfortunately, an unannounced one. Was in my room at the time, drafting a sharp note to the editor re the inexplicable substitution in this week's column of the name Stephen for Simon, when I heard the unmistakable sound of someone moving around downstairs in the kitchen.

Though a lifelong advocate of a man's freedom to protect his home – or in this case his sister's home – against unwarranted intrusion by strangers, I am only too aware of how easily personal confrontations can get out of hand, and have no intention of sharing a prison cell with a gun-toting farmer from Norfolk. Tiptoed into P's bedroom and rang the police.

It is unfortunate that John Julius has not inherited my dress sense and will insist on draping himself in baggy imitation combat trousers and T-shirt. Ditto that he has shaved his head so that he looks like Joan of Arc on her way to the stake – though even she drew a line at eyebrow rings. Had he been looking halfway respectable, the police might have been more prepared to accept that he was my son and not an opportunistic sneak thief on the lookout for a free meal.

It was also unfortunate that they arrived on the scene as quickly as they did, otherwise I might have had a chance to spruce myself up and cut a more authoritative figure. As it was, I was still wearing my towelling dressing gown when they came charging through the front door, and when I explained that it was all a silly mistake and I knew J J, they got it into their heads that I was implying some degree of intimacy and that he was a disgruntled erstwhile partner who had returned to rob me and teach me a lesson.

At all events, we both finished up at the local police station giving statements in separate rooms. On reflection, it was perhaps unwise of me to have given a false name, which I took to be normal procedure when celebrities are arrested – though the police chose not to view my explanation in quite the same light. Nor were they convinced when I told them that Hugh Bryant-Fenn was one of my *noms de plume*.

The upshot of this absurd misunderstanding is that I have now been charged with assuming a false identity, which I am told carries a maximum penalty of a year in prison. In the same cell as that Norfolk farmer, knowing my luck.

P arrived eventually to bail me out. Could not have been more humiliated.

To add insult to injury, bail was set at a mere £100.

Friday, April 7th

Have asked P if JJ can come and stay with us for a few days, until he gets over the shock of yesterday's events. While I have no objection per se to him living with his mother and her paramour, it means I see precious little of him, and although we do not always have a lot to say to one another, it is important to keep the lines of communication open at all costs.

Also, now that he's at music college in the middle of London, he doesn't need to add the daily agonies of commuting to the strains that are already placed upon his vocal chords. Indeed, the thought has crossed my mind that his decision to be a counter-tenor (what used to be known as an alto when I was in the Fenton School Choir) might well result from some latent psychological trauma rather than a God-given talent, as Mollie Marsh-Gibbon insists.

Am glad to say that everyone concerned has given my suggestion the nod and he is moving in sometime over the weekend.

Saturday, April 8th

The new au pair's grasp of English even more rudimentary than I had at first supposed. Not only is every remark greeted by a look of blank incomprehension, followed by a sudden pulling down of the corners of the mouth, puffing out of the cheeks and lifting of the shoulders, but even when no one is speaking to her she looks bad-tempered. The only time she displays any signs of animation is when she rings her family in Rouen, which she seems to do most evenings and at considerable length. Even then she sounds as if she's having an almighty row with them.

The other day I asked her if everything was all right. She looked at me as if I were speaking fluent Martian.

'OK?' I said with a reassuring smile, throwing in a thumbs-up for good measure. '*Tout va bien?*' She promptly burst into tears and ran into her bedroom, slamming the door behind her.

She is also experiencing considerable difficulty getting my name right. When first introduced, she called me 'Creep' until P explained that it was 'Crisp', as in chips. Ever since then, and despite my efforts to persuade her otherwise, she has insisted on calling me 'Mr Chips' – or, rather, 'Meester Cheeps'. Wouldn't mind so much if she didn't tack it on every time she greets me. If she says 'Hallo, Meester Cheeps' one more time when I arrive at breakfast, I think I'll go potty.

As French names go, Marie-Celeste could not be more apt. There is quite clearly no one aboard.

Sunday, April 9th

John Julius arrived at tea-time, looking extraordinarily scruffy even by his standards. Union Jack motif on what passes for hair not a success. Nose ring ditto. When I asked him whether his mother approved, he shrugged and said, 'Why shouldn't she? She's got two. And another one you can't see.' Did not like to ask where.

Was relieved to see that he had brought only a hold-all. Said as much, to which he replied, 'Oh, Guy's bringing the rest in a minute. He's just trying to find a parking space.'

Five minutes later there was a ring on the front doorbell. Opened it to find the doorstep piled high with hi-fi equipment and boxes of tapes and CDs, and Guy the Gorilla wearing one of his physique-enhancing T-shirts on which were printed the words IMPRESSED? YOU SHOULD SEE THE REST OF ME!

'Where do you want this lot put, then?' he said. 'I could suggest a few places that'd make your eyes water.'

I don't know what sets my teeth on edge more: his

ghastly line in so-called jokes or his tightly curled hair.

At that moment P appeared and started simpering and fawning all over him like a lovesick schoolgirl.

When she finally pulled herself together, she said, 'I don't know where you're going to put all this stuff,' and, before I knew what, I found I'd agreed to move out of my room and into the tiny boxroom where she and Chad store the junk for their Serendipity stall.

Have heard of writers living in garrets, but no garret could possibly be as cramped as this.

P said, 'I don't see the problem. You could kneel on the floor and type on the bed.'

I said, with undisguised irony, 'I could kneel on the bed and type on the floor.'

'Whichever you find more comfortable,' she said, and went downstairs to resume her mating dance with Guy.

The sooner I find somewhere of my own to live, the better for all concerned. Especially me. Where, though, I cannot for the life of me imagine. A cardboard box would be preferable to this.

Monday, April 10th

Have always liked the cut of Chaucer's jib. Whatever the situation, he manages to hit the nail on the head every time. 'Whan that Aprill with his shoures soote / The droghte of March hath perced to the roote.' Has anyone managed to capture more perfectly the essence of an English spring day? I think not.

Stupidly made the mistake of declaiming the lines at breakfast this morning, using the authentic Nevill Coghill pronunciation. Chad said, 'I never knew you could speak Dutch.' 'Sounded more like double Dutch to me,' said P and everyone laughed, including Marie-Celeste.

Personally I blame my sister for egging her on. She seems to derive a curious pleasure from making me look foolish.

To do so in front of junior members of the family, even if they are eighteen like John Julius, is embarrassing enough, but to implicate the au pair is frankly unacceptable. I do not believe she could have had the foggiest clue what she was laughing at. But then that's the French for you: always trying to muscle in on everything. The more one knows about them,

Whan that Aprill with his shoures soote *Je men fiche*

Have always admired the cut of Chaucer's jib

the more it explains why so many turned collaborator in the war.

Tuesday, April 11th

Was coming downstairs this morning just as Marie-Celeste was going out of the front door.

Said, 'Good morning, Marie-Celeste.'

She said, 'Goodbye, Meester Cheeps,' and closed the door behind her.

She is either dimmer than I thought, or much more *au fait* with our language and literature than she lets on and is having a good laugh at our expense. Cannot for the life of me decide which.

Wednesday, April 12th

The older one gets, the more life seems to be one long round of worries. Have suspected for many years now that there's a lot less to bottled water than meets the eye. I blame the French, of course, but the Scots are as much at fault as anyone for persuading us to waste money on so-called 'spring' water. To my mind most of it tastes rather more like 'late summer' if not 'early autumn'. Yet, no matter what I say, hardly a day goes without Priscilla staggering up the front path beneath the weight of yet another case of plastic bottles which she has acquired at a special knock-down price from some supermarket or other.

Today she came home with something called 'Balmoral'. It has a picture on it of the Queen's Highland home and suggests that this is the same water that Her Majesty drinks when in residence.

Oddly enough, as she came into the house I happened to be reading an article in the *Daily Mail* by 'a leading environmentalist' saying exactly what I had been saying all this time – namely, that each week we in Britain drink millions of gallons of bottled water which is exactly the same in every respect as the stuff that comes out of our taps – except that it costs anything in excess of 60p or 70p a time.

Could not resist rubbing P's nose in it. She said, 'Yes, I read that earlier.'

I said, 'So all that stuff about London tap water being

riddled with hormones as a result of half the female popula-
tion being on the Pill was a red herring after all?'

She said, 'You obviously haven't got as far as the bit about
all the hormones that are extracted and dumped in the North
Sea.'

'*Now* what are you trying to say?' I said.

'Nothing,' she said. 'Only that a lot of sea creatures are
undergoing strange sex changes and that you like to go swimming every day when you stay with those friends of yours in
Swanage.'

My sister has always had a penchant for the dramatic. Even
so, one can never take anything for granted these days. Is it my
imagination or am I a little chubbier round the chest area than
I used to be?

Thursday, April 13th

Might think more kindly of Chad if he did not take such a
holier-than-thou attitude towards his so-called work. There is
nothing particularly admirable about selling junk off a stall in
a market in Clapham Junction. It does not, as he is so fond of
claiming, fulfil some vital need in the lives of the less well-off
citizens of transpontine London. How can it at the prices he
charges?

Nor does dressing like an agricultural labourer, wearing
one's hair in a pony-tail and reading the *Independent* automatically confer some moral advantage over one's fellow men, as
he tries to suggest.

Indeed, morally speaking, he seems to me to be skating on
very thin ice indeed. I do not know where he acquires his 'merchandise', but after dropping in on P one day when she was
'holding the fort' and finding my collection of Carroll
Gibbons LPs being offered for sale at a specially reduced price
of 50p each, it wouldn't surprise me to wake up early one
morning to the sound of the Flying Squad breaking down the
front door.

My feelings towards the man my sister will insist on referring to as 'the love of my heart' might also be a little warmer
if he did not insist on using my so-called bedroom as a repos-
itory for his dubious wares. He seems to derive inordinate
pleasure from knowing that I can hardly climb in and out
of bed for the rubbish that he blithely piles up around it

on a more or less daily basis.

This morning, woke to find I had lost all feeling in my feet as a result of some heavy object he had clearly deposited under the eiderdown at the bottom of my bed in the small hours – almost certainly for the sole purpose of annoying me.

Threw back duck feathers to find self face to face with enormous buffalo head. Admittedly it was stuffed and mounted, but it was none the less shocking for that.

Lying next to it was a large stuffed otter. When I made my feelings known at breakfast, he said, 'It's an otter you can't refuse!'

Thursday the 13th, in every sense!

Friday, April 14th

Never mind incipient breasts, am now beginning to wonder if there's something wrong with my brain. Called in at the super-market on my way home this evening and filled my basket with half a pound of Country Parsonage Extra Mature Cheddar, a packet of Jonsson's Swedish Crispbread, a hand of seven 'ripen-in-the-bag' bananas, a tin of cock-a-leekie soup and a dozen eggs. Five items – in my book, anyway.

Hurried to check-out desk marked FIVE ITEMS OR LESS. Luckily, had it to myself.

Could not resist pointing out to cashier that, grammatically speaking, the sign should read FIVE ITEMS OR FEWER. The next thing I knew she had interrupted me to say that in point of fact I had six items not five and shouldn't have been at that checkout in the first place.

Added the items up again to my satisfaction, but evidently not to hers. Told her I had no intention of moving to another location where the queues were much longer and people were pushing trolleys piled high with goods.

She said, 'I'm only doing my job,' and rang a bell on her till.

A man with a face like a duck appeared from behind Jams and Preserves and introduced himself as the manager. Quickly put him in the picture, only to be told that, had I bought a box of a dozen eggs, it would certainly have counted as one item, but that two half-dozen boxes count as two sep-arate items.

I said that, in my book, a dozen eggs is a dozen eggs. He said, 'Grammatically you're right, numerically you're wrong' and sent me off to join the back of one of the other queues.

Thirty-six minutes it took me to get through. To add insult to injury, arrived back at the car to find a traffic warden sticking a parking ticket on my windscreen with only one minute of penalty time on the dial. Had no compunction about snatching it off, tearing it up into tiny pieces and throwing it to the four winds, like so much cheap confetti.

The warden said, 'Waste of time, mate. It's all down on the computer.'

I said, so would he be by the time I'd spoken to a few people.

I may take this further or I may not.

Saturday, April 15th

Am becoming increasingly concerned about Mother. Her so-called 'boyfriend', Bill Redvers-Mutton, who must be eighty-five if he's a day, rang shortly after eight o'clock this morning to say that she is becoming increasingly absent-minded.

It seems that he went round to the house early yesterday afternoon to take her out to tea with the Brown-Bouveries only to find she had forgotten all about it. She popped upstairs to change, and when she didn't reappear for ages he became worried and went to look for her, to find her sitting in front of her dressing-table mirror in her nightie, her face covered in cold cream, putting in her curlers.

Frankly, I don't believe half of what Bill says. A couple of weeks ago he rang to say he had been appointed traffic warden at his local church. When I laughed and asked him if his duties included handing out tickets to parishioners who arrived late

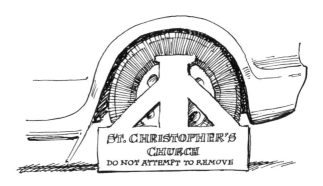

for matins, he said, 'Don't be ridiculous; how could I possibly do that when I'm clamping illegally parked cars by the lych-gate?'

Lynch-gate, more likely, by the sound of it. Those two are as bad as each other.

Feel I should be more worried than I am. The trouble is, my own memory is not quite as needle sharp as it once was. Poured myself a whisky and soda this evening and sat down to watch a programme to find I had already poured myself one. Had no memory of it at all. Is it hereditary, I wonder?

Sunday, April 16th

This evening, John Julius came into the sitting room, threw himself on to the sofa and said, 'God, I'm exhausted.'

When I enquired what he had to be exhausted about he was outraged.

'Bloody hell, Dad,' he said. 'I've been up all day.'

Monday, April 17th

Was in the middle of my bottled-water piece for next week's 'Up Your Way' when Sheila Hollingsworth-Palfrey rang to say that in future would I kindly send all my pieces by e-mail.

I said that unfortunately my PC is not equipped to send e-mails.

She said she was sorry, it was general policy and everyone was being asked to comply.

I said, 'Even that woman who does the Vet and Dry column?'

'Even her,' she said.

I said, 'Would the *Mitch & Toot* be prepared to give me a modem?'

'We're not made of money,' she said.

She can say that again.

Rang the people who were so helpful when they supplied my PC ten years ago, only to find they have moved to some-where in the Midlands and the shop has been taken over by a firm selling exotic cheeses. Needless to say, the man with the French accent I spoke to had no forwarding address for them nor any suggestions as to how I might trace them.

Following a frustrating hour with directory enquiries (it is no accident that they are not called 'directory solutions'), finally ran them to ground in Market Harborough.

They were every bit as courteous and helpful as I remember, but unable to help since my machine is apparently too old-fashioned to be connected to the Internet. They have suggested I upgrade to a more state-of-the-art model.

Is there any aspect of modern life that does not involve vast expense?

Tuesday, April 18th

To Compu-Warehouse near Redhill to buy a new PC. I gather from Bryant-Fenn that it's the biggest and best computer store in the south of England. He said he buys all his stuff from there and couldn't recommend it more highly.

After spending a couple of hours considering the merits of half a dozen machines of different types, sizes and prices, and listening to a salesman with a very bad wig called Dave, speaking in what might just as well have been Serbo-Croatian, for all the sense it made, about 'servers' and 'search engines', finally picked one.

The brand name is not one that I have ever heard of before, but then, as Dave pointed out, what on earth is the point in my spending a lot more money than I need merely for the sake of having a famous brand name when I can enjoy exactly the same advantages and benefits in a machine costing half the price?

Could not agree with him more. It would be a different matter if I were planning to set up a 'dot.com' company (what P will insist on referring to facetiously as sit.dot.com), or launch a magazine, or do a lot of research on the Internet.

Cannot think of any item of information that is not immediately available in my *Arthur Mee's Children's Encyclopaedia*, or in my local library.

As I told Dave, all I am looking for in a PC is a typewriter with e-mail facilities. This machine will do precisely that, and if I feel like browsing the World Wide Web from time to time, I can do that as well.

For £850, including a workmanlike printer and, as Dave put it, 'all the singing and dancing', I feel I am now equipped to face the world of modern communications in no uncertain terms.

It may be nothing more than a small step forward for some people, but for me it is a giant leap in every sense.

Wednesday, April 19th

Am very glad I turned down Dave's offer to arrange for an engineer to visit at great expense and set my new computer up for me.

Was talking last night to Vanessa, who said that she had bought exactly the same machine and had set the whole thing up herself in less than an hour.

She said, 'The whole point about modern technology is that it is foolproof.'

Have challenged her to prove it and she is popping over tomorrow evening to do so, lured no doubt partly by the prospect of a bottle of champagne and a pizza supper, but mainly, I suspect, by the opportunity to show off.

Thursday, April 20th

Maundy Thursday. Turned on television to find no mention of this on any channel. Like all our most ancient royal ceremonies – even those that have their origins in Our Lord Himself – it is evidently no longer considered 'cool' in New Labour Britain. And I thought Blair was supposed to be a Christian.

Vanessa arrived shortly after seven and immediately started complaining that I hadn't even unpacked the machine.

Told her I did not wish to deprive her of a moment's pleasure.

An hour later she emerged from the sitting room, shaking her head and grinning in that irritating way people do when wishing to express mild incredulity.

'Well?' I said.

'Nothing,' she said. 'Everything's up and running.'

'No problems?' I said.

She said, 'Only that they've forgotten to include the cable that connects the computer with the printer. Can we eat? I could murder an American Hot.'

I could murder Compu-Warehouse.

On the plus side, have saved myself fifty quid. Minus, of course, one bottle of champagne (non-vintage) and a couple of pizzas. Including an extra helping of pepperoni.

Friday, April 21st

Had been planning to attend Good Friday service at St Botolph's. My attendance record over the year is unlikely to have them dancing in the corridors of Lambeth Palace. On the other hand, have always been a firm believer that one cannot hope to experience the joy of Easter without having first lived through the agony of Good Friday: to wit, three hours of gloomy hymns, a lot of depressing sermonizing and jolly hard seats in what must be one of the coldest churches in Christendom.

Was literally on my way out of the front door, prayer book in hand, when the telephone rang. It was Barry from Features to say that, because of the holiday, they were getting next week's paper ready earlier than usual and where was my piece on bottled water? Was I sure I had sent it? Said that not only was I sure, but, with the holiday looming, had delivered it by hand, as requested by Sheila Hollingsworth-Palfrey. If they didn't believe me they could check with Reception.

Barry rang back a few minutes later to say that Reception had no recollection of my coming in. Would I mind running off another copy and taking it round by hand?

The matter could have been rectified in a matter of moments (a) had I bought my new computer a day or two earlier, (b) had I not neglected, for reasons that I cannot explain, to save a final version of the piece on a floppy disc, and (c) had my stupid machine not taken it into its head, for some equally inexplicable reason, to lose the rudimentary draft that I thought I had saved on my hard disc.

By the time I had rewritten the thing from scratch and delivered it by hand – again – it was two fifteen and the journey to Calvary was almost at an end. And not just for Our Lord. Decided to forget church and went for a walk on Mitcham Common instead to have a good think. It probably amounted to much the same thing. One does not need to be on one's knees in church to hear the Christian message. After all, what is God if not the Creator of the natural world, and what is Mitcham Common if not a manifestation of His feelings for us? Knowing God, I think He'd have understood.

Saturday, April 22nd

To Kent for Easter Saturday lunch with Mother, and to see for myself whether she is really as absent-minded as Bill Redvers-Mutton makes out. More to the point, whether she is still capable of living on her own.

Delighted to find her standing on the doorstep, looking as bright and welcoming as ever. My fears that she might have forgotten I was coming immediately allayed.

'I'm glad you came early,' she said. 'You can take me shopping.'

Drove to new out-of-town shopping centre near Ashford and sat in cafeteria while she went off with basket hanging from one arm, peering at shopping list, just as she did when we were young.

An unfortunate incident occurred while she was away. Was sitting alone at table for two when bulky man loomed up carrying tray containing cup of coffee and plate with two ring doughnuts and plumped himself in the other chair.

He drank the coffee, ate one of the doughnuts, then got up and walked away.

Am not a cake-and-fancies man per se. On the other hand, cannot abide waste, and the thought of a perfectly good doughnut being scooped up by some dim table-clearer and chucked into the gubbins along with half-eaten portions of pizza, used drink cartons and cigarette ends was more than I could stomach.

Looked quickly around, but there was no sign of the man, whose eyes were obviously bigger than his stomach and, evidently not being of the generation that was brought up in the austere atmosphere of the early Fifties, thought nothing of wasting good food.

Finally reached across, took doughnut, and was on point of sinking teeth when suddenly realized man was standing there holding another cup of coffee.

Explained I thought I had spotted fly on doughnut and was taking closer look.

He said, 'If you want a doughnut and can't afford one, I'll treat you to one.' I thanked him very much and said that actually I had to go and look for my mother, who was going a bit funny in her old age.

He said, 'It obviously runs in the family.'

Finally ran Mother to earth in Cold Meats and Delicatessen. I said, 'Are you getting on all right?'

She said, 'Why shouldn't I be? People are always asking me if I'm all right these days. Anyone would think I was going doolally.'

To prove she isn't, she not only dealt efficiently and briskly with the girl at the checkout desk, but pointed out that she had failed to ring up one item. Not that she got any thanks for it.

'Got everything?' I said as we prepared to drive home.

'I think so,' she said.

I started the engine. 'Home,' I said.

'Hadn't we better wait for Simon?' she said.

Sunday, April 23rd

Woke before dawn with a sick feeling in my stomach, and lay there for ages worrying about poor Mother. She seemed bright enough when I left her, happy even; but how can she be if she doesn't know who anyone is? What are we, after all, if we do not have our memories?

Before I knew what, my thoughts had turned to the whole nature of existence. Are we really anything more than a complicated arrangement of bone, muscle, fat and nerve endings? Is the brain merely the engine that drives the machine we call the body? If so, is there such a thing as the soul? And what price everlasting life?

Am beginning to think that all that matters is what we leave behind for others. Is it any wonder I am so keen to plant a footstep or two in the sands of time before it is too late?

As Shakespeare said, 'Tomorrow and tomorrow and tomorrow creeps in this petty pace from day to day.' Could not have put it better myself.

By the time the pips went for the seven o'clock news was in such a state of gloom that, for the first time in my life, could not bring myself to join in the words of the Easter hymn 'Jesus Christ is risen today'.

Indeed, cannot remember an Easter when the alleluias have seemed so irrelevant and meaningless.

Chad was reading the newspaper after dinner when he suddenly called out, 'Here's something that's right up your street, Sim. The Dull Men's Club web site. "A haven where the dull and pedantic can share thoughts and experiences free from the pressure to say something interesting."'

He said, 'The current warm potato under debate is airport carousels. Which conveyor belts move in a clockwise and which in an anticlockwise direction. Boston, Istanbul and Terminal Three at Manchester are all clockwise; Guam and Manchester Two are anticlockwise.'

There was a pause, then he said, 'Bad luck, you've just missed National Folding Maps Week, but if you're quick you'll just be in time to add your voice to Egg Salad Week.'

Did not grace his remarks with a response. Funnily enough, have often wondered if there's a special way of folding maps.

Monday, April 24th

Woke with a shock to realize (a) that it is Easter Bank Holiday; (b) that for the first time in thirty years of office life this is not a cause for celebration; and (c) that there's less than a fortnight to go before my birthday. Though it is by no means a landmark, I suddenly feel overwhelmed with a desire to entertain my friends to a surprise party.

Have not made out a guest list yet, beyond deciding to make it a family-free event, but will definitely be having it at the Botticelli. Can already hear Bryant-Fenn giving his well-known hollow laugh and saying something like 'Keeping in with your old clients, then?' But the fact is I would choose the Botticelli any day of the week for the simple reason that it happens to be very good, and Carlo happens to be a very old and very dear friend.

Am only sorry he wasn't in when I rang, but whoever it was I spoke to promised to tell him I'd called and assured me that he would get back to me as soon as possible

Stayed in specially all morning, but heard nothing. Called again just before one and got the same man again. He said, 'Carlo is busy with the lunchtime service right now. Can you call back this afternoon?'

Rang again after lunch, though to judge from the background din of conversation and laughter and the clatter of cutlery on china, it seemed an awful lot of people didn't have offices to go to. Same man answered. He said, 'May I tell him what it is about?' I said, 'Just tell him it's Simon Crisp.'

He put the receiver down and I could hear him calling out, 'Carlo!... Carlo!...' and then nothing happened for ages and then I heard those familiar velvety Tuscan tones saying, 'Ristorante Botticelli. May I help you?'

I said, 'Carlo, you old rogue! Trying to pretend you're run off your feet in the middle of the afternoon! The oldest trick in the world. I should know, I taught it to you.'

Carlo said, 'Who am I speaking to, please?'

'Come off it,' I said. 'It's me. Simon.'

'Sorry?'

'Simon Crisp. Who did you think it was? Simon the brother of Andrew? How many Simons do you know?'

Carlo said, 'Yes, Mr Crisp. What can I do for you?'

I said, 'You can begin by calling me Simon.'

Carlo said, 'This is Carlo Bambino speaking. I don't believe we have met before.'

I said, 'I'm sorry. I thought I was speaking to Carlo Genovese.'

'Mr Genovese has returned to Siena. I am the owner of the Botticelli now.'

Disguising my disappointment beneath a veneer of bonhomie, I said, 'And I *was* your public-relations consultant. Welcome aboard. It's nice to know that there's a new skipper at the helm and that in my own small way I was responsible for the craft being as ship-shape as it is today.'

He said, 'You are very welcome here any time you wish.'

There was no mistaking his drift. I thanked him and said that, as it happened, I was planning a small birthday celebration on May 5th with a dozen or so friends and that perhaps we might come to some accommodation?

He said that of course he would be only too happy to book a table for twelve. Would eight thirty be convenient?

Decided we had shilly-shallied long enough and said that it would be even more convenient if he could see his way to some sort of discount. How did twenty per cent strike him?

He sounded genuinely surprised and said it was not the Botticelli's normal practice to offer discounts to customers who did not patronize the restaurant on a regular basis.

Reminded him that time was when lunchtime at the Botticelli was not the same unless I was sitting at table six.

He said, 'That was then; this is now. We run a very successful operation here and we turn people away every day of the week. Indeed, there is a waiting list of at least three days for a good table in the main part of the restaurant.'

I pointed out that the reason the restaurant was so success-ful was due in very large part to the efforts of TCP Public Relations and me in particular.

He said, 'Do you want me to book you a table or not?'

I said, 'I wouldn't book a table in the Botticelli if it was the last Italian restaurant in London.'

'*Grazie*, Signor Crisp,' he said, and put the phone down on me.

The upshot of this thoroughly disagreeable episode is that I have booked for twelve at the O Sole Mio, where they are delighted to have my custom and offered me a five per cent discount without a murmur.

I suppose I shouldn't be surprised at Bambino's behaviour. Loyalty is not a word that features in many Italians' vocabu-laries – as Mussolini found to his cost. Or intellectual rigour, come to that. It is surely no coincidence that, when taking part in a recent NATO exercise, instead of invading fellow member Norway, the Italian army invaded neutral Sweden by mistake.

And to think these are the same people who gave us Dante, Michelangelo and Claudia Cardinale.

Tuesday, April 25th

Spent all morning ringing round with invitations to birthday beanfeast. Tim and Vanessa (though not as a couple, of course), Theresa and Philippe de Grande-Hauteville, Hugh Bryant-Fenn, Mollie Marsh-Gibbon, who could not resist a snide elitist joke at my expense, the Varney-Birches, Paula and Roland Batty, Charlie Kippax and yours truly. All my oldest and, I should like to think, my best friends. Plus Piggy, of course.

Had thought about inviting Chad but, knowing how chippy he gets whenever my 'smart friends' are mentioned, feel he might have trouble fitting in. John Julius and Marie-Celeste are going to see *Scream 3* and wouldn't have wanted to come anyway.

Naturally, everyone can order what they want. However, do not wish hurly-burly of commercial transactions to spoil the evening's pleasure, so have given Franco my credit card details and he will fill in details as and when. Have also taken the precaution of arranging for six bottles of his best Villa d'Este red and six of white to be open on the table and three of champagne (non-vintage) to be on ice for when people arrive.

Somebody once said that old friends are like old pullovers. Slip them on and you immediately feel comfortable with them. What an apt metaphor that is. Am beginning to experience a warm glow already.

Wednesday, April 26th

I can't believe it's possible. My piece on the meaning of Easter has been reduced to a couple of meaningless paragraphs. Decided enough was enough and rang the editor shortly before ten to put my feelings into words in no uncertain terms. He was not in his office, but Sheila was and I had no hesitation in explaining the nature of my call. I said that if it happened again I should have to give serious consideration to my position. She could not have been more sympathetic and promised to put my message at the top of the editor's list.

She said, 'Is it my imagination, or did you tell me you're a Christian?'

'Not any more,' I said.

Had just put the phone down when who should call up but

Barry, to say that our regular monthly restaurant critic, Gervaise, has just announced he's going to be in Australia for the whole of May and would I fancy deputizing for him at the Royal Grill?

Am not the type who gets excited at the prospect of a free meal or at the mention of a famous West End restaurant. In the course of a long career in marketing and public relations, I have seen the inside of more expensive eateries than most people can shake a fist at. Indeed, I can think of one or two very so-called exclusive establishments where I have been known to shake my own fist as a result of poor service, sub-standard cuisine and, on one memorable occasion, offensive behaviour by *le patron*, culminating in an entire pot-roasted guinea fowl in a wild mushroom and truffle bouillon with braised cabbage being deposited over the marketing director of Harley Preston's Giorgio Armani suit, followed almost immediately by a fricassee of kidneys with morels and spinach.

On the other hand, it is some months since I last came face to face with a *menu gastronomique*, and the opportunity to give my taste buds an outing was not to be sniffed at. At the same time, did not wish to appear too eager.

I said, 'Do you mean just me, on my own?'

Barry said, 'No, no, make a night of it. Take a friend. If you've got one that is, har har. Thousand words. Talk it up a bit. No fee involved, but feel free to eat your way through the card. Drink, too, as long as you get your piece in on time.'

Have said I'll give it a go.

'Copy by Tuesday the 16th?' he said.

'Fine by me,' I said.

Rang Sheila to say that my faith had suddenly been reaffirmed and would she be very kind and treat my message to the editor as if it had never existed?

She said, 'I suspected all along you were one of us. One sometimes needs these little moral crises to make one pull one's socks up. Now if I promise to do this for you, can I beg a favour for you in return?'

'Ask and it shall be given you,' I said. 'John 23, verse 8.'

She said, 'Our group are having a little get-together on Sunday evening at my place. Just to say "Hi" to Jesus and chat things over with him. It's all very informal. Coffee and biscuits. I think you'd enjoy it. And, by the way, it's Matthew 7, verse 7.'

I said I was sure I would; the only thing was I was a bit tied up on Sunday. She said, 'If Our Lord could rearrange His diary, I'm quite sure you can. Imagine where the Christian religion would be today if He had turned down the invitation to the Marriage at Canaa in Galilee on the grounds that He had a previous engagement.'

'Since you put it that way,' I said.

She said. 'I live at 43 St Paul's Way, Theydon Bois. It's on the Central Line. Shall we say half past seven?'

'I'll do my best,' I said.

'Me, too,' she said.

'God moves in mysterious ways,' I said.

'Doesn't He just?' she said.

P seemed rather less excited by the prospect of an outing than I had anticipated.

'It *is* the Royal Grill,' I reminded her.

'All right,' she said. 'As long as we won't be too late.'

I said that gastronomy, like love-making, was not something to be rushed if one wanted to get the most out of it. This was a heaven-sent opportunity to get one's foot into a very different door. One did not know where it might lead.

She said, 'If I know anything about your love-making with your ex-wife, the spare room.'

I said, 'Well at least you didn't have to listen to it like I do every time you and Chad decide to make a night of it.'

She said, 'Chad is an actor and an artist. His instinct is to express himself.'

I said, 'The railway analogy could not be more apt.'

She said, 'If you don't like it here, you know what you can do.'

I said, 'Eleven latest.'

She said, 'Ten.'

'Fifteen?' I said.

'Done,' she said.

Have booked a table for two for Wednesday, May 10th. Did not mention who I am. One doesn't want them laying on anything special and trying to give a false impression.

Thursday, April 27th

Was cycling with W on the Common this afternoon, minding my own business, when suddenly from behind came the unmistakable sound of trainers on gravel. Normally try to ignore joggers. Would certainly have given this one a wide berth had he not called out 'Good morning' in a loud voice.

Turned to find myself face to face with a very small, very fat Indian, dressed in a white-and-purple shell suit. Had no alternative but to return his greeting.

Had assumed that was the end of that, but no such luck.

'Excuse me for asking,' he said, 'but what kind of dog is yours? Don't tell me. She is a big poodle.'

I said, 'Actually *he* happens to be a rare example of the West Dartmouth Sharp-Toothed Terrier.'

He wobbled his head and said, 'Well, he looks just like a poodle to me.'

Began to cycle off, but he sped up until he was running parallel to me.

He said, 'Mine is a Heinz 57 variety. Very good dog. Very easy to train.'

I said, 'So is mine. Intelligent, obedient, behaves well in public . . . '

Thought we had pretty well shot our bolts as far as dog small talk went, but no. The next thing I knew he was wanting to exchange names. His is called Tendulkar, after the famous Indian cricketer.

'Woodhouse,' I said. 'After Barbara, rather than Plum.'

At that moment the fool animal took it into its head to wander off.

'Heel, Woodhouse,' I murmured. 'Good boy.'

Explained to the jogger that he tends to lose concentration if I get waylaid by something or somebody.

The jogger said, 'Excuse me for asking, but your face is very familiar. Have we met before somewhere?'

I said I thought it was unlikely, but that it was possible he might have seen a photograph of me in the *Mitcham & Tooting Times*.

'Crisp,' I said. 'Simon Crisp. I'm their star columnist and, as of this week, their guest restaurant critic.'

The jogger threw both hands in the air. 'What a coincidence!' he exclaimed. Because I am . . . '

Did not discover who he was or why it was such a coincidence because Woodhouse suddenly caught sight of a squirrel bounding between two trees and chased after it, barking loudly. Called to him to heel, and even gave several blasts on my 'One Man and His Dog' High-Pitched Whistle, but I might as well have been whistling at a brick wall.

'Intelligent, obedient and behaves well in public,' said the Indian, grinning and wobbling his head.

Pretended I had not heard and set off after Woodhouse. Unfortunately, in my eagerness to get away, my foot slipped and I caught my shin painfully on the pedal as it came round. I don't think he noticed.

Friday, April 28th

Came out this morning to find a skip parked outside the house next door and the pavement littered with empty polystyrene cups. Uh oh.

Saturday, April 29th

Was putting last touches to kedgeree to the accompaniment of a performance by the Wind Ensemble of Prague of the rarely performed Octet in B flat major by the sadly under-rated Czech composer Mysliweczek when Priscilla marched in and promptly switched the radio off.

'Excuse me,' I said. 'I was listening to that,' and switched it back on again in a meaning way.

She said, 'Are you doing anything?'

'You mean, apart from cooking kedgeree and trying to listen to Radio 3?'

'Only the thing is,' she went on as if I had not spoken, 'I'm rather worried about John Julius. He's changed.'

'Changed?' I said. 'In what way?'

'He's become much more moody,' she said. 'And secretive. And he's got much worse round the house lately. He doesn't lift a finger to help. He sits around being waited on hand and foot. His room's a pigsty. The other day he actually had the cheek to ask Marie-Celeste to change his sheets.'

Asked her what she wanted me to do about it.

'Speak to him,' she said. 'Man to man. Well, father to son, anyway. I'd do it myself, but, as you know, I help out at Katie's t'ai chi class on Saturday mornings and I'm running late.'

I said I felt that subjects like washing up and bed-making were more her province than mine, and was about to elaborate further on the subject of familial responsibility when John Julius's voice came wafting down the passage.

Try as I might, I still cannot warm to the counter-tenor voice. There is something inherently disturbing about someone with the build of a second-row forward, shaved head and three days' worth of stubble opening his mouth and sounding like Kathleen Ferrier. On the other hand, have to admit that my son does have a way with Purcell, and his rendering of 'Welcome, Then, Great Sir' had the hairs rising on the back of my neck in the best possible sense.

As he walked in, P went into her Mother Earth routine, cooing and fussing over him as if he were five years old instead of eighteen.

If John Julius derived any gratification from his aunt's solicitude, he certainly gave no sign of it. Indeed, apart from a single grunt, he did not even acknowledge her presence. Had he treated Belinda in a similarly off-hand way, she would have made her feelings felt in no uncertain terms, but then that's an army upbringing for you – as I know to my cost. P, on the other hand, drifts around the place as if this were still the Sixties, she were still the Flower Petal of East Kent, and John Julius were Donovan on a flying visit from his Hebridean commune.

John Julius stared at the radio. 'Who's the band?' he said.

'Prague Wind Ensemble,' I said. 'Mysliweczek. Octet in B flat major.'

'Safe,' he said.

'Thought you might recognize it,' I said.

'Never heard it before in my life,' he said, and pressed the waveband button.

Rap music boomed out.

'I happened to be enjoying that,' I said.

He said, 'What's that funny smell?'

'It's kedgeree,' said Priscilla. 'Your father's just cooked it.'

'Cooked an aboriginal musical instrument?' he said.

I said, 'Kedgeree is a mixture of lightly smoked haddock, hard-boiled eggs, butter and basmati rice. It's a standard breakfast dish in all the best English country houses.'

'Rough,' he said. 'What's it doing here, then?'

I said that I thought it would make a nice change from the usual dull round of Shreddies, Coco Pops and Swiss muesli, adding that Evelyn Waugh loved it.

John Julius said, 'I don't care if she ate raw goose liver for

breakfast, I'm not touching it.' And he poured himself a large bowlful of Shreddies.

At that moment Katie came in, to be greeted with more gushing from P. Anyone would think she was home after a year's backpacking round Australia instead of lying around in bed, reading.

'What's the book?' I enquired.

'Stephen Hawking,' she said. '*A Brief History of Time.*'

By an extraordinary coincidence, happened to be reading an article about him only the other day in the *Telegraph*.

'Good for you,' I said. 'What do you make of it?'

She said, 'I like his idea that a no-boundary universe might replace the Big Bang theory, but of course the black hole controversy's pretty much up for grabs these days.'

'Well, yes and no,' I said, and picked up the oven gloves.

P said, 'Eat up your muesli, Katie, or you'll get a brief history of kedgeree.'

John Julius said, 'What's all this with fancy food, then? You're not going in for *Ready, Steady, Cook,* are you, Dad?'

Before I could say a word, P chipped in with, 'According to your father, we could be looking at the next Loyd Grossman.'

'Really?' said John Julius. 'Through the keyhole?'

'No, John Julius,' said P. 'In your father's case, through the cakehole.'

'More likely through his . . .' Katie began to say, before she was cut short by P.

At that moment, Marie-Celeste came in, looking like nothing on earth and brandishing a loo-paper holder.

P said, in her best French accent, '*Ah bonjour, Marie-Celeste. Ça va?*'

Marie-Celeste said, speaking very fast, '*Il n'y a plus de papier hygiénique. Il faut en acheter plus.*'

Understood perfectly well what she was saying myself, but P obviously completely flummoxed.

'English, please, Marie-Celeste,' she said as if addressing a nursery-school class. 'That's why you're here.'

Marie-Celeste thought for a moment and then very slowly said, 'No possible wipe bum.'

I said, 'Sorry, Marie-Celeste. It is *not* possible *to* wipe *my* bum.'

Marie-Celeste looked at me and frowned. 'Why I wipe your bum?'

P said, 'It's all right, Marie-Celeste. I've put it down on the shopping list. Now then, breakfast. Something typically English this morning. Katie, would you mind passing the kedgeree to Marie-Celeste?'

Marie-Celeste looked at it, sniffed loudly and said, '*Mais c'est dégueulasse!* Katie, you want?'

Katie said, 'No fear. It smells like the loo at school.'

Seized the opportunity to broach not-ungermane topic.

I said I realized that, strictly speaking, it is none of my business. I am merely a lodger in the house and, as such, have no say in the warp and woof of domesticity. On the other hand, that does not disqualify me from holding opinions, and in my view someone had become unusually heavy-handed of late with the lavatory paper, leaving the rest of us distinctly *empty*-handed.

I said, 'I had the same trouble when I was married to Belinda, but that was nothing compared to the present situation. I have replaced the roll in the downstairs loo four times in the last two weeks. In ecological terms, that is roughly the equivalent of a medium-sized birch tree every fortnight.'

I concluded by asking if anyone had any theories.

Katie said, 'A black hole?'

Everyone groaned, but I think I made my point.

Sunday, April 30th

What should have been a happy, relaxing, family day spent agonising over whether or not to go to Sheila's religious soirée in Theydon Bois.

On the one hand, I did do a deal with her and, indirectly, with God. After three days have still not had a cheep from the editor, which would seem to suggest that she, at least, kept her side of the bargain. One cannot, of course, speak for the Almighty, but, as anyone who saw the recent film of Graham Greene's *The End of the Affair* will know, one makes deals with Him at one's peril.

On the other hand, Greene was a Roman Catholic, and I cannot imagine that God is quite so tough on us C of E types as he is on the Romans.

Were I to go to the meeting, these theological nuances could probably be sorted out in a matter of moments – though, Central Line or no Central Line, Theydon Bois seems an awful long way to go to find out if I should be there in the first place. I do not recall Our Lord having any sharp comments to make about people who say they will do their best to be in a certain place at a certain time and then discover at the last minute that, owing to unforeseen circumstances, they can't make it.

Besides, it's not as if I am a committed Christian. If I were, God might have some justification for giving me a theistic clip round the ear for taking His name in vain. As it is, He has no more demands on me than I on Him.

On the other hand, do not wish to hurt Sheila's feelings, and *certainly* do not want her to decide that what's sauce for the goose is sauce for the gander and spill the beans to the editor.

Decided in the end, therefore, that I would ring her on Monday morning and explain that I had set out for Theydon Bois with every intention of having my hand round a coffee mug by 7.30, but was taken ill on the train between Buckhurst Hill and Loughton and, not wishing to upset what promised a marvellous evening, had turned round and gone home again.

However, on the off-chance I might have got caught out by a tube strike or a flash flood in Snaresbrook, thought it prudent to make the actual journey.

By an extraordinary coincidence, suddenly came over queer just as we were pulling out of Liverpool Street, and by the time we had reached Bethnal Green had very nearly been sick three times.

Am now home in bed writing this and still feeling slightly queasy, though happy that when I ring Sheila tomorrow morning the story I tell will be the truth, the whole truth and nothing but the truth. Except, of course, that I will now have to substitute Liverpool Street and Bethnal Green for Buckhurst Hill and Loughton.

Never mind taking the Lord's name in vain; I am far from convinced that Jesus wants me for a sunbeam anyway.

May

Monday, May 1st

Would have jumped out of bed at six and given full throat to my traditional May Morning rendering of 'Sumer is icumen in, / Lhude sing cuccu! / Groweth sed and bloweth med, / And springth the wude nu', but in the event woke at eight forty-five feeling decidedly unsummery after a largely sleepless night.

Felt even less inclined to sing 'cuccu', or anything else for that matter, when, in epicurean mood, I went all the way to my local bookshop to buy a copy of Artemis Cooper's excellent biography of Elizabeth David, which has been such a talking point in gastronomic circles in recent weeks, only to discover it was shut because of the May Bank Holiday, if you please.

Could not believe my eyes. This is the second bank holiday we have had in as many weeks. Not only must it be costing the country a fortune in lost revenue, but, when I was young, May Day was always very much a Commie event. Have always blessed my stars that I was born in this country and not in Russia, but the way things are going it would seem that there is precious little difference.

Tuesday, May 2nd

I yield to no one in my admiration for Carol Vorderman. She is a television presenter after my own heart. Lively, amusing, good-looking and blessed with an intelligence quotient that many of today's so-called 'brains' would give their eye teeth for, there is not a programme to which she does not add distinction and sophistication. Am only sorry I cannot be as enthusiastic about her choice of wardrobe, but we all have our little Achilles' heels.

Like her, I am a keen and, though I say so myself, quick anagrammatist (interestingly enough, itself an anagram for 'I'm a star gnat, ma'), and though my mental arithmetic is not always at its lightning best these days, there is nothing that cannot be put right with a little cerebral workout and no earthly reason why I should not be a front runner to take over from her on *Countdown*, were she ever to feel like moving on to higher things.

Richard Whiteley is also very much a man with whom I am convinced I could make the verbal sparks fly in no uncertain terms.

It gives me no satisfaction, therefore, to report that Carol has slipped badly in my estimation after her unfortunate showing on last night's *Celebrity Who Wants to Be a Millionaire?*

It is hard enough to believe that someone with an IQ like hers could possibly get stuck on the £8,000 question and have to ask the audience who killed Billy the Kid. Ditto that she did not know that the city to which Muhammad departed from Mecca, thereby inaugurating the Muslim era, is Medina, and had to phone a friend. (The fact that the celebrity 'friend', Richard Whiteley, did not know either surely raises uncomfortable questions re the chairmanship of *Countdown*, and a letter to the producer may not be out of the question.) But not to know that Sir Toby Belch is a character in *Twelfth Night* beggars all belief.

Mind you, P was convinced it was *Macbeth*, but then anyone who thinks *Hamlet* is a small cheroot can be forgiven anything. John Julius plumped for *King Lear* on the grounds that it's the only Shakespeare play he could think of that has a lot of wind in it. Needless to say, Katie got it straight away. Trust a twelve-year-old to make Miss Vorderman sound like the village idiot.

Incidentally, for the record, when I said that the film in which Quentin Tarantino plays Mr Brown is called *Reservoir Hamsters*, it was meant as a joke. I think Whiteley would have got the point – though after his showing on the Medina question, nothing can be taken for granted.

Cable connecting computer and printer finally arrived, for all the good that will do me. I now find that my system is incompatible with the *Mitch & Toot*'s and every time I tried to send my piece today I got a message saying that a 'system error' had occurred and delivery was not possible. Find I am also unable to browse World Wide Web.

Rang Sheila to explain and to ask what I should do.

'What I always do when things don't go my way,' she said. 'Pray.'

She may have a point, especially if, as I am beginning to suspect, this is the Almighty's way of paying me back for mocking Him the other day.

Offered up silent prayer while watching *Newsnight*, though remained seated.

Wednesday, May 3rd

Am beginning to think I may be in God's good books after all. Was browsing through an old copy of *Radio Times* when out fell a leaflet containing details of the BBC's new talent contest.

As a practising journalist, would not normally dream of entering such a thing. It would be like Isaiah Berlin applying to join an Open University course. On the other hand, the whole point of opportunities is that they are there to be seized. John Ogdon, Vladimir Ashkenazy, Bryn Terfel – all got their first breaks by winning competitions, and who am I to gainsay them?

The opportunity to help shape the BBC of the future is not one that presents itself every day, and I shall seize it with both hands.

Unfortunately, have missed the closing date for sitcom writers. It's probably just as well, since I have never felt comedy to be my forte. Or the BBC's, to judge by some of the damp squibs that attempt to pass themselves off as comedies nowadays. On the other hand, have always thought of myself as a natural when it comes to presentation, and had I not made the unfortunate mistake of hooking my arm over the back of the studio couch during that debate on the taxing of business expenses nearly twenty years ago, and had my stupid shoulder not decided to go into spasm, I have no doubt I would have made a more positive splash than I did.

I felt then, as I still feel today, that the television studio is as much my natural habitat as it is Paxman's or Whiteley's, and I cannot wait to experience once again the soft touch of the make-up brush, the faint hint of under-arm sweat as the floor manager adjusts my lapel mike and the friendly glow of the red light atop the camera.

I see that auditions in Bradford and Birmingham have

already been and gone and Cardiff start theirs today. Cannot imagine there are many nuggets of talent gleaming in the dull rock-face of any of those cities, so will wait until phone lines open in London on May 12th.

Auditions are to be held in the Odeon Cinema, Leicester Square. By an amazing coincidence, that is where I felt the first intimations that I was destined for a life in show business. It happened during a film starring Ian Carmichael and Kay Kendall which, coincidentally, was a comedy about a couple working in television. A good omen or what? And the day after tomorrow is my birthday. Everything is suddenly falling into place – and not before time.

Thursday, May 4th

Oddly enough, happened to catch part of a radio programme in which one of the people in charge of the search was being interviewed and asked what qualities they were looking for in an auditionee.

'Raw talent,' she said.

This was music to my ears. If there is one thing I have in abundance it is talent – for people, for language and, above all, for communicating. It goes without saying that, after twenty-five years in the public relations industry, rawness is not a quality that features high on my list of executive skills. *Tant mieux*. Given the choice between a raw amateur and a smooth professional, I know which I'd rather hire. I have little doubt the BBC share my thinking on this.

The BBC woman also explained what an audition comprises – notably, reading from a prepared script and explaining in forty seconds what I believe would make me stand out as an individual.

If I can't do both of those standing on my head, I want my bottom smacked.

Friday, May 5th

What should have been a red-letter day will surely go down as one of the blackest of my life to date.

Everything started off so well, too. Cards from everyone – including Mother. Her choice of fluffy bunny rabbits playing football well meant, if a little odd, given that I have never

taken the slightest interest in the round-ball game since receiving one full in the face at St Osmo's when I was eight.

She claims the incident is a figment of my imagination, which is surprising. Had always understood that one of the odd features of Alzheimer's is that although victims may not be able to tell you what happened yesterday, or even five minutes ago, they have total recall of events of fifty years ago or more. Not, of course, that she has been diagnosed as a sufferer, but everything seems to point in that direction.

Lots of presents. A CD of *The Best of Mysliweczek* from John Julius, a half a Camembert from Marie-Celeste, and a hideous wooden box with a lid from Piggy. It had an Indian look about it.

'I thought it might be useful for putting things in,' she said.

Nothing from Chad, needless to say. Not that I expected or wanted anything.

An inconsequential day of the sort that often seems to occur on the most momentous occasions. It wouldn't surprise me if the Queen Mother finds her 100th birthday more humdrum than she expects.

Wanted restaurant gathering to be a surprise for P, so pretended all day that we were going to have a quiet drink at home and then slip round the corner for a pizza. In reality, of course, I was going to whisk her off to O Sole Mio to join in the fun.

Was about to open a bottle of cold Pinot Grigio when she walked into the kitchen and said, 'Oh I forgot to tell you earlier that Camilla Standish rang to say they are going to the theatre this evening, but they wanted to have a drink with you first. Could you possibly pop round at about six? They've got to leave just before seven.'

I said, 'Why don't they come and have a drink here en route?'

P said, 'Firstly because they're expecting you there, and secondly it's out of their way.'

I said, 'We mustn't be too late, or we won't get a table.'

'In the Pizza Pomodoro?' she said.

'It can get very busy,' I said. 'Anyway, I'll be back by seven fifteen.'

'There's no hurry,' she said.

To the Standishes in Claypole Avenue to find Roger struggling with a champagne cork and Camilla putting bits of smoked salmon on tiny slivers of – to my way of thinking – rather stale brown bread.

They seemed unusually delighted to see me and in no rush to get off to the theatre. Asked them what they were going to see.

'*Copenhagen*,' said Roger.

'*Lady in the Van*,' said Camilla.

'Sounds the perfect recipe for an evening out,' I said.

Camilla said, 'I don't know why I said *Lady in the Van*. We saw that last week.' I said I thought they had also seen *Copenhagen*. In fact they were the ones who recommended it to me.

'We liked it so much,' said Camilla, 'we're going again.'

'Did you go?' said Roger.

'No,' I said.

'Ah,' he said.

'What time is your curtain-up?' I said.

'Seven thirty,' he said.

'Are you sure?' she said.

'Absolutely,' he said.

'Shouldn't you be getting a move on?' I said.

'Doesn't matter if we miss the opening,' he said.

'We've seen it already,' she said.

After several minutes of pointless chit-chat, I said, 'Well, I've got somewhere to go if you haven't' and we all laughed and I left, clutching a bottle of malt whisky and a birthday card which had a drawing of Ratty, Mole and Toad and a joke about 'feeling ratty' which I felt didn't quite come off.

To my surprise, they were still standing on the doorstep when I drove away.

Got back later than expected to find both sides of road jam-packed with cars and no space to park a bicycle. Drove up and down a couple of times in hope someone might be going out somewhere – to a dinner party perhaps, or the theatre. Fat chance in this part of the world.

Finally found a space three streets away and walked back into the house. Opened the sitting-room door to be confronted by a crowd of beaming faces who broke into a ragged rendering of 'Happy Birthday to You'.

Was so taken aback that at first I didn't recognize anyone, but then gradually familiar features snapped into focus from out of the grinning blur: Priscilla, Chad, John Julius, Marie-Celeste, Mother and, most unexpected of all, Roger and Camilla Standish – all pulling faces and pointing at me in the way people do when a victim of *This Is Your Life* has just been caught by Aspel clutching the famous Big Red Book.

Did not know who to speak to first and stood there for a while feeling rather foolish. In the end, Roger called out, 'Speech!' and then everyone joined in.

Mumbled something about what a surprise it was and how lovely to see everybody, and then P came up and kissed me in her rough, sisterly sort of way, and Roger seized me in a bear hug, which was embarrassing and actually rather painful, and then Mother came over and grabbed hold of my arm and said, 'Who's a silly chump, then?'

The next thing I knew, P was pushing a glass of sparkling Chardonnay into my hand and saying, 'Well, don't just stand there. Come and eat something.'

Was piling my plate with cold cuts and rather dreary salad when I suddenly remembered that eleven of my oldest and dearest friends were at that very moment standing in O Sole Mio, sipping champagne, eating expensive canapés and wondering how soon they could get stuck into Franco's home-made pastas and top-of-the-range Italian wines. In my absence and, more to the point, at my expense.

Made a mumbled excuse about suddenly remembering I had to ring the paper, rushed out into the kitchen and called the restaurant. A voice I did not recognize answered. In the background I could hear the sounds of braying laughter and clinking glasses.

I said in a low voice, 'This is Simon Crisp.'

'*Momento*,' said the voice, placed the receiver beside the telephone and disappeared. The bellows of laughter were even louder. After a while someone picked it up again.

'*Pronto!*' said another voice.

I said, 'It's Simon Crisp here. May I speak to . . . ?'

Before I could even get Franco's name out, the voice said, 'He no here.'

'What do you mean?' I said. 'He's the owner, he must be there.'

'*Momentito*,' said the voice. I could hear him calling out, 'Signor Crisp! Signor Crisp!' above the hubbub. Why these Italian waiters can't be bothered to speak proper English – better still, understand it – I can't for the life of me imagine, but there it is. I could heard Tim Pedalow's voice shouting, 'Tell whoever it is that if he sees the silly bugger to tell him to get a move on. We've all started.'

Finally the voice came back on and said, 'Sorry. Signor Crisp no here.'

I said, 'I know that. He's here. I'm Crisp.'

The voice said, 'Ah, Signor Crisp!'

I said, 'I've been held up. I'll be there as soon as I can. You haven't opened all the wine yet, have you?'

He said, '*Si, si*. The wine. I open it now.' And he put the phone down.

Hurried back into the sitting room. P looking decidedly the worse for drink. I said, 'There's been a crisis at the paper. I've got to go in. I'll be back as soon as I can.'

'What sort of crisis?' she said.

'Major,' I said.

Ran to the car, to find that some fool had double-parked leaving me no room to get out, front or rear.

Sat there for a while with my hand on the horn, but might as well have been playing the penny whistle for all the effect it had.

Got out, ran to the main road and waited for a taxi. Never realized until that moment how far out of central London my sister lives and how few black cabs find their way to this part of the world.

Finally flagged one down. 'Merton Road and step on it,' I said.

'You can step on it,' he said. 'I'm going up west.'

Finally arrived at O Sole Mio three quarters of an hour later to find the party in full swing. Practically everyone had finished eating, the table was stiff with half-empty champagne and wine bottles, two waiters were distributing cigars, liqueurs and brandies, and Bryant-Fenn was lounging back at the head, opening yet another bottle of champagne and asking anyone who wanted to 'party on' at The Lizard Lounge to raise their right hands. It was all on me.

Franco seemed genuinely surprised that I was not delighted at the news that he had virtually emptied the contents of his cellar on my behalf.

I said, 'This was meant to be a quiet birthday party for friends. It looks like the end of prohibition.'

He grinned and said, '*Si, si*. Everybody very happy.'

I asked him who he thought was going to pay for it, but he just went on grinning and saying how happy everybody was. Not *everybody* I wanted to say, but did not have time to get the words out as at that moment Hugh caught sight of me and shouted, 'Here he is. Better late than never. Grab a pew and have a drink.' Anyone who didn't know might have supposed that he was hosting the event. Thinking of the size of the bill I was about to be landed with, I only wished he was.

To compound his offensive manner, he then led the company in a ragged, drunken chorus of 'Happy Birthday to You'.

Never mind 'happy'; I was beginning to wish I had never been born.

Managed to raise a weak smile and said I'd be right with them; I had something urgent that needed dealing with first and would Hugh be very kind and act as host in my absence.

I meant it to sting and, despite his languid 'No problem', I think it did.

Rushed out and arrived back at Priscilla's, having been forced to park even further away than before, expecting everyone to be really concerned for me, but all P said was, 'I've left a plate of food for you in the kitchen.'

On the way out, bumped into Mother coming in the opposite direction wiping her mouth with a napkin. No sign of aforementioned plate, only empty bottles and a sink piled high with dirty crocks.

Returned to sitting room and confronted Mother.

She said, 'Waste not, want not. Anyway, you're getting far too fat for your age.'

Had not realized how long it takes to wash up after twelve people. Nor how hungry one can be at the end of a long day without anything to eat or drink.

Nor, more importantly, that P had taken it upon herself to invite Mother to stay 'for as long as she wants'.

Saturday, May 6th

Franklin D. Roosevelt summed up the Japanese attack on Pearl Harbor as 'a day of infamy'. The same words sprang to my mind when I woke up this morning with aching limbs on the sofa in the sitting room and remembered that my bed is being occupied – for the foreseeable future, anyway – by Mother.

I do not begrudge her the smallest pleasure in life, but fail to understand why I am the one who is expected to sacrifice what little comfort remains to me in this already far from comfortable house, and why nobody thinks it at all odd that my son, aged eighteen, is still occupying what was, until he arrived on the scene, my room.

Cannot imagine the Queen being asked to vacate her room in Balmoral and doss down in one of the ballrooms whenever her mother comes to stay. But then, of course, the Queen Mother has her own house next door, as she does wherever she visits them, be it in the Scottish Highlands or Windsor Great Park.

Sunday, May 7th

Review pages full of nothing but Kingsley Amis's collected letters. One would think that nothing else was being published this spring. Everyone seems very complimentary, and I could not be more pleased for the Amis family and their friends, though sadly cannot share their enthusiasm for his sense of humour.

The word 'bum' is all well and good in its place, but to use it as a valediction in every one of one's letters to one's oldest friend, as Kingsley did to Philip Larkin (e.g. 'I shall/shall not be accompanied by my bum'), seems to me to smack of the bike sheds in the playground.

At the same time, curiously inspired by the thought of collecting my own correspondence over the last thirty years with a view to publication. My letters to friends like Tim Pedalow and Mollie Marsh-Gibbon may not be as riddled with famous names as Kingsley's, nor theirs to me, but they are none the less interesting for that. Indeed, can imagine reviews in the Sunday papers by the likes of Anthony Thwaite and Gyles Brandreth praising the volume for its very ordinariness. Have made a mental note to ring depository in Croydon where all my stuff is stored and get collating.

At lunch today, Mother said to me, 'You're looking very old. How old are you?'

When I told her, she said, 'Good God, you look twice that! When's your birthday?'

At the rate she's going, it looks as if I could be getting my bed back sooner than I thought.

Monday, May 8th

A beautiful sunny day, and one that makes me realize how unsuited I am to city life. I am a country boy at heart and always have been. Only the other day, as I was walking down a road in Fulham, found myself humming a tune that sounded strangely familiar. After a few bars, realized it was that old favourite of countrymen up and down the land, 'To be a farmer's boy'. Before I knew what, had burst into full song. An elderly passer-by looked at me as if I was mad.

So overwhelmed was I by *joie de vivre* that, like a frisky lamb, I gave a sudden skip in the air and grabbed at the lower branch of a tree in one of the gardens, meaning to pull off a fresh green leaf and savour the unmistakable odour of English springtime at its best. Unfortunately, slightly misjudged my aim and pulled the whole branch down, tearing it away from the trunk. The passer-by stared at me, so I pulled it off completely. At that moment the upstairs window flew open and a young woman stuck her head out and asked me what the hell I thought I was doing.

'Pollarding,' I said, and walked on down the street.

Since she was clutching a baby at the time and, if I am not mistaken, feeding it at the breast, I felt there was little likelihood of her pursuing me, but broke into a gentle lope, just to be on the safe side.

Frankly, if people who live in places like Fulham will insist on trying to invest their suburban Victorian villas with the trappings of the English countryside, they must learn to expect the odd natural disaster. If they cannot come to terms with country ways, they have only themselves to blame.

Tuesday, May 9th

By way of preparing my taste buds for tomorrow's *soirée gastro-nomique*, ate nothing all day but fruit and raw vegetables and drank nothing but water. By tea-time had one of the worst headaches I have ever known. P said it must be all the poisons in my system fighting their way out.

Better that than my brains.

Speaking of which, have finally admitted defeat re computer and have arranged for engineer to come and sort the whole thing out. Explained to woman at Compu-Warehouse that we are talking about a little hiccup in the system, not a major overhaul, and that I hoped their charges would reflect that.

She said, 'No problem.'

Replied that there *is* a problem, which is why I called them, but that it is only a small one.

She put the phone down on me. Hope engineer more civil. No joke intended.

Wednesday, May 10th

To the Royal Grill by taxi. Typically, P worried about the unusual expense and said that the tube would be fine by her. I said that if I have learned one lesson in life it is that if a thing is worth doing it is worth doing well, and that, anyway, the *Mitch & Toot* were picking up all my expenses on this one.

Unfortunately, got stuck in a jam for twenty minutes near Oval station, thanks to burst water main. Had we gone by tube we would have been there in half the time and at a fraction of the expense. Was so relieved to arrive that in gratitude handed the cabbie a generous tip, only to realize too late that, instead of a fiver, I had given him twenty. No wonder he was so pleased.

As we approached the famous revolving doors, reminded P that anonymity was the watchword for the evening. The slightest hint of who I was and they'd start laying it on, thereby ruining the whole exercise – though, as she said, the whole point about places like the Royal Grill is that they lay it on whoever you are.

Was quite surprised, therefore, when the maître d' – a superior type called Antoine – showed us to what he described as 'a nice quiet table for two', but was in fact a poky little table for one stuck behind a pillar.

'You won't be disturbed here, sir,' he murmured. Or served, I felt like saying.

I explained that actually Priscilla and I were not together in the accepted sense.

'Quite understand, sir,' he said in a slightly suggestive tone of voice.

I said coolly, 'I'd rather sit over there,' and pointed to a larger table nearer the centre of the room.

Antoine said he was very sorry, but that table was already

reserved. Decided this was the moment to make it clear that I was not just anybody. Reached into my inside pocket and pulled out my notebook. What I did not realize was that it was the same pocket where I had put my money, and out with the notebook came another £20 note which fluttered past Antoine's chest.

'Thank you very much, sir,' he said, catching it and slipping it into his trouser pocket. 'I'm sure the gentleman in question won't mind sitting somewhere else.' Before I knew what, he was helping P into her chair.

She said, 'Money certainly talks. Particularly when it's someone else's.'

I said, 'I have eaten in places like this before, you know.'

She said, 'And don't think it doesn't show.'

Am sorry that she had to let me down by ordering a glass of water as an aperitif. There is no better way of ensuring cavalier treatment from a head waiter than by appearing to be a cheapskate.

Ordered a champagne cocktail for myself and, while we scanned the menu, toyed with interestingly flavoured nibbles.

Jotted the words 'elegant' and 'stylish' in my notebook.

I said, 'One feels that at any moment one might look up and see Noel Coward coming through the door. Or Marlene Dietrich.'

She said, 'That would certainly put everyone off their dinner.'

When I asked her why, she said, 'They're both dead.'

Extraordinary how one's nearest and dearest can be so out of tune with one's wavelength.

Waiter arrived with drinks and small plate of tiny pastries.

Pointed at nibbles bowl and said, 'These are delicious. What are they, exactly?'

'Dried flowers,' he said.

Detecting a faint French accent, I cried *'Formidable!'* His face lit up.

'Ah! Mais vous parlez français!' he said.

I shrugged. *'Un peu,'* I said.

One of the problems of not speaking a language as often as one might wish is that when it is sprung on one, one's ear is not sufficiently attuned to pick up every word. So I didn't quite gather what he said next.

'La carte,' he said.

At that moment, light dawned. I said, '*Aha! Oui, oui. La carte. Le* notebook. *Moi journaliste.*' I lowered my voice. '*Critique gastronomique, mais très* hush-hush*? Comprendez?*'

P said, 'He wants to know if you've chosen. From the menu.'

I said I was perfectly aware what he was saying; I was merely making gastronomic small talk.

'*Excusez-moi,*' I continued. '*Votre accent. Vous êtes du sud* perhaps?'

'Well spotted,' he said. 'Hastings, actually.'

I said, 'I didn't know people spoke French in Hastings.'

'My family came over with the Conqueror,' he said. Via the Thames estuary, to judge from his accent.

Would dearly like to have chatted further. Am quite a genealogist in my own quiet way. But it was not to be. Business came first.

P said she would start with an omelette.

'*Une omelette,*' said the waiter. 'Followed by . . . ?'

I said, 'That's a bit unimaginative, isn't it? An omelette?'

The waiter said, 'The Omelette Rudyard Kipling is the speciality of the Royal, sir.'

Talk about teaching one's grandmother to suck eggs.

Being in rather more adventurous mood myself, my eye lit up at the word 'carpaccio'. How, though, did the *chef de cuisine* prepare this classic dish?

'Plain and simple, sir,' said the waiter.

'Good,' I said. 'Just the way I like it. The very word reeks of sunshine and garlic and the honest sweat of generations of peasant women slaving over the stove for their hardworking menfolk.'

The waiter said. 'Excuse me for interrupting, sir, but carpaccio is raw beef sliced very thin. I think you may be confusing it with gazpacho.'

Not wishing to embarrass the poor chap, I laughed and said, 'Well done. Just testing. Do we honestly look like the sort of people who don't know our gazpacho from our carpaccio?'

'Far from it, sir,' he said.

P then went completely off the rails and ordered fish and chips. Could not believe my ears. I said, 'Oh for goodness' sake, Piggy, do try.'

She said, 'Oh all right then. *Le Cabillaud Rôti et Gâteau de Crabe avec Pommes de Terre.*'

'*Le Cabillaud*,' the waiter repeated, with what I can only describe as a smirk.

'With vinegar,' said P.

If I didn't know her better, I could have sworn she was trying to flirt with him.

'*Mais bien sûr, madame*,' the waiter said solemnly and kissed the air with his fingers. There was no doubting the innuendo.

'*Et pour moi*,' I said, '*les côtes d'agneau sur cèpes et échalotes.*'

'The lamb chops,' said the waiter. 'Certainly, sir.'

To accompany them I chose a Château Calon-Ségur 1985 – claret at its very best, as the sommelier was the first to agree.

P could not resist a quiet snigger as I was going through my usual tasting ritual, but I did not allow it to distract me from what is, to me, one of life's great pleasures. You can never lavish too much love and attention on a great wine, and as I lowered my nose into the glass and breathed in, my whole head seemed to be filled with the scent of strawberries and blackcurrants and the warmth of the rolling St-Estèphe hills.

It was unfortunate that the assistant sommelier had a rather larger nose than most. Had I spotted it, my enthusiasm might have been a little more restrained. On the other hand, cannot believe that I am the first Royal Grill customer who has exclaimed 'What a massive nose!' in his presence. Were he really as sensitive about it as P suggested, he would surely have chosen a different profession.

Her suggestion that he over-egged the bill for the purpose of cheap revenge is sheer fantasy – though I must admit it was a good deal steeper than I had anticipated.

However, a hole in my bank account of £210 was the least of my problems. Was dozing in the back of the cab on the way home when I was suddenly woken by P calling my name.

Looked up to find we were at some traffic lights somewhere in Upper Tooting Road. She said, 'Do you see what I see?' and pointed out of the window at a brilliantly lit sign on which glowed the words ROYAL GRILL TANDOORI AND TAKEAWAY.

Luckily Barry was on late duty in the office when I rang him on P's mobile.

He said, 'What Royal Grill did you think I meant? The one up west?'

Laughed and said what did he take me for? Explained I was just double-checking and wondering how many words he was expecting etc.

Told P I'd quite understand if she wanted to go straight home, but that I would very much appreciate it if she kept me company. We wouldn't have to eat anything. I could make the whole thing up, have a cup of coffee, check the menu, recce the toilets and be out and home in ten minutes.

Entered the hottest, noisiest and most crowded restaurant I have ever encountered in my life. Was on the point of suggesting we come back tomorrow when I suddenly heard a voice shouting at me from the far side of the room, 'Welcome to the Royal Grill, my dear friend. I know why you are here. Intelligent, obedient, well-behaved in public, eh?'

Have never tried a Maharajah's Banquet before, and have no plans for doing so again. Lost count after course number seven, but P assured me the final tally was twelve, including banana splits.

'One hundred and twelve pounds and seventy-five pee,' I groaned as we emerged an hour later.

'He did throw in the after-dinner mints for nothing,' she said.

Too exhausted to respond.

Arrived back at the house to hear the telephone ringing. Owing to porch light still being broken, was unable to fit key in lock and finally picked up receiver to be greeted by loud disengaged sound.

Took Woodhouse out for widdle, had a large Alka-Seltzer and was in pyjamas and on way to bed with water and headache pills when the phone rang again. No response from P's room, so stumbled downstairs in semi-darkness, stubbing toe painfully on carpet en route.

Picked up receiver to hear sounds of party in progress. Realizing it was a wrong number, was about to replace when a man's voice came bellowing down the line, 'Are you coming or not?'

I said, 'I think there must be some mistake.'

The voice said, 'There certainly is. You were meant to be here hours ago.'

After a certain amount of misunderstanding all round, the caller revealed himself to be my cousin Dudley, wanting to know where I was and why I wasn't in Streatham Vale.

'Don't say you've forgotten,' he shouted. 'It's my fiftieth, remember? Cheese fondue and fizz. We're all waiting for you. Aren't we?'

Could hear a roomful of people all shouting 'Yes' at the tops of their voices.

Meant to explain that we had both been taken ill with food poisoning and wouldn't be able to make it, but in fact heard myself saying that we had been held up through unforeseen circumstances.

'OK,' he said. 'Well, get here as soon as you can. We've got a lot of fondue to get through. And fizz.'

P was asleep with her light on, a Joanna Trollope paperback across her chest and her mouth wide open.

Luckily for both of us, it was even wider open an hour later when, having been the life and soul of Dudley's party, she suddenly threw up straight into the cheese fondue and we were able to go home and get to bed at last

Have never been more grateful to anyone in my life.

Was mulling over the events of the evening in P's room at around ten this morning when there was a knock on the door and in marched Katie followed by John Julius carrying a tray covered with a cloth and singing 'Blow the Wind Southerly' at the top of his voice.

He laid the tray on the bed and whipped off the cloth to reveal two huge platefuls of food. He pointed to each of the items in turn. 'Bacon, eggs, tomatoes, mushrooms, baked beans, black pudding and a little kedgeree. Who says I don't do anything round the house?'

Thursday, May 11th

What should have been a day of joyful creativity, regaling my readers with gastronomic highlights, spent largely in lavatory. Was browsing through a back number of *The Week* and came across the following quote from Woody Allen: 'I do not want to achieve immortality through my work, I want to achieve it through not dying.'

What an original mind there is beating beneath all that flip New York Jewish wisecracking humour. While Allen is around, not a moment is ever wasted. Even on the lavatory.

On the other hand, must admit I am sorry not to be going to Bankside tonight to grand opening of Tate Modern, rubbing shoulders with the likes of Mick Jagger, Sir Paul McCartney, Jerry Hall and Yoko Ono and, more excitingly still, mingling with some of the young unknown artists and sculptors who may one day be the new David Hockneys and Antony Gormleys.

Friday May 12th

Papers full of the cultural event of the year. According to *The Times*, modern art has not been so much fun since Duchamp unveiled his urinal in a Paris gallery all those years ago. And we art lovers know what fun that was!

If Duchamp was right, and art is the unlikely object placed with aesthetic care in the unexpected setting, the greatest work of art yesterday in the Tate Modern was Her Majesty the Queen.

Am only sorry Serota and his cohorts saw fit to take her on what they considered to be a 'safe route' through the gallery, avoiding the Gilbert and George, the Damien Hirst and the Chapman Brothers' latest creation. One does not get to be Queen of England for nearly half a century and travel half the world without coming face to face with a limp male organ or two.

One doubts whether any of the organs she has seen have been connected to a hammer driven through a brain, though knowing how many Leonardo drawings she owns, one can't be entirely sure.

At all events, cannot wait to make my own Grand Tour of Britain's newest, and possibly greatest, temple to the arts. The sooner the better.

Meanwhile, have pressing artistic demands of my own and immediately after breakfast rang BBC to book audition for presenter job, only to be told that lines did not open until midday. On tenterhooks all morning and unable to concentrate on anything else. Rang as noonday pips were sounding on Radio 4, but line already engaged. Continued to call at five- and then one-minute intervals for the next three-quarters of an hour with similar results. Finally got through at 12.50, to be informed that all the audition slots had been filled.

Pointed out that I had rung the number forty times and that this was the first time I had managed to get through. The woman on the other end said she was very sorry, there were obviously far more members of the public wishing to give the BBC the benefit of their talent than they had realized.

I said there would have been even more had they included the people who hadn't managed to get through.

She said it had been done on a first-come-first-served basis.

I said what if the last-come-last-not-served caller turns out to be the new Jeremy Paxman?

She said, 'Since the list is now closed, we'll never know, will we?'

I said that I thought that was a typical example of the short-sighted policy that has made the BBC what it is today.

She said, 'You may be Alan Titchmarsh, Mark Lawson and Alastair McGowan rolled into one, for all I know, but we're just going to have to live without you.'

A sad day for the BBC, for Britain, and for me.

Saturday, May 13th

Another unlucky 13th for me. Was woken at two thirty this morning by the telephone ringing. Stumbled downstairs and picked up receiver. A man's voice with a rough regional accent said, 'Do you offer late-night service?'

Said I didn't think he'd find anything open at this hour. Had he tried calling the AA?

The phone went dead and I went back to bed. Was on the point of nodding off when it rang again. A different voice said, 'Do you give discipline?'

I said, 'Are you sure you don't want a garage?'

The voice said, 'Do you mean electric dungeon?'

I said I didn't know anything about dungeons, but if he was having trouble getting started there was nothing to beat a good pair of jump leads.

At this he became thoroughly offensive and put the phone down on me. Suddenly began to wonder if I was swimming in deeper and murkier waters than I had hitherto imagined. There must be a way of dealing with unexpected enquiries of a deviant nature at three in the morning. If so, I should like to know what it is.

Sunday, May 14th

Several more calls last night. Two requested electric dungeon. Joke about jump leads went rather better.

Monday, May 15th

A largely sleepless night. For this I have to thank the dozen or so sex maniacs who evidently cannot survive the wee small hours without feeling an overwhelming need to be abused and ill-treated by women. Fortunately, most of us get all the abuse and ill-treatment we can handle at home – though some of the treatments requested would have been beyond even my ex-wife's lively imagination.

Not that I ever discovered exactly what was involved in 'Badminton Horse Trials' or 'doggie in the basket', since the moment I attempted to engage any of the callers in conversation they immediately hung up on me.

By four o'clock, demand had fallen off sharply and there were no more calls after four thirty. Even so, woke feeling as if I had been through not only the entire Badminton card, including cross-country and dressage, but also the Grand National, the Cheltenham Gold Cup and the Horse of the Year Show.

A lorry arrived first thing this morning with a crane on it and deposited a huge pile of bricks and other building materials in next door's garden. What on earth the owner is planning to do with it all I can't imagine. Build an electric dungeon, perhaps.

Finally finished Royal Grill piece, though am still in two minds about correct spelling of *bhajee*. Am not entirely convinced by Tim Pedalow's story that the dish was named after a nineteenth-century Thames lighterman who retired to India and became head curry cook to the Nizam of Hyderabad. But then, having been brought up in India, he ought to know what he's talking about.

Engineer arrived at three thirty to sort out computer. After a while he said, 'Blimey, who set this thing up? The PG chimps?'

Asked him if I looked the sort of person who would entrust a delicate piece of equipment to anyone other than an expert.

'Pass,' he said.

Did not wish to get off on wrong foot by antagonizing him, so went downstairs and left him to it.

He finally pronounced himself satisfied just before six, but not before treating me to further gems from his Little Book of Insults, and left me with egg on my face and a bill for £95, not including VAT.

I may kill Vanessa.

Tuesday, May 16th

Sent piece through to *Mitch & Toot* via e-mail without a hitch.

I said jokingly to Sheila, 'This machine may change my life.'

She said, 'Machines don't change lives. God does.'

To Kent late morning by train to check Mother's house is still in one piece. It all took rather longer than I'd anticipated. Everything in the place is cocooned in elastic bands. There must be some deep-seated psychological reason for this, but I'm blowed if I know what it is.

On the train coming home, a youngish woman spent half an hour on her mobile at the top of her voice putting her child to bed. I'm surprised she didn't read him a bedtime story while she was about it.

I thought if she blew one more little kiss down the phone I'd go stark, staring mad. Made my point by saying, 'Give him a big kiss from me, too.'

The woman looked at me as if I had made some improper suggestion.

She said, 'Do you mind not listening in to my conversation? It's private.'

The sooner Mr Prescott introduces Telephoning and No Telephoning carriages throughout the network, the better for all concerned. But then, of course, he himself probably never travels on trains.

Wednesday, May 17th

Whether Pedalow knows what he's talking about re Indian food is irrelevant, since the entire anecdote has been cut. Amazingly, the rest survived untouched. It was unfortunate that the word 'paratha' ended up as 'piranha'. Even so, the fact that they ran the piece at such length means I stand a better chance of recovering at least some of the expenses I incurred over and above the £112-odd I paid in the Indian restaurant – though quite how much is at this stage very much a matter of conjecture. £286.00 for a couple of taxi rides is excessive, even at today's prices.

Thursday, May 18th

To the South Bank in good time for Bryant-Fenn's Eye party. Met in café, as instructed. Hugh was being his usual, noisy self, making a great fuss about buying everyone coffees, soft drinks, biscuits etc. In the excitement it escaped his notice that we were supposed to be standing in a queue waiting our turn to 'board', along with everyone else. When we tried to push through, we were told we had missed our turn and that we should go to the back of the line and wait until we were called.

Hugh got frightfully hot under the collar and started throwing his weight about (which is considerable these days) and trying to pull rank. But the more he protested, the more his entreaties fell on deaf ears. Fortunately for him – though not for me – none of the Fleet Street luminaries he had mentioned had been able to make it.

Indeed, was unable to recognize a single member of our party.

Actual 'flight' might have been enjoyable (a) if I hadn't stupidly decided to go the the loo at the last minute, (b) if the Australian youth collecting the tickets had not taken it upon himself to ban me from joining the rest of the party, and (c) if I had not been joined at the last moment in an otherwise empty 'pod' by a large group of elderly American tourists.

It was annoying enough that they all crowded to the windows so that I could barely see a thing, but one of them who seemed to have appointed herself tour leader proceeded to identify various well-known landmarks and get every single one of them wrong.

'That's Prince Charles's official residence,' she said, pointing at Horse Guards.

She told them that Waterloo station was Victoria, Blackfriars Bridge was London Bridge, and St Margaret's, Westminster, was St Clement's and that you had to be born within the sound of its bells to be a cockney.

Decided to confuse them even further by telling them that Buckingham Palace was the Tower of London.

The woman said, 'I don't know what part of the world you come from, but if I were you I'd buy myself a decent guidebook.'

She could not have got a bigger laugh if she had told them that the Mayor of London is Dick Whittington.

Hugh's guests even more full of it than the Americans. Afraid I was unable to share their enthusiasm

As we mingled afterwards, a large and over-excited woman whose name I hadn't quite caught said didn't I think it had been an experience to remember?

I replied, 'Noel Coward once said that television was better to be on than to look at. I think the Eye is quite the reverse.'

She said, 'I always thought Noel Coward was a pompous prick and I think you are, too.'

Hugh suggested we should all 'adjourn' to what he likes to call his club, but is really just a drinking establishment in Soho. Not wishing to appear a party-pooper, agreed to go along, though after my conversation with Hugh's female friend, would rather have had all my teeth drawn.

'What happened to Melvyn, then?' I said in a pointed way as we headed north in a taxi.

'He's sitting next to you,' said Hugh, indicating a man I had never set eyes on in my life.

Am sorry to say was rather colder towards him than I might have been, but then Hugh said, 'Melvyn and I were at Cardiff University together. He's deputy head of presentation at Chiltern Television.'

Hope my sudden interest in my new acquaintance was not too obvious. Anyway, he was very happy to accept my business card which he examined with interest.

'The *Mitcham & Tooting Times*, eh?' he said, and put it in his top pocket.

Could not tell from his tone whether this was a good move on my part or not.

An embarrassing thing happened in the Spike Club. Was suddenly hailed by a man I have met several times at the Pedalows, but whose name at that moment had me groping. Was therefore unable to introduce him to my host.

Managed to survive several minutes of awkward conversation when the man announced he had to go and 'strain the greens'. The moment he was out of earshot, apologized to Hugh for not introducing him and explained why.

'No problem,' said Hugh. 'Leave it to me. I'm used to handling delicate situations like this. I'll have a quiet word in his ear. He'll never suspect a thing.'

When the man returned, Hugh took him by the arm and leaned forward confidentially.

'I'm very sorry,' he said in a loud voice, 'but Simon Crisp here has completely forgotten your name.'

Friday, May 19th

Was on my way out this morning when a black Golf GT drew up next door and out stepped one of the most beautiful women I have ever seen in my life. She strode up the path on long brown legs and stood on the front doorstep, fumbling in her handbag.

'Excuse me,' I said. 'I'm afraid there's no one living there at the moment.'

She said, 'Yes, there is. I am,' and took out a key and let herself in.

I don't know why I should suddenly be feeling thirty years younger, but I am.

Monday, May 20th

Was browsing Net this evening and, out of interest, logged onto www.dullmen.com. I see that June has been designated National Accordion Awareness Month, and why not? The accordion is a sadly under-rated instrument and about the only good thing to have come out of France since Margaret of Anjou.

Sunday, May 21st

More sex callers last night. Unfortunately, Mother happened to be wandering through the hall at about one thirty when one of them rang. Came out to hear her inviting him round to fill her hot-water bottle.

'What a nice man,' she said when I replaced the receiver.

Shortly before three was on point of engaging fellow with rough Glaswegian accent on subject of piercing when P appeared in the doorway in crumpled kimono.

'I'll deal with this,' she snapped, and snatched the receiver from my hand.

'Where did you get this number from?' she demanded. The caller immediately hung up.

I said, 'It must be your winning telephone manner.'

She said, 'I'll answer it next time. You go back to bed.' And she went and got a blanket and pillow and settled down in the armchair in the hall.

'It's a magazine called *Whips and Thongs*,' she told me at breakfast. 'Someone must have put our number in by mistake.'

Needless to say, Chad was all for buying a copy and doing a bit of telephoning himself. Felt like saying the way my sister was looking at three o'clock this morning he probably got everything he wanted at home, and more. But at that moment John Julius appeared with Mother, so held my tongue.

While they were all occupied with breakfast, sneaked out of the house and headed for the newspaper shop. Scanned the top shelf for several minutes, but was unable to locate publication in question. Suddenly heard Mr Rathna's voice enquiring politely if I needed any assistance.

I said, 'No, I'm fine, thanks. Just doing some professional research.'

'Ah yes,' he said. The innuendo did not escape me.

Eyes finally alighted on magazine in question. Thumbed quickly through, but could find no sign of personal pages.

'Are you sure I can't help you?' Mr Rathna persisted.

'No, honestly,' I said. 'I just need to look up a phone number.'

He said, 'The magazines are for sale. This is not a library.'

'I know this sounds silly,' I said, 'but our telephone number got put into an ad by mistake.'

'I quite understand,' he said.

Returned to my task, but still with no success. Suddenly realized that the sort of people who make those sort of phone calls may not necessarily confine themselves to recent issues of the magazine. Indeed, I am sure there is quite a market in well-thumbed back issues, and if our number did appear in one by mistake, it may have happened months, if not years, ago.

Called out, 'I think I'll leave it,' and was putting the magazine back on the shelf when I realized that my glamorous next-door neighbour was standing at the counter looking at me and giving me what I can only describe as a conspiratorial smile.

She said, 'You look like a man who knows what's what. I could use your help. Ring my bell one evening. If you want to, that is.' And she walked out of the shop.

Mr Rathna wobbled his head and said, 'Who needs magazines?'

Had not planned on spending any money, but in the circumstances felt I should leave him in no doubt of the seriousness of my quest, so bought the first thing I could see on the counter, which happened to be a copy of *Hello!*

'Full of beautiful women,' said Mr Rathna, wobbling his head even more.

Am beginning to think I may have to take my custom back to Mr Patel – possibly in some sort of disguise. As a Glaswegian lorry driver, perhaps.

Meanwhile, do I take our new neighbour at her word or not? Life is one long round of moral brain-teasers.

Monday, May 22nd

Am still reeling from the death of Dame Barbara Cartland. What a character she was, and what a contrast to the sleazy underbelly of society into which I was obliged to dip my toe yesterday. Just reading her obituary this morning made me feel slightly grubby. Not the obituary, of course, but the memory of where I had been and what I had been doing.

Cannot pretend that I am one of the Dame's biggest fans. Indeed, I do not believe I have ever finished one of her books – or even started one. Never mind; like her I am a firm believer that deep down all women long for chivalrous men and old-fashioned family life.

She is an example to all of us who toil in the vineyard of creativity, and her passing reminds me that it is high time I started a novel. Some people may think that I have left it a little late to begin writing fiction, and I certainly do not see myself producing 723 books and selling a billion copies in 35 languages – even if I live to the age of ninety-eight. If anyone succeeds in wresting the record for the longest *Who's Who* entry from her grasp, it will certainly not be me.

On the other hand, Mary Wesley did not become a novelist until she was well into her sixties, and it did not stop her selling in thousands.

Am wondering if I should try dictation. Vanessa doesn't have a lot on her plate these days, or in the bank. First things first, though: I must try and think of a story.

Incidentally, happened to notice that the flautist Pierre Rampal has also died. How unfortunate that he should have chosen to do so at the same time as Dame Barbara. A day or two later and he would have enjoyed a much more lavish obituary. Not, of course, that he is enjoying anything much now.

Tuesday, May 23rd

Lunch with Tim Pedalow at his club. His father – and, as I have to keep reminding myself, my ex-father-in-law – has not been at all well this year. No one seems to know quite what the trouble is. Something vaguely degenerative, I gather.

Alyson has decided what he needs is a holiday and is taking him off on a Mediterranean cruise.

Was telling Priscilla about it later and happened to mention that one of the places they'll be stopping at is Sicily, which was where he got his MC.

She said, 'How awful. You'd think he'd want to give it a very wide berth, seeing how ill he's been.'

At first I thought this was her idea of a joke, but I honestly wonder.

Wednesday, May 24th

Was in a little shop in the Charing Cross Road, buying a bon-voyage card for Claud and Alyson, when I happened to notice they sold nylon watch straps. My faithful old black-and-yellow one is very much on its last legs, so took the opportunity to pick up a replacement. Finally plumped for one with maroon-and-dark-blue stripes.

Was attaching it to watch when an elderly man behind me said, 'I hope you're not thinking of wearing that.'

When I asked to give me one good reason why I shouldn't, he said, 'Those are the colours of the Brigade of Guards. Is that good enough for you?'

Fortunately, am someone who can think quickly on his feet. I said I knew very well what they were and had chosen them deliberately in memory of my father, who had fought his way through North Africa with the Grenadiers and been killed at Anzio.

The man's face crumpled. 'I'm most frightfully sorry,' he said. 'Naturally, had I known . . . ' It was as much as I could do to stop him paying for it.

I suppose I should be feeling guilty, given that my father, being a chicken farmer, was deemed to be in a reserved occupation and therefore not liable for military service, but I'm afraid I'm not and that's all there is to it.

Thursday, May 25th

The builders' foreman next door has suddenly taken to greeting me in the street as if we are old friends. How he has managed to find out my name is a mystery, since I am not in the habit of giving out confidential information to strangers – certainly not now that I am a household name in the Mitcham area. Can only assume his glamorous client has been shooting her mouth off – unfortunately not to my advantage in view of his regular daily greeting of 'Morning, Cripps!'

Am not a man who is often at a loss for words, but must admit that, for once in my life, was rendered speechless. Was strongly tempted to point out that in the circumstances 'Mr Crisp' might be a more appropriate form of address, or possibly even 'sir'; but that if he insisted on toeing the matey, Blairite, 'I'm-as-good-as-you-are' line, and addressing me purely by my surname, then the least courtesy he could pay me would be to get it right.

Unfortunately, by the time all these thoughts had finished racing round inside my head and I had finally formulated a response that was firm, tactful and friendly, he had disappeared up the garden path and in through the front door, leaving me standing in the street feeling thoroughly foolish. Is it any wonder that, however hard one tries to get on terms with these kinds of people, one finishes up wondering why one bothers?

On the plus side, have had a letter from the police to say they have decided not to proceed in my ridiculous false-identity case. This is a huge weight off my mind. Am only sorry local council not prepared to take a similarly conciliatory line re my parking ticket.

Friday, May 26th

Wonders will never cease. James is back. He arrived from Darwin first thing this morning after living in the middle of Australia for six months with a tribe of Aborigines. He looks well – very brown and lean: not unlike an Aborigine himself, but didn't like to say so.

Mother had no such misgivings. 'You look like a native of Bongo-Bongo Land with that hair.'

When I tried to shush her, James said, 'It's all right, Uncle. I take that as a compliment. Thank you, Granny.'

Katie was so excited at seeing her brother after all this time, she could hardly contain herself.

'I'd kill for that tan!' she squeaked. 'Is it all over? Did you walk everywhere in the nude carrying a spear and your boomerang? Can you stand for hours on one leg? Did you wrestle with crocodiles and eat snakes and things? Can you play the didgeridoo? Can you kill people a mile away by shouting very loudly?'

James laughed and said, 'The only things I carried were a notebook and pencil.'

P said, 'I hope you've brought back lots of artefacts. We're rather low on stock at the moment.'

James said, 'Sorry, Mum. All I've got is what I stand up in.'

'Not even the teeniest spearhead?' said P.

James said, 'It is good to collect things, but it is better to go on walks.'

'Rimbaud?' said Katie.

'Anatole France,' said James.

'Of course,' she said.

At breakfast I said, 'You must be quite a good singer by now.'

He looked at me as if I had suddenly broken into Classical Greek.

'Isn't that how the Aborigines get around in the outback?' I said. 'By singing?'

He said, 'I presume you are referring to what Europeans call the Songlines or Dreaming Tracks and the Aborigines call the Footprints of the Ancestors.'

'What else?' I said.

'They're not strolling troubadours, you know,' he said. 'They don't march along singing highlights from *The Sound of Music*.'

I laughed and said I realized that. I meant singing in the Aboriginal sense.

James said, 'I think you just wanted to make a cheap joke.'

'Not at all,' I said. 'I happen to be very interested in primitive people and was once a regular subscriber to *Anthropology Today*. I assume you travelled down the Songlines.'

James said, 'Our nature lies in movement; complete calm is death.'

'Pascal,' said Chad. 'From his *Pensées*, no?'

'Got it in one,' said James.

Mother said, 'What *am* I doing here?'

Katie said, 'Now that's definitely Rimbaud.'

P said, 'It's definitely time someone had a bath.'

Trust her to bring the conversation down with a bump.

I said, 'He may prefer to get the Hoover bag out and cover himself with dust.'

Mother said, 'Don't be sillier than you have to be.'

And I thought the Aborigines were odd.

Saturday, May 27th

Am feeling as though I have spent a night on Ayers Rock. In the last few weeks, thanks to the arrival of John Julius and then Mother, I have been demoted from the reasonable comfort of the guest bedroom to the boxroom and thence to the sofa bed in what Chad will insist on calling the lounge. I have now suffered the final indignity of being offered a choice between his camper van and my old scout tent in the garden.

Having seen some of the things my sister and her partner transport to and from their Serendipity stall in that van of theirs, had no hesitation in plumping for the comparatively salubrious pleasure of a night under canvas.

Unfortunately, far from being transported back to childhood, as expected, spent the entire night wide awake, tensing and untensing to the sounds of various footsteps on the pavement only a few feet from my head, and wondering how long it would be before I found myself sharing my accommodation with an urban fox or, more likely still, an urban mugger.

On the other hand, 28 Bermuda Avenue is no more my home than it is John Julius's, and I would be a poor father indeed were I to endanger his vocal cords and possibly jeopardize a brilliant career on stage and concert platform by exiling him to the dank darkness of a suburban garden.

Sacrifice is the *sine qua non* of parenthood. I have done little enough for my son over the years, and though he is hardly a child any more, I feel sure he has suffered as much as anyone from the divorce. It's all very well Vanessa trying to persuade me that guilt is the most useless of all emotions, but the least

I can do for the poor boy is ensure that he has a warm bed to sleep in.

When I told him my plans, all he could think of to say was 'Cheers, Dad,' but I think he appreciated the gesture.

Sunday, May 28th

Was woken last night by what I took at first to be a heavy shower, possibly of hail, but on investigation turned out to be the bulk of the contents of the stomach of a young and surprisingly well-spoken drunk. He was still leaning over the wall and spitting as I stuck my head out between the tent flaps. Indeed, I only just missed receiving a second helping straight in my face.

'Sorry about that' was all he could muster by way of an apology. 'Didn't realize anyone was in there.'

Much of what remained of night spent spraying tent with garden hose. Stupidly neglected to close flaps. Am more sorry than ever now that I chose to position pillow where I would derive the most fresh air.

Am considering contributing a few words to Dull Men's Club web site on subject of small tents. It could provoke some lively correspondence.

Monday, May 29th

One of the most important talents a journalist requires is the ability to spot a good story when one sees one. This morning was a case in point. Was idling through the *Daily Mail* when what should I come across but an item about a new television series called *Video Vacation*, to be introduced by Gaby Roslin, in which members of the public make a video of a typical family holiday. This is then judged by professionals and the winner gets to make a real film, to be shown as a one-off special over the Christmas period.

Not only does this offer me a chance to get my foot in the televisual door, it is also a perfect opportunity for the whole family (not including Mother, of course) to do something together, to have an adventure, to get to know one another and, most important of all, to have some real fun for a change.

My idea, which was inspired partly by talking to James and partly by my recent experiences under canvas (though without

the unwelcome grace notes, obviously!), is that we should buy a couple more tents, buy or rent a camcorder, hop over to France, and made a video of a family camping holiday in somewhere like Normandy or Brittany.

The weather forecast for next weekend looks promising, and the sooner we get our story in the can the better.

Am thinking of giving it a slightly surreal Buñuel *La Charme discrète de la bourgeoisie* feel.

That or *Carry on Camping*. It could go either way.

Tuesday, May 30th

P was away in Sussex all yesterday at what she describes as a 'country-house auction' (car-boot sale, more likely), so unable to broach subject of video. Mentioned it first thing this morning, but she said it was quite out the question – someone had to stay and look after Mother.

Asked John Julius, who said, 'This isn't one of these father-and-son bonding things, is it?'

I said, 'Certainly not.' He said, 'Well, you don't have to sound quite so pleased.'

I said that if any bonding were needed, I certainly wouldn't dream of doing it in a tent in a Normandy camping site; did he want to come or not?

He said OK, but could we take Marie-Celeste? I suggested

it might be a bit of a busman's holiday, but he said, 'Not at all. She's got relations in Abbeville. We could go and visit them. It would add a whole extra dimension to the film.'

I can't imagine why he thinks that. I am perfectly capable of making myself understood in several languages, but, not wishing to strike a discordant note at this stage of the proceedings, have suggested he go and ask her.

Needless to say, she has leapt at the chance to go back to France, even though it is only for a couple of days. I sometimes wonder why she bothered to come to England in the first place. Nothing that any of us eat, drink, watch on television, think is funny, buy in the shops, wear, say or even think compares with France. It wouldn't surprise me if, the moment we get there, she doesn't ask for political asylum.

Anyway, now James has suddenly announced he wants to come as well. And Katie. Am quite excited suddenly. Unlike my sister.

Wednesday, May 31st

Is it my imagination, or is Marie-Celeste giving me what Mother used to call 'old-fashioned' looks? Am not one of those middle-aged men, like Beddoes, who go round thinking that every woman who smiles at them wants to go to bed with them. In his case, of course, most of them do, and if they don't, he wastes no time putting the idea into their heads.

Marie-Celeste is not one of nature's more obvious beauties, and long frizzy hair normally has the effect of setting my teeth slightly on edge, but I must admit she does have a certain *je ne sais quoi* which you often find in Continental women, and I have noticed that whenever I come into the room when she is there she gives me a look which is, frankly, roguish.

She is also the only person in the house who seems to appreciate my satirical sense of humour.

She even laughs at things that aren't meant to be a joke. Today at breakfast, for example, I asked her, in French, if she had had enough toast. '*Etes vous pleine?*' I said, at which she shrieked with laughter, went red in the face and left the room.

'Well done, Simon,' said Katie.

When I asked what she meant, she explained that to ask a woman if she is '*pleine*' is to enquire if she is pregnant. The correct wording is '*Est-ce que vous avez eu assez à manger?*'

I presume she was pulling my leg. I know the French can be dreadfully flowery when they want, but I cannot imagine anyone coming out with all that complicated syntax in order to express a simple enquiry about toast.

I only hope that by including Marie-Celeste in the production I am not raising false hopes in her ample Gallic breast.

Was devouring the Books and Arts section of the *Telegraph* when P marched in and asked me if I had spoken to John Julius yet re his attitude to family life. I said that actually I was working, but would try and do so later.

She said, 'Most people would say that reading the morning papers is synonymous with relaxation.'

I said, 'Most people would say that staring out of the window is staring out of the window. Writers call it thinking. In fact something like eighty per cent of a writer's working life is spent thinking.'

She said, 'In that case, I am sure your brain can divert the other twenty per cent to the subject of John Julius.'

There was no point in arguing further. When my sister has got something on her mind she's like a terrier with a bone. Put down the interesting piece I was reading about Alan Bennett and Proust and went upstairs to find John Julius.

Could hear his rendering of 'Where the Bee Sucks' from the bottom of the stairs. Tiptoed along the corridor and knocked quietly on his door.

'Yer?' he said. I never cease to marvel at the contrast between his singing and speaking voices.

I said, 'May I come in?'

'Who is it?' he said.

I said, ' Michael Tilson Thomas and the entire string section of the London Symphony Orchestra.'

'Tilson Thomas doesn't conduct the LSO any more,' he said.

'Look,' I said, 'I'm sorry to disturb you. I know what it's like to have one's concentration snapped . . . '

'Doesn't bother me,' he said.

I said, 'Anyway, the thing is, I have been wondering – or, rather, your aunt has been wondering – whether you could, you know, pull your finger out a bit more in the household department. A bit of table-clearing, bit of washing-up, bit of dustpan work now and then. You know.'

'No problem,' we said.

Should have left it there, but felt I had not quite got to the heart of the matter. I explained that, like all mothers, P is a worrier and so am I.

John Julius said, 'Yer. Cheers.'

I said that on the other hand, as flesh and blood, one does have certain responsibilities, family-wise, if he got my drift.

'We talking condoms here?' he said.

'Sorry?' I said.

He said, 'No, honestly. It's OK. Message received and understood. Flesh and blood and responsibilities and all that. Don't worry, I'm covered in that department. No joke intended.'

Was on the point of pressing him further on his love life when I heard a loud bang from inside the room, as if something heavy had been dropped.

When I asked what it was, he said it was nothing. I thought I could hear the sound of whispering, so I said, 'Have you got someone in there with you?'

'What?' he said.

Was not about to stand any more nonsense. Opened door to see Marie-Celeste standing on the other side of the bed, holding a duvet up to her chin.

'*Bonjour*,' I said.

'I change the sheets, yes?' she said.

Call me old-fashioned, but ten o'clock on a Wednesday morning seems an odd time to be changing someone's sheets.

Am beginning to have serious doubts about this trip.

June

Thursday, June 1st

Rang Eurostar to be told all car places taken for tomorrow, so have booked us on noon crossing from Folkestone to Dieppe. Nothing like a sea breeze in one's face and a teak deck pitching beneath one's feet to remind one that, for all our lip service to Brussels, we are still a proud island race. *Of* Europe, perhaps, but not *in* Europe.

To misquote the Bard, 'Fair stands the wind for France.'

Was planning to buy a camcorder, but luckily Chad had one which he'd found at the bottom of a box of personal effects in a jumble sale in Epsom. It is not exactly top-of-the-range, but he assured me it 'does the bizzo'. He said he and P had recently used it to make a pornographic home video with outstanding results – though whether filmically or otherwise he chose not to divulge.

I think I know my sister a bit better than to be taken in by titbits that are obviously intended to get a rise out of me. However, before I go any further I intend to give it a good rub all over with Dettol.

Friday, June 2nd

Woke to rain and high winds. Drove to Folkestone to find the sea lashing the harbour wall and all crossings cancelled until further notice.

Can think of many people who in the same situation would have thrown up their hands and abandoned the whole project – my four passengers among them. However, am the kind of person who can find something good in even the worst setbacks, and, as I reminded the sullen quartet, *Apocalypse Now* got made in the worst conditions possible, yet it is considered not only one of Francis Ford Coppola's masterpieces, but one of the greatest movies of all time.

Katie said, 'Given a choice between Cambodia in the monsoon season and Folkestone on a wet afternoon in June, I'll take Cambodia every time.'

I said, 'Given a choice between sitting here and moaning, and making the best of a bad job, which would you take?'

John Julius said, 'What do you have in mind?'

I said, 'Why don't we make the film in the garden at home?'

Must confess my offer came as much of a surprise to me as it obviously did to the others, but actually the more I thought about it, the more it seemed to me to provide the perfect solution to our problems. One tent in the rain is much like any other, whether it's in the corner of a French camping site or in a garden in Mitcham. Ditto French food and wine. It's practically all you can ever buy in English supermarkets these days, anyway. We were also lucky enough to have a real French person with us in the shape of Marie-Celeste, who I felt sure would be happy to play the part of a Normandy peasant girl who befriends us, takes us shopping and describes some of the local tourist attractions. We could even ask some of her au-pair friends to take walk-on parts as local villagers etc.

James said, 'You'd never get away with it.'

I said of course we could, no one would know the difference. It would be like *Capricorn One* all over again.

Naturally they all looked blank, so I gave a quick synopsis of the plot: astronauts set off for the moon, the whole world sees them bouncing around the lunar surface in their space suits, but actually they haven't gone at all – the whole thing's been mocked up on a film set.

'Wicked,' said Katie. 'What happened?'

Unfortunately, was unable to remember rest of story. Have a feeling it all ended in disaster, but this was not the moment to be negative, so devised a happy ending instead.

James said, 'What's in it for us?'

'The chance to be on prime-time television?' I said.

He said, 'I've just spent six months living with people whose greatest aim in life is to be part of one huge family, to contribute as much as possible to others, and to share in the universal spirit of the living and the dead. Making a prat of myself on television is not high on my list of priorities right now.'

I said, 'Put it this way. By taking part in this experiment, you will have the satisfaction of knowing that you have contributed to the physical and mental well-being of this family in no uncertain terms. You will also get to drink as much top-of-the-range French wine as you can get down you.'

'And beer?' said John Julius.

'If you insist,' I said.

'Stella Artois,' he said. 'None of this gnat's-pee stuff that passes for beer in most French cafés.'

Am seriously beginning to wonder if my son is turning into an alcoholic. He seems incapable of getting through a day without beer. I asked him the other day how much he expects to drink on a Saturday night when and his friend Rats go to the pub.

'Pubs, you mean,' he said. 'Six or seven pints. Why?'

I said that seemed an awful lot for one evening. He said, 'What do you mean? That's per pub.'

Decided this was not the moment to become embroiled in a major moral debate and have agreed to his demands.

As usual, Marie-Celeste was completely out of her depth, and seemed astonished when I told her that we were not going to France after all. When I added that we were going to make the film at home instead, she threw her hands in the air, blew out her cheeks and made one of those '*bouff*'-ing noises the French always produce whenever they are asked to do something that doesn't suit them.

Though very much a Euro-sceptic at heart, I do not believe my worst enemies could call me a xenophobe. Some of the happiest times of my life have been spent in small French *estaminets*, eating bread and cheese, quaffing an honest *vin du pays*, playing *boules* and sharing a joke or two with the locals. So, much as I would like to have put Marie-Celeste across my knee and given her a good spanking (in the purely non-sexual way, of course), felt it my duty, both as head of family and *in loco parentis*, to explain my thinking and generally put her in the picture.

Reminded her that the whole point about being an au pair is that for several months you become a member of the family and, as such, are expected to join in all their activities willy-nilly. It's the only way to discover how other nationalities live, how they think, and how to speak their language.

She shrugged her shoulders, pulled a face and said, '*Mais vous êtes complètement fou.*'

I said, 'In English, please, Marie-Celeste.'

She said, in a bad stage-French accent, 'You are completely med.'

'Mad,' I said. 'Not med. Med is a sea. It is short for Mediterranean. Mad is the word. Try saying mad.'

'Med,' she said. 'Completely med.'

No one can say I don't make an effort.

Could not help noticing in reflection in car window that she made a vulgar gesture in my direction, opening her mouth, putting a finger on her tongue and pretending to be sick. Pretended not to notice. Am wondering if the signals she has been giving me are quite what I imagined. But then, of course, the French are notoriously duplicitous when it comes to feelings.

Took a few establishing shots of waves breaking over harbour wall, sailing boats rocking, and the steamer moored at the quayside, plus a couple of shots of our party with rucksacks on their backs, heading purposefully towards the check-in. Unfortunately, Marie-Celeste and Katie could not resist giggling, which set the others off, so had to do it a couple more times before calling 'Cut.'

Luckily there was an empty tape in there already, so did not have to fiddle about in rain inserting new one.

Arrived back in London in mid-afternoon to find the house empty and a note from P on the kitchen table to say that she and Chad had taken Mother to Kent to stay with Bill Redvers-Mutton for the weekend.

She could not have done me a better service if she'd tried. She would almost certainly have found some reason why I should not be doing what I'm doing, and Chad – though he might have added extra texture to the story as a rough fellow camper – would only have interfered and made a general nuisance of himself.

Could not help noticing that he has started eyeing Marie-Celeste in an unhealthy way, and any opportunity to keep him well away from temptation is to be seized at all costs. Not that she has the remotest interest in him – and who can blame her?

Afternoon spent erecting tents. On my own, mainly. When

the boys finally deigned to put in an appearance and I asked them where they had been, they said, 'Buying the beer, of course.'

Katie looked at the tents and said, 'You're not expecting us to actually sleep in those, are you?'

I asked her why on earth not.

JJ said, 'When we've got perfectly good beds a few yards away? You can't be serious, Dad.'

I pointed out that the getting-ready-for-bed and the waking-up-in-the-morning scenes were vital in order to give the film some sense of time passing.

Katie said, 'The whole point about films is that they aren't real. They're made up of lots of little bits taken from here and there and edited together.'

I said I knew perfectly well how films were made.

She said in that case I could shoot a sequence showing us all going to bed, then we could all have a good night's sleep, then I could shoot another sequence tomorrow morning showing us all getting up and no one would be the wiser.

I said that wouldn't be quite the same thing.

JJ said, 'This whole thing isn't the same thing, anyway. We're in Mitcham trying to pretend we're in Brittany.'

'Normandy,' I said.

'Wherever,' he said.

Decided to cut cackle and agreed they could all sleep in the

house on condition they came for a typically French meal at Chez Gaston in Colliers Wood High Street.

They grudgingly agreed, and I was able to get some very convincing footage of them eating *steak pommes frites* and pretending to enjoy the house red. It's unfortunate that Gaston himself does not exist and that *le patron* neither eats there nor speaks one word of French, being a retired taxi driver from East Sheen. However, persuaded him to move his lips while I dubbed in a few appropriate phrases from behind the camera, like '*Bonsoir, mesdames et messieurs*' and '*La spécialité de la maison ce soir est le steak pommes frites.*'

Cannot pretend that my accent is authentically Normand, but doubt Gaby will be up to spotting the difference.

Lights-out scene less successful than I had hoped, owing to sounds of drunken passers-by on their way home a few yards from 'camp site'. Had considered possibility of sleeping in Mother's bed in her absence, but decided to tough it out in tent. If I don't set an example, who will?

Had barely dropped off when woken by sound of people talking very loudly just above my head and objects landing on tent. Stuck head out to see a group of teenagers of mixed sex, sitting on wall only a few feet away, drinking beer out of cans. One of the boys emptied last of beer down his throat and tossed empty can over his shoulder on to tent.

'Excuse me,' I said. 'Would you mind not doing that?'

To my astonishment they carried on talking as if I were not even there.

'Excuse me,' I said again, this time much louder. A couple of them turned round and looked at me. If I had been a garden snail they could not have appeared less concerned.

I said, 'Would you mind going and sitting on someone else's wall? And please don't throw cans on my tent.'

One of the girls said, 'Are you John Julius's dad?'

I said that I was.

'Thought so,' she said.

And they all stood up and walked off down the street.

Quite unable to get back to sleep. Was just dozing off when I heard what sounded suspiciously like water being dribbled on to tent and muffled giggling.

Did not give them the satisfaction of thinking I cared.

And to think that today is the forty-seventh anniversary of the Coronation of Queen Elizabeth II.

Saturday, June 3rd

Up early and off to Maison Brigitte for a dozen freshly baked croissants, to find shop has completely disappeared and been replaced by boutique called Horsebox. Bridge rolls from supermarket not the same thing at all, but a step up from sliced Hovis, I suppose.

Returned at nine to find camp site as deserted as when I left it. Had stupidly given my front-door key to JJ the previous evening, so was unable to get into house. Rang front doorbell but to no effect, so tried throwing stones up at James's bedroom window. In my efforts to ensure sound was loud enough, managed to break one of the panes. It would not have mattered so much if some nosy-parker neighbour – no prizes for guessing who – had not taken it upon himself to ring the local police station.

When I told the policeman I thought things had come to a pretty pass when one could not do what one wanted in the privacy of one's own garden, he said, 'Is this your garden, sir?'

Said that, technically speaking, I was not the owner and was going on to explain situation, but, before I knew what, found myself being interviewed ('grilled' might be a more accurate description) and having to justify not only my actions but my very presence at 28 Bermuda Avenue.

It was my bad luck to have fallen foul of a bear of very little brain for whom the idea of filming a travel video in one's own garden was difficult enough to grasp, but that I should be doing so while pretending I was in France could not have been more baffling had I tried to explain Einstein's General Theory of Relativity.

The upshot was that it was not until after midday that I was finally able to rouse my fellow campers, and nearly two by the time I got them up and reasonably *compos mentis*.

Is it my imagination, or did Marie-Celeste's bed look suspiciously unslept-in? As my old flatmate Beddoes would doubtless have reminded me at this point, it is one thing for the father to sleep with the au-pair girl, but when the son starts muscling in on the action it threatens the very foundation of family life as we know it.

Managed to persuade them all to act as if they had just woken up to a glorious Normandy day – clambering out of their tents, yawning, stretching, scratching their heads etc. – ditto to nibble at rolls and sip at tepid mugs of coffee while studying map and pretending to discuss their itinerary for the day.

Was beginning to congratulate self on how well things were going when entire project ran slap into buffers.

Need I say who was responsible? Must admit Marie-Celeste's au-pair friends not the saucy French sex kittens of popular myth, but as Normandy dumplings they fitted the bill very well. Was in the middle of setting up establishing shot of the four of them walking across middle of Mitcham Common and had explained how I wanted them to walk past the camera, chattering away to each in French, when Marie-Celeste said, 'Is not possible.'

I said it was perfectly possible, provided they didn't trip over anything or look at the camera.

She said, 'Is not possible to speak French.'

When I asked her why on earth not, she said, 'We are not permitted to speak French. We are here to learn English. You say we must always speak English. Never French.'

I laughed and said these were very special circumstances, and promised I would never tell her to speak English again as long as she stayed with us. Marie-Celeste said, 'I not believe you. You say we go to France, we not go to France. You say we make film at home, eat good French food, drink good French wine, we eat bad food, not French at all, and we drink bad wine, give us tummy squits. You not say truth. You never say truth.'

Was not about to take that sort of thing from anyone, let alone a bolshy and spoilt French teenager, and made my feelings known in no uncertain terms.

As usual, the French are better at dishing it out than taking it on the chin and she burst into tears and said she wanted to go back to France immediately. Am not one of those men who is incapable of admitting when he is in the wrong, nor do I fancy having to cope with the backlash she might create in the event of her carrying out her threat to leave, so did my best to mollify her, but to no avail.

As last resort, played the vanity card and sat everyone down in front of the television and ran VTR, as they say in the business.

Did not realize I had filmed so much already. Tape ran back for what seemed like ages. Pressed PLAY button to be confronted with sight of Chad and my sister, in bed, in the nude, grappling each other in what looked like a *tableau vivant* of Heracles and the Nemean Lion.

'*Ça alors*,' said Marie-Celeste. Did not attempt to correct her.

Sunday, June 4th

Were I an Etonian, I would today be decorating my boater with wild flowers, opening a bottle of champagne and drinking a health to King George III on the occasion of his birthday. As it is, I am sitting here with a cup of lukewarm coffee in one hand and the property pages of the *Sunday Telegraph* in the other, staring out of the window at my tent, wondering if the rain will eventually wash off the combined beer, sick and urine stains with which it has become adorned in the last few days.

Am obviously very disappointed that my film had to be abandoned. But then, Orson Welles spent half a lifetime trying to make a film of *Don Quixote*.

Monday, June 5th

To dinner at the de Grande-Hautevilles'. Vanessa there. She has had a face-lift, of all things. Never mind looking like somebody else: she now looks like two different people.

Tuesday, June 6th

The anniversary of D-Day. Another reason to be proud one is English. Not that that would mean anything to the Cool Britannia brigade. The only Monty they've ever heard of is the full one.

Thursday, June 8th

To Kent to pick up a few more bits and bobs for Mother and check the house is in one piece.

Decided on a whim to make a detour via Great Barham – one of the great stamping grounds of my youth. It is forty-two years since I attended my first teenage dance there at The Fiddler's Elbow, and was intrigued to see how much the old place had changed in the intervening decades.

Arrived shortly before lunch and parked outside Fiddler's. Could not believe my eyes. It was exactly as I remembered it. The picture-postcard village green, the charming old cottages, the shops clustered round the duck pond.

What a joy and a relief it is to realize that, in the midst of so much change, something of the old England remains untouched by the heavy hand of commercialism, artificiality and New Labour. The opening words of my next column began to spring ready-formed into my mind.

At that moment a little old lady wearing a hat and lavender gloves emerged from one of the cottages. Seeing me, she gave a little smile.

'Good morning!' I cried. 'Miss Marple, I presume?'

She stopped and said, 'I beg your pardon?'

I gestured at the surroundings and said, 'It's just that this village is so marvellously . . . well . . . villagey. It's almost as if I had walked into a detective story and, lo and behold, here's Miss Marple, come to life.'

She frowned and said, 'Yes, I *am* Miss Marple.'

I said, 'You mean that's your real name?'

She said, 'It was when I got up this morning.'

Shook my head and said, 'I don't believe it.'

'I can't help that,' she said.

Said waggishly, 'The next thing you'll be telling me is that there's been a murder at the rectory.'

She said, 'How did you know?'

Happy Days CARD CO.

'Know what?' I said.

'About the murder at the rectory,' she said. 'It happened only last week. The Rector was found in the library with a dagger sticking out of his back. The police were baffled.'

I said, 'You must be joking.'

She said, 'I can't imagine why you should think I would joke about a dear old friend being murdered in such a horrible way.'

'No, of course not,' I said, trying to keep a straight face. 'I presume you solved the mystery?'

She looked at me and scowled. 'Don't be ridiculous,' she said. 'How could I possibly solve a murder mystery? I'm a retired schoolmistress, not some sort of amateur sleuth.' And she turned and walked off down the village street.

She may have been pulling my leg or she may not, but the first rule of investigative journalism is not to be 'fazed' by the unexpected.

To Village Shop next. Old-fashioned bell on spring tinkled reassuringly as I entered, transporting me back to an age of long-lost innocence. A nice-looking man of sixty-something was standing behind the beautifully polished wooden counter. He was in shirtsleeves and an old-fashioned grocer's apron. A pair of half-moon glasses dangled by a chain from his neck. Stood there for a moment or two just looking around, drinking in the atmosphere. It was everyone's idea of what a traditional village shop should be. Shelves filled with colourful jars of this and that, old-fashioned scales with weights, wooden draws with the words 'Rice', 'Flour', 'Sugar', 'Salt' etc. painted on them.

I said, 'Some things in England never change,' and ran my hand lightly over the polished wood of the counter. 'There's nothing to beat good English oak.'

'Yes,' he said. 'It is clever, isn't it?'

'Clever?' I said.

He said, 'It's some sort of composite material, I gather. A chap knocks it up by the yard in Camberwell.'

Could not conceal my surprise and disappointment. I said, 'What happened? Did the original get worm?'

'What original?' he said.

I said, 'Well, as I remember it, this shop was one of the oldest in the village. Victorian? Possibly earlier.'

He said, 'It was built about 1957, I gather. Mind you, it didn't look like this when I bought it. It had a lino floor,

Formica counter, frosted-glass shelving – absolutely ghastly. I had to tear everything out and start again.'

I said I could have sworn it looked just like it does now.

He said, 'That's memory for you. Actually, it was my interior designer's idea, this Olde World look. Personally I think it's rather naff. Smacks too much of TV costume drama, for my taste. The customers seem to like it, though. Not that they're here that much, except at weekends.'

I said, 'So you're not a local, then?'

He laughed and said, 'Good Lord, no. Who is these days? No, I was in corporate finance for years. Couldn't stand it. Took voluntary redundancy about five years ago. Always fancied myself as a shopkeeper. Can't imagine why. Bloody awful job, slicing ham all day. Hardly man's work. No money in it, either. One's chums try to support one, but most bring their grub and gargle down with them. Can't blame them, I suppose. It's half the price at Waitrose. In fact I'm thinking of chucking in the towel and moving back to town. Colliers Wood. Do you know it? SW19. One tries to keep one's SW low, but one can't be too choosy at my age.'

'I know it well,' I said. 'Nice village atmosphere. Meanwhile, you still sell traditional country fare, I take it?'

'Depends what you call traditional,' he said. 'Our prosciutto and pecorino mousse is made from a sixteenth-century Veronese recipe, and our *pâté de poisson aux asperges et fines herbes* is mentioned by Alphonse Daudet in his *Lettres de mon moulin.*'

I said, 'Actually, I was thinking more in terms of farm eggs, stone-ground bread, locally made sausages, freshly gathered field mushrooms – the kind of things one might expect to find in a typical farmhouse kitchen.'

He looked at me for a moment, then said, 'You've been watching too many TV commercials.'

Bought a tin of sardines to show willing, and went off for lunch at The Fiddler's. Had been looking forward to a good honest ploughman's and a pint of Kentish ale, but had to settle for seared scallops. They were quite tasty, though £12.95 seemed an awful lot of money for four bits of rubbery bi-valve – even if they had been hand-plucked from the seabed off the Irish coast

Was walking back to the car when a herd of cows came down the street with a young cowman in charge. Stood back on the pavement to let them through. At that moment two

tweedy women with hair like corrugated iron emerged from the Post Office. I smiled at the traditional country scene and took a deep breath.

'Ah,' I said. 'The sweet smell of the swollen udder!'

At that moment one of the cows dropped a huge pat right in the middle of the road.

'Well, really!' said the first woman loudly.

'So unattractive,' said the second.

'And so sloppy,' said the first.

'One tries to keep the place clean,' said the second, 'but one wonders why one bothers.'

Decided to put these two obvious townies in their place and called out to the cowman as he passed, 'Morning, drover. What price are milkers fetching on the market these days?'

'Don't ask me,' he said. 'I'm just a sociology student trying to earn some pocket money in the holidays.'

Got back to the car to find I had been given a parking ticket. Am seriously considering withdrawing my support from the Countryside Alliance.

Friday, June 9th

At dinner last night at the Varney-Birches', sat next to a plump woman with grey hair tied in a bun who said, 'You don't remember me, do you?'

Was completely taken aback, since I had never to my know-ledge set eyes on her in my life, and though I had been intro-duced to her when we arrived, had already forgotten her name.

'Liz Stobart,' she said. 'Liz Muspratt-Johnson as was.'

I said I was very sorry, but she had the advantage of me.

She said, 'Oh, don't be so pompous. You must remember. Oak Tree Lodge Summer Ball 1965. You came over on a coach with the Fenton boys and landed me for the Supper Dance – worse luck for you, though not for me.' And she nudged me playfully – and rather painfully – in the ribs.

I laughed and said, 'Oh dear, I'm afraid I wasn't very good with girls in those days.'

'*Plus ça change*, apparently,' she said.

'Actually,' I said, 'I have been married, but I'm divorced.'

'Oh, goody gumdrops,' she said. 'Me, too.'

Had a sudden vision, not dissimilar to that of Saul of Tarsus on the Damascus road, of a large, unwieldy creature swathed in pink taffeta suddenly stopping in the middle of a quickstep, seizing me by the shoulders and saying, 'I'll be man now!'

I said, 'Actually, I'm quite tied up these days.'

'Ooh,' she said. 'Naughty, but nice!'

I said, 'I mean, I'm very busy. I'm a writer. I don't have much time for anything else.'

She said, 'That's what you said that evening when I sug-gested we should sit out the next few dances on the lacrosse pitch.'

I said, 'As I remember, I was hoping to become a barrister in those days.'

'And did you?' she said.

'No,' I said.

'I didn't think you would,' she said.

Do not believe my worst enemies could accuse me of social ineptitude, but could see no future in continuing this pointless discussion with a woman whose only point of connection with me was that I had once danced a quickstep with her in Sussex nearly four decades ago. Was on the point of turning to Paula Batty on my left when I suddenly heard Liz saying, 'You probably remember my brother, Harold. He was at Fenton at the same time as you.'

I said, 'I remember him very well. "Prat" Johnson. Good heavens, I haven't thought about him in years. Whatever became of him?'

She said, 'He's about to become deputy features editor of the *Daily Telegraph*.'

Can imagine that a lot of people in my position who, suddenly faced with this information, would have started back-tracking madly and remembering that, for all his little faults, he had once been their best friend. However, was in no mood for party games.

'Good for him,' I said.

She said, 'And for you, too, if you play your cards right. Could you pass the salt please?'

I can't imagine what she has in mind, if anything. All I know is that every time I turned in her direction she winked at me. If she seriously thinks that I am interested in taking up ball-room dancing again after all this time, she's got another think coming.

On the other hand, one has one's future to consider – whatever that may be.

Was saying goodnight to Verena Varney-Birch when I felt a hand fumbling with my jacket. Turned to find Liz looking coy.

'Slow, slow, quick, quick, slow,' she said.

In the car, found a note in my jacket pocket with a telephone number on it. Was interested to note it was an 0208 number. Oh dear.

Saturday, June 10th

Great excitement. The Millennium footbridge across the Thames was opened today by the Queen. As a landmark in the cultural, social and commercial life of this great city, it is second to none.

Have been one of Norman Foster's biggest fans ever since being stuck in Stansted Airport for three hours when my flight to Guernsey was delayed due to fog. No one knows how to make use of indoor space more imaginatively than Norman, and though I have not yet had a chance to see the Reichstag in Berlin, I understand from those who have that it is even more impressive than Stansted.

Am less familiar with Ove Arup's work, though have always thought of him as a prince among structural engineers. The Prince of Denmark, one might say!

At all events, cannot wait to get down to the City and straddle Old Father Thames in person.

Sunday, July 11th

Interesting footnote to London Garden Squares Day on Dull Men's Club web site to the effect that, while Belgrave, St James's, Trafalgar and Manchester are truly square, Sloane, Eaton, Chester, Grosvenor, Berkeley, Onslow and Ladbroke are in fact rectangular.

Monday, June 12th

I can't believe it. They've closed the Millennium bridge already. Apparently it wobbles when you walk on it – so much so that some people were staggering from side to side, as if drunk, children were screaming with terror, and pensioners were falling on their knees and praying to God for help.

Mollie Marsh-Gibbon said, 'Trust Ove to make a balls-up of a simple job. The Scandinavians know as much about foot-bridges as my plumber knows about the metaphysical poets.'

Tuesday, June 13th

My concern for Mother increases daily. In Sainsbury's in Streatham High Road this morning we were standing by the cold meats, trying to weigh the merits of 'oak-smoked' ham against those of 'honey-roasted', when she suddenly seized my forearm and said in a loud stage whisper, 'Don't look now, but that woman over there slept with my husband on the first night of our honeymoon.'

Since the only other shopper in sight was an elderly black lady in headscarf and slippers, can only assume that Mother is finally going round the bend. Am not aware that Dad ever had an affair with anyone – certainly not on his honeymoon night, and certainly not with a black lady in Streatham.

After she had gone to bed with a tray, suggested to P that perhaps we should seriously consider looking at some old people's homes in the neighbourhood.

James said he had never heard anything so awful in his life. In Aboriginal families it is considered an honour to have one's grandparents living under same roof as everyone else. Indeed, the older generation consider it their duty to pass their wisdom on to the younger members of the family. In this way they play as full a part in family life as everyone else.

I said I did not think that the words that Mother comes out with these days are either wise or suitable to be passed on to her grandchildren.

James said, 'The Aborigines believe that wisdom is in the ear of the listener.'

I said that no one has more respect for the Aborigines than I do, and that I perfectly understood the regard in which he held them, but reminded him that this was Mitcham, not Wagga Wagga, and, fast as I believe society in this country is falling apart, I thought we are still some way from the Stone Age.

He promptly got up and left the room. I think I made my point.

Wednesday, June 14th

Apropos last night's little cultural ding-dong, was in local bookshop browsing through an excellent new history of the Thirties when I came across a very interesting section on King George V – another great man that Mr Blair and his New Labour pals have doubtless airbrushed from English history.

Fascinated to discover that, despite his many European cousins, he had no time for abroad.

'Amsterdam, Rotterdam and all the dams. Damme if I'll go,' he said once. And who could blame him? Went to Rotterdam myself once. Never again.

How very refreshing to find that I am not alone in thinking there is nothing odd in wearing one's favourite old clothes. Were I to wear detachable collars, can quite imagine that I, like His Majesty, would put in the same collar stud I had used since adolescence.

Formality in dress and behaviour is very much pooh-poohed nowadays in this laissez-faire, let-it-all-hang-out and damn-what-anyone-else-thinks shambles we call modern Britain, but we could all do worse than take a leaf out of the old King's book. And, though I feel that not allowing people to wear spectacles indoors without permission might be taking formality a little too far, one can quite understand his being shocked at the sight of Mahatma Gandhi toddling around Buckingham Palace with his knees showing.

Do not know whether Queen Mary really was as much of a kleptomaniac as the author suggests, but the fact remains that the crowds along the parade route at the 1935 Silver Jubilee were so dense that dozens fainted, and when the King died a million people queued for hours to pay respect to his body as it lay in state in Westminster Hall.

Mind you, those were the days when the first question in the army exam for officers was, 'How many times in each twenty-four hours are the bowels of a mule moved?'

Tony Blair may sneer, but it was knowing things like that that made Britain great.

Thursday, June 15th

Am beginning to think national decline more rapid than I had imagined. Went to bed last night in tent to find complete stranger curled up in my sleeping bag. When I asked him what on earth he thought he was doing, he said, 'Trying to get a good night's sleep like everyone else.'

I said, 'Don't you have a home to go to?' He said, 'If you can call a cardboard box behind the Savoy Hotel a home.'

In normal circumstances would have given him his marching orders in no uncertain terms, but suddenly into my head, unbidden, came the story of the Good Samaritan. For two pins would have invited him in for a meal and told him to make himself comfortable on the floor, but was afraid that Mother might wander down in the night and stumble over him, and in her present mental condition there's no knowing who she might think he is. Our Lord Himself, knowing her.

Was also, frankly, not very keen on the idea of sleeping in the same bag where he had just been.

Left him where he was, and slept on floor myself. Much less well, I may say, but do not feel in the circumstances I have any reason to complain.

Friday, June 16th

Am not one of those journalists who sees everything that happens to him in life and everyone he meets as potential copy, but am suddenly very excited about the idea of devoting next week's piece to homelessness in London. In normal circumstances would do a straightforward 'think' piece, but on this occasion have decided to experience life in a cardboard box for myself and tell it as it really is.

First things first, though. Must find a suitable box.

Saturday, June 17th

To Sainsbury's first thing to pick out a box. Size is what matters most, though am naturally concerned that any brand or product names should give the right impression. To bed down beneath the name of a gourmet food – potted shrimps, say, or ready-to-eat veal hongroise – may not send one's fellow dossers quite the right message. Similarly, a box that until recently contained a duck-down duvet or a 24-inch television set could lead them to suppose that one is not quite one of them.

Decided, therefore, to go for something completely uncontroversial, like lavatory paper or washing-up liquid.

In the event, all they could offer me were empty wine cartons. How they imagine anyone could sleep in a space reserved for a dozen bottles of Chilean Chardonnay is beyond my comprehension. Unless one were a Japanese businessman, of course.

Tried Safeway with similar lack of success.

Am very glad I decided to write this as a documentary feature. Until one has actually tried to sleep rough, one has no idea of the unexpected problems it throws up.

In the end had no alternative but to go to local dump. Man at gate directed me to next available skip. Explained that I had come to look for something.

He said, 'Are you trade?'

'No,' I said, 'social services.'

'Take your pick,' he said.

Looked in all the skips, but could see nothing but black plastic bags, broken chairs and dead foliage. Was beginning to despair when spotted man hauling flattened pile of what looked suspiciously like old removal cartons out of back of newish Volvo.

Called across, 'I could use those if you don't need them.'

He said, 'Help yourself. Moving, are you?'

'In a manner of speaking,' I said.

He said, 'I've got a old black-and-white telly and a rather out-of-date, but perfectly serviceable, music centre in the back of the car if you're interested. I know only too well what a drain on the purse a move can be.'

I said, 'Actually, I'm planning to sleep rough. Behind the Savoy. Do you know where I mean?'

'Ah, well,' he said, 'a television and a music centre won't be much use to you, then. You could always try and sell them, I suppose. Anyway, good luck.'

Suddenly realized that he had got hold of the wrong end of the stick. Went to explain, but he was already in the driving seat and reversing out. Funnily enough, my own music centre has shown signs of going on the blink recently.

Waited till the coast was clear at about eight p.m., dressed in clothes from jumble bag and Mother's mittens, and sneaked off to the Savoy, taking carton, sleeping bag that John Julius carried round India, Thailand and Australia during his year off, discarded blanket from dog's basket, a couple of old cushions, a medicine bottle full of whisky, and some cheese sandwiches wrapped in copy of Chad's *Independent*. Parked Polo on Embankment and made my way up side street next to world's most famous hotel.

Confronted by depressing sight of assorted shelters made of plywood and cardboard with square holes cut in sides, some of them covered with old blankets, bed covers, sacks and black plastic sheeting. Inside, could make out shapes of bodies curled up under more old blankets, sleeping bags etc. Several men and women dressed in ancient overcoats held together with string and woolly hats were sitting around in a circle, smoking roll-ups, drinking out of plastic cups and staring empty-eyed into the darkness.

The voices of gay young things in tails and feathers or elaborate fancy dress, bursting from the River Entrance after some smart debutante ball, laughing and joking and saying 'Let's go on to The Four Hundred!', echoed in my head as I stood there surveying the scene.

Approached group and said, 'Mind if I doss down for the night?'

No one said a word, or even registered my presence. Repeated my question.

One of them said, 'I don't mind if you jump in the river. I do from time to time. Doesn't help, though.'

Erected my pathetic shelter in the only available space and made up bed inside as best I could. Although it was a warm

June evening, a cold wind swirled round the corner, blowing litter about. Was glad I had put on extra T-shirt.

Sat down cross-legged in empty space and took bottle out of overcoat pocket.

'Whisky, anyone?' I said.

One of them, a large man with a huge bushy beard and a mass of tangled hair, said, 'Blended or single malt?' in a surprisingly educated voice.

'It's only Sainsbury's best, I'm afraid,' I said.

'That's fine by me,' said the man. 'I was afraid you were going to say Johnnie Walker. Can't abide Johnny Walker. Red label or black.'

'What a lucky escape,' I said.

He said, 'Are you trying to be funny?'

'A mere pleasantry,' I said.

'I don't like pleasantries,' the man said. 'And I don't like you much, either. There's something not quite right about you. Not quite genuine.'

Some of the others muttered in agreement.

One said, 'You're not doing this for a bet, are you?'

I said nothing could be further from the truth.

Another said, 'He could be one of them nosy-parker, churchy buggers, come to tell us Jesus loves us.'

I gave an airy laugh. 'Do I honestly look like a churchy type?' I said.

He said, 'You can never tell with them churchy types. One minute they're just like you and me, the next they're asking you if you're saved and other likewise bollocks.'

A third said, 'Perhaps he's another of those newspaper people, come to take the piss out of us.'

I laughed again.

'Let's hope you're not, otherwise you'll be laughing on the other side of your face.'

'Like that last one who came,' said the second man.

'He didn't come back in a hurry,' said the third.

The man with the educated voice said, 'Don't I know you from somewhere? Your face looks familiar.'

Delighted though I was at the sound of the words that every aspiring media figure hopes to hear, did not like to suggest he might well have seen my face in an old copy of the *Mitch & Toot* – possibly crumpled inside one of his boots.

Decided to play it safe by saying it was perfectly possible,

I'd been on the streets for quite a while, chances are we'd dossed down together in a shop doorway somewhere.

The man said, 'Frankly, I couldn't give a bugger. Are you going to let me have some of that whisky or not?'

By the time it had been round the entire circle two or three times, there wasn't a drop left. Can't say I was sorry.

Decided to withdraw while I was winning, and crept away to my box. Oddly enough, it was rather more comfortable than the tent, and for a brief moment I could see the attractions of life as a down-and-out. Companionship, complete absence of responsibility, and no one peeing on you while you're asleep. They have a special place in the corner for that.

Was fast asleep when woken shortly after eleven by the sound of voices and a certain amount of metallic clanking. Poked head out of rudimentary doorway to see a crowd gathered around a couple of women who appeared to be dispensing something from a large round metal container on top of some sort of trolley.

One of the women spotted me and headed in my direction.

'Hot soup?' she said. 'It's cream of vegetable tonight. Yum yum. Very good for you. I made it myself.'

Suddenly realized to my horror that I knew her. It was none other than my erstwhile fiancée and the daughter of my one-time boss and chairman of Harley Preston, Amanda Trubshawe.

Tried to scramble back inside the box, but too late.

'Simon!' she shrieked. 'What on earth are you doing here?'

Gesticulated to her to keep her voice down, but she always was a noisy girl, and women in puffa jackets and headscarves who do charity work rarely become quieter with age.

By now my fellow derelicts were looking across in my direction and talking among themselves.

'I'm undercover,' I whispered.

She said, 'I can see you're under cover, but why? What's happened to you?'

One or two of the men had begun to shuffle over to see what was going on. 'Can't talk now,' I said.

'Why not?' she said. 'Is there something wrong with your voice? What's happened to you? This is dreadful.'

One of the men said in a menacing tone, 'Do you know this fellow?'

'I did,' she said. 'I was once engaged to him. He was young

and good-looking and full of promise in those days. Oh, this is dreadful!' And she burst into tears and walked quickly away to join her companion.

I said, 'She must be thinking of someone else.'

The man said, 'We were all someone else once,' and they drifted away.

Soon afterwards the two women packed up and prepared to leave. Suddenly Amanda ran across.

'I'm so sorry, Simon,' she said, and thrust a piece of paper into my hand. Discovered after she had gone that it was a £20 note.

Decided enough was enough. Folded box, but before stealing away, went over to where men were still sitting and handed one of them the money.

He said, 'I knew there was something odd about you the moment I set eyes on you.'

I said, 'We're all brothers under the skin' and left.

That gave him something to think about, I'll bet.

Sunday, June 18th

Morning spent writing column about my low-life experiences. Have titled it, intriguingly, 'Down and Out at the Savoy'.

Coincidentally, a fellow chronicler of *la condition humaine 2000*, Martin Amis, was on *The South Bank Show* this evening. Apparently he is a lot smaller than one might think, though this is not evident from his many television appearances, since he is nearly always sitting down and, more often than not, in close-up. Am wondering if too much smoking has stunted his growth.

Have not got round to reading his autobiography yet, but have read all the interviews and reviews and extracts, so feel I know enough about it to be able to keep my end up at dinner parties in this neck of the wood, if not further afield.

Interested to read about the tricky relationship he had with Kingsley. Cannot imagine what it feels like to be in competition with one's father. But then, of course, Dad wasn't a famous writer. Indeed he wasn't a writer at all: he was a chicken farmer, and not a very famous one at that. The most I ever saw him write was a cheque, and that was obviously a huge effort. Hope he would have been proud of what I have done in my life, and feel sure he would have found it easier to express pleasure in my efforts than Kingers did in Martin's.

On the other hand, have no difficulty empathizing with M's guilt over his divorce. Like him, I swore I would never repeat my parents' mistakes, and blow me down if I haven't ended up as a divorcé myself. Can only hope John Julius will not be tempted to follow my example.

Cannot see myself marrying an exotic American writer, like Amis *fils*, and starting a new family, or being described as the Cliff Richard of the literary world, or being able to command the princely advances he does. On the other hand, see no reason why, when I am gone, John Julius should not be as proud of me as Martin is of Kingers.

First things first, though, I must get down to a novel. Have got an idea simmering away about tramps and derelicts, though am also seriously tempted to start a children's story. J. K. Rowling has had it all her own way for far too long now. A little serious competition won't do her any harm. As Martin himself said in an interview, it is through our children that we learn about ourselves.

Realized as I was dropping off to sleep that today is Father's Day. John Julius had evidently forgotten, too. Like father, like son.

Monday, June 19th

Woke up to realize that I knew exactly who the tramp with the educated voice was last night. It was Charlie Ibstock. We arrived together at Fenton as New Squits in Footer Term 1961, but did not remain quite as close as we might have done – thanks largely to my being made a Top Swine a term ahead of him and being obliged to give him a Double Jankers for coming into House Convoc wearing a jockstrap on his head. Have not actually set eyes on him since we both left – I to the University of South Northants, he to join Brook Partridge to train as an accountant.

Had supposed from the frequent accounts of his exploits in the *OF News* that he had made his way in the world in no uncertain terms. At one point, I seem to remember, he was quite a big cheese in Crédit Belge First Chicago in Abu Dhabi, but clearly something must have gone seriously wrong somewhere along the line.

Despite our differences at school, would not dream of including his name in the 'Where Are They Now?' section of *OF News* willy-nilly. On the other hand, feel it would be a kindness to his many OF friends, who must be wondering why he has disappeared from view, to let the secretary know that he is still alive and, as far as one can make out, kicking.

Have therefore penned a note, marked Private and Confidential, to Tommy Thompson, describing my meeting with Ibstock – or Ibo, as he was known to everyone in Toggers' Room – and suggesting that if anybody is interested in contacting him, he is to be found in a cardboard box behind the Savoy Hotel. Feel I have done my duty by Ibstock, by my fellow OFs, and by the principles by which we lived at Fenton all those years ago and still do to this day. *'Conjuncti Perstamus'* – 'We Stand Together.' What is the point in a school having a motto if one does not cleave to it?

Am only hoping that Amanda Trubshawe does not feel obliged to inform her family and friends of what she mistakenly perceives to be my own fall from grace.

Tuesday, June 20th

The first day of Royal Ascot. Am not a racing man per se, but have not missed a Royal Procession in years. It is one of the glories of our national life, and one that Mr Prescott and his pals sneer at at their peril.

According to the woman who was hired to describe the fashion on BBC television, the 'in' colours this year are grey, biscuit, fuschia and pale sorbet pink, and feathers and flowers are the inspiration for most people's outfits.

Glad to see that, as usual, the Queen is no slave to fashion. Her lime-and-yellow viscose-and-cotton dress by Hardy Amies a triumph. However, am far from convinced that Princess Margaret looks her best in apricot.

The Queen Mother played safe in pale blue.

Very much like the cut of Edinburgh's jib on these occasions. The black coat and topper so much more elegant than Wales's more conventional grey. He always looks as though he is on his way to a wedding – and often is, of course.

Much talk in the papers of Prince William's eighteenth birthday – though why the Queen chose tomorrow as the day on which to throw a party to celebrate her family's various milestones is a mystery to me. The Queen Mother's long anticipated 100th is on Aug. 4, Princess Margaret's 70th is on Aug.

21, Princess Anne's 50th is on Aug. 15 and Prince Andrew's 40th was on Feb. 19. Prince William – or Wills as my sister will insist on referring to him with unjustified familiarity – is the only one whose birthday actually falls tomorrow, yet he's the only one out of all of them who can't be there. Surely HM must have known he'd be revising for his A-levels? Perhaps she is more out of touch with everyday life than we realize.

Not that it makes a scrap of difference to me when they pull the rug back and kick their legs in the air, since I have not received an invitation and do not expect to. I have no particular desire to be there, but one would have liked to have been asked.

Wednesday, June 21st

Prince William's eighteenth. Happy birthday, Your Royal Highness, and long may you reign. Not that I shall be here to see you crowned, more's the pity.

Royal Procession well up to standard. Queen charming in coral, Queen Mother gracious in pink, Princess Anne in blue. 'Her lack of vanity is very attractive,' said female commentator. Could not agree more. Have always had a soft spot for her and have never quite been able to make out what she sees in Tim Laurence. But then what can Priscilla possibly see in Chad?

Commentator herself wearing pink nightdress and felt Stetson.

No sign of my piece, however. Rang Sheila at office to ask what had happened. She said she'd enquire and ring me back.

When she did, it was to deliver the astounding news that the editor thought it was too far-fetched and why didn't I tackle a subject people could relate to, like traffic wardens?

No comment.

Thursday, June 22nd

Papers full of last night's do at Windsor. Not surprised the Royal Procession was late arriving. All the usual suspects on the guest list – the Spains, the Greeces, the Frosts – plus one or two surprise names, including Colin Montgomerie, the golfer.

Not entirely clear which 80 out of the 600 invitees were invited to dinner. Am also wondering whose idea it was to invite the bulk of the guests at ten, ply them with canapés and then serve them with breakfast.

No one is readier to tackle a full cooked English than yours truly, and though I have never acquired a taste for black pudding, I would be the first in the queue, spooning on the scrambled eggs, sausages and bacon with the best of them. Not at eleven thirty at night, though. Perhaps everybody held back and there was a rush just before two when the cry went up for last orders.

Incidentally, would be very interested to know how the royal chef does his kedgeree.

According to Mother's *Daily Mail*, at one point during the dancing Sir Tim Rice sprang on to the stage, seized the microphone, and gave a spirited rendering of 'It's All Over Now' by the Rolling Stones. Whether this was by Royal Command or merely a spur-of-the-moment birthday tribute is not entirely clear, but cannot help feeling that, given the ages and identities of the two older birthday girls, he could have chosen a number with a slightly more tactful title.

Dread to think what George V would have had to say.

Friday, June 23rd

Midsummer's Eve already. It hardly seems possible. Mentioned it to Mother. She said, 'The nights will soon be drawing in.'

Royal Procession somewhat diminished. Queen in lilac with chiffon overblouse and Freddie Fox hat. The Dean of Windsor was in the third carriage, which was surprising – though not, presumably, for him.

The female commentator said, 'Friday is always a young people's day and this year there are lots of short legs.'

Short brains too.

Came in after tea, following a more than usually hectic walk with Woodhouse, to find a message from P on my desk saying that a Robert Harbinson had rung from the *Daily Telegraph* and that he needed to speak to me at the earliest possible opportunity. The Weekend Section is involved in a major new project, but they are missing one important element and I am the only person they can think of who can possibly fill the gap.

This is the best news I have had all year. Robert is one of the *Telegraph*'s most influential editors, and though I would not claim close friendship, we got on very well when we met at the

Varney-Birches' Christmas party. Was sorry he did not feel able to use my idea for a series on Britain's Best Country Hotels. It certainly didn't seem like a hackneyed theme to me. However, he did promise to get back to me and he has been as good as his word. Do I detect the hand of Miss Muspratt-Johnson in this?

Cannot imagine what this big project can possibly be, unless it has something to do with country hotels. It would certainly explain why he is so keen to get hold of me.

Unfortunately, have not been able to get hold of *him*. Have rung several times, only to be greeted by his 'voicemail'. I must have left at least four messages, the last one just before eight o'clock, so it doesn't look as though he will be getting back to me today, or indeed this week. Cannot remember when I was last so frustrated.

Said as much to P who said, 'How about last week when you turned on to watch that late-night programme on Channel 5 about sex films and found they'd put on a football match instead?'

I pointed out that there is the world of difference between sex films and adult entertainment.

She said, 'There's certainly a world of difference between a sex film and a semi-final between two unpronounceable clubs in central Europe.'

When I asked her to name them, she said, 'I've just told you: they're unpronounceable.'

Went to bed in an even worse mood than before, if such a thing were possible.

Saturday, June 24th

Bit of a drama with Mother last night. She will insist on sleeping surrounded by what Priscilla and Chad are pleased to call their merchandise and anyone else would call junk.

Why on earth they think anyone would be remotely interested in wasting good money on a theatrical costume of a nineteenth-century general I cannot for the life of me imagine. It is moth-eaten, sweat-stained and extremely smelly, and I do not believe for a moment that it was once worn by George Grossmith in a production of *The Pirates of Penzance*. Neither, I suspect, will even the most gullible of the punters who spend their Saturdays and Sundays picking through the rubbish that passes for 'antiques' in Lavender Lane market.

The fact that the uniform is displayed on an equally unsavoury-looking tailor's dummy merely shows up its many faults.

Whether Mother was aware that it had been left in her room I can't quite make out. All I know is that she woke up in the middle of night, saw this figure standing by her bed and thought it was a burglar, if not worse.

Being still exiled in the tent, was not ideally placed to reassure her, nor, unfortunately, to prevent her ringing 999. The first I knew about it was when a police car came screaming to a halt outside the house, blue light flashing, siren blasting. At least it wasn't the same team I had trouble with over the John Julius incident.

The upshot is that Mother is now under sedation in Mitcham General. The doctor has assured her that she is only suffering from shock and this is merely a precaution; she should be out again in a couple of days. However, have a feeling he is more worried than he lets on. It's more than can be said for Chad, who said that he didn't think it was fear that had got her into such a state as much as excitement at the sight of a strange man in her room in the middle of the night.

'She must have thought her luck had changed,' he said.

It's a pity his hasn't. The sooner my sister recognizes him for the boorish sponger he is, the better for all concerned. Also, as I have had cause to mention earlier, I don't care for the way he looks at Marie-Celeste. Luckily, she seems not to have noticed. But then she doesn't seem to notice an awful lot of what goes on in this house.

Sunday, June 25th

Life continues to be one long round of worries. Most worrying of all is why I seem to be the one in this family who has to shoulder them all.

Have moved into Mother's room while she's in hospital and was enjoying my first real night's sleep for as long as I can remember, when was roughly awoken by P wanting to know if John Julius was with me. It was four o'clock and he still wasn't in. Did I know where he was?

Said that her guess was as good as mine. As I understood it, he was going to a birthday party given by a cor-anglais player at the music college and that we were to expect him when we saw him. Was there a problem?

She said it was only that she thought she had heard the front door open and what sounded like a taxi driving away, but that when she had gone to make sure he was all right there was no sign of him. Where did I think he was?

I said I hadn't the faintest idea. Perhaps he'd been abducted by a mad taxi driver. She said she didn't think that was the sort of thing one should joke about. London is full of weirdos these days and one is always reading about young people who disappear without trace, never to be seen again.

I said I thought she was being ridiculously melodramatic, but that if she was really worried I would come and take a look for myself.

Hunted high and low in the house, but no sign of him anywhere. Surprised to find front door unlocked, suggesting that someone really had come in and, presumably, gone out again. But who? And where?

Was suddenly rather worried. P said, 'Why not try ringing him on his mobile?'

Did so and was enormously relieved to hear his voice. Asked him where the hell he was.

He said, 'Outside in the street. Walking up and down. Getting some fresh air.'

Asked him how long he was planning to spend there.

'Back any moment,' he said.

'There you are,' I said to P. 'All that fuss over nothing.'

She looked suitably sheepish, and we both went back to bed.

Was woken half an hour later to find her shaking my

shoulder and saying, 'He still hasn't come in. Shouldn't you go and get him?'

Got up again, pulled on dressing gown, and went out into street. No sign of anyone. Walked round into Honeysuckle Grove and glanced casually into semi-darkness. Was able to see nothing at first and then spotted large shape on ground about halfway along. Ran up to it to find it was John Julius, curled up on his side in the gutter, completely out for the count.

Somehow managed to shake him into consciousness. He opened his eyes and said, 'Oh hi, Dad. It's not time to get up yet, is it?'

Had almost got him on his feet when I stumbled and fell and, before I knew what, was rolling in the gutter myself.

John Julius roared with laughter and said, 'I think you're more pissed than I am.'

At that moment looked up to see our glamorous next-door neighbour walking past, dressed up to the nines, presumably on her way home from some fancy nightclub.

'You two look as though you've been having fun,' she said, and before I could say a word she had rounded the corner and disappeared.

It's bad enough that a woman I was seriously thinking of asking round for a drink now thinks she's living next door to a couple of alcoholics, but finally got JJ indoors to discover that, without bothering to ask first, he had borrowed my Aquascutum double-breasted pinstripe which was, until now, in pristine condition and is now impregnated with the smell of dog doings.

Where have I gone wrong?

Monday, June 26th

Tried all morning to get through to Robert Harbinson, but without success, so decided to take bull by horns and go down to the *Telegraph* in person. This was not the sort of opportunity I could afford to miss.

Got there much later than anticipated, thanks to the Docklands Light Railway breaking down twice – and that was before we had actually got out into the open.

Had a bit of an argy-bargy with the commissionaire at Canary Wharf, who absolutely refused to let me in, even though I assured him that I was a bona-fide journalist and even invited him to strip me naked if he seriously believed I was carrying a bomb.

In the middle of it all, Robert came strolling out of the lift with some colleagues. I called out his name and he broke off and came over and shook me warmly by the hand. Could not resist giving the commissionaire a look.

'What brings you to this Tower of Babel?' Robert said, for all the world as if he didn't know. Had no intention of playing his game – whatever that might have been – so said casually, 'I'm just on my way to a meeting with one of the features editors at the *Independent*, actually. We're hatching a little idea which I think might work very well. So does he.'

When he asked who, exactly, I pulled out the first name I could think of.

'Adam Vickers,' I said.

'That's odd,' he said. 'He's just left to work for us.'

I laughed and said, 'Not on one of your projects, by any chance?'

'No,' he said.

He was about to walk off when I said, 'By the way, did you leave a message on my answering machine?'

He said, 'Oh, so I did. We're doing a feature on country-house hotels and of course I immediately thought of you.'

I said, 'I do have quite a lot on my plate, but I'd certainly be very interested in giving a helping hand.'

He said, 'Good man. The thing is, you remember you were telling me at the Varney-Birches' about that old umbrella stand your uncle left you in his will?'

'The one in the shape of a rattan duck?' I said.

'That's the one,' he said. 'We're photographing some typical items that sum up English country houses and wonder if we could borrow it for a couple of days?'

Was reminded of the famous scene in *Sunset Boulevard* when Cecil B. de Mille sends for Gloria Swanson and she turns up at the studio where she was once a star, thinking he is going to offer her a part and revive her career, only to discover he just wants to borrow her car.

Mind you, in Gloria's case there had been a career to revive.

Tuesday, June 27th

The *Daily Mail* has an interesting article by that excellent writer Ray Connolly about going with his screenwriter son to the Glastonbury Festival.

Have never met Connolly or his son or been to Glastonbury or ever considered doing so. Perhaps I should. To judge from the photograph of the two of them standing there smiling together like old friends, it could be a perfect opportunity for John Julius and me to let our hair down together and get to know each other as people.

The more I thought about it, the more the idea of spending a day or two in the magical land of King Arthur and his knights, living in a tepee, painting one's face, and swaying with the crowd to the sound of Rolf Harris with his didgeridoo singing 'Stairway to Heaven', seemed irresistible.

When JJ emerged this morning, I came straight out with it.

'Would you be at all interested,' I said, 'in spending a couple of days with me at Glastonbury?'

'No,' he said.

One can but try.

Afternoon spent hunting for rattan-duck umbrella stand. Finally spotted it at very back of cupboard in spare room, buried beneath a pile of Serendipity junk. After much struggling, pulled it out to find head had come off.

Am a firm believer in casting one's bread on the water, but only if one can be certain it will float first.

Mother still in hospital. Went to see her this evening.

She said, 'Oh, there you are.'

Had a long chat about this and that. As I was leaving, she said, 'You don't happen to have seen my son anywhere, I suppose?'

And she's due out any day now.

Wednesday, June 28th

Do not know who it was who said about life that when one door closes, another one opens, but in my experience when one door closes, the next one slams shut in your face. However, today could prove the exception to the rule.

Was riffling through last week's copy of the *Mitch & Toot* when my eye was caught by a item announcing that the ITV *Antiques Road Show*-type programme, *So What's It Worth?*, is coming to the Colliers Wood Masonic Rooms next Saturday. Anyone who has an object of some sort which he or she thinks might be of value or of interest to the team of experts – a picture perhaps, or a piece of china, or an item of furniture – is asked to turn up with it at the main entrance at nine o'clock.

Would not normally consider attending such an event. However, the questing mind of the journalist never rests. Not only is this a natural for next week's column, but who knows where it may lead? It is not unheard of for members of the public to catch the eye of a producer and find themselves being asked to leave their names and addresses.

Ted Moult, Irene Thomas, Edward Enfield – these are just a few of the legendary broadcasters who were mere members of the public one moment and stars the next, for no other reason except that they caught someone's eye. Or in their case, ear.

Spent rest of day in the cellar looking out one of our most prized family heirlooms – a large and rare bronze head of Lord Nelson.

Mother came home in the evening. Delighted and relieved to find she is quite her old self again. Showed her head of Nelson and she greeted it as though it were an old friend.

She said, 'We're related, of course, through my mother's side.'

Am surprised she has never thought to mention this before – though, funnily enough, have always suspected that my adventurous spirit must have its wellspring in some rare figure in history, and the news that I have the blood of one of Britain's greatest heroes coursing through my veins confirms it in no uncertain terms.

If this does not guarantee me and my head many minutes of valuable air time, I don't know what will.

Pleasure at having Mother back in family fold somewhat diminished by having to abandon comparative comfort of boxroom bed for rough embrace of sleeping bag and musty odour of soiled canvas.

Thursday, June 29th

Just when one thinks life can't hold any more surprises, another comes along to make one wonder if we have been taken over in the night by extraterrestrial beings who have turned our brains into Christmas pudding.

According to a full-page article in the *Daily Mail*, the reason the Millennium bridge wobbles is because when people walk on it they do so in the wrong way. Instead of strolling across normally, they suddenly, for no reason at all, start marching in perfect unison, as if taking part in Trooping the Colour. This appears to have come as much of a surprise to Foster and Arup as it has to everyone else. They say the bridge is going to be closed for the foreseeable future. Like half the nation's intellects, apparently.

Friday, June 30th

Speaking of which, came down to breakfast this morning to find Mother sprinkling washing-up powder on her All-Bran.

Oh dear, oh dear.

July

Saturday, July 1st

Up early and off to Masonic Rooms, carrying head in Sainsbury's bag. Arrived to find long queue of amateur collectors clutching pathetic items which have obviously been gathering dust for years in cellars and attics and which they fondly imagine are going to be revealed on television as unexpected treasures.

Woman behind me could not wait to show me her hideous Victorian chamber pot. Was strongly tempted to say that those sort of things are two a penny, but decided joke would be lost on her.

Was about to show her head when handle of bag broke and it fell face down on pavement.

She said, 'I knew Nelson sustained a lot of injuries, but I never realized he broke his nose,' and shrieked with laughter. Did not feel inclined to join in.

Doors opened by plump young woman with clipboard who directed us towards wooden tables to have our objects evaluated by a team of 'experts'.

When it came to my turn, she pointed me to a table marked Knick-Knacks. I said I thought there must be some mistake.

When she asked me why, I said I would hardly call a rare bronze head of Lord Nelson a knick-knack.

She said, 'We'll be the judge of that.'

Was waiting my turn, holding head under arm, when I heard a voice say, 'Not that dreary old thing, surely?' Turned to my left to find Priscilla standing in the next line clutching a small plastic bag.

When I asked what on earth she was doing there, she said, 'Same as you, presumably. Trying to make some money.'

She rummaged in the bag and produced a square china egg-cup covered with hideous, brightly coloured, geometric designs.

I said I couldn't imagine a prime-time television programme was going to waste its viewers' time or its advertisers' money on some nonsense she had picked up for a quid from a bric-a-brac stall.

She said, 'Actually, it was 50p, and I think it's rather special.'

At that moment her part of the queue was redirected to a table on the far side of the hall.

Man in bow tie at knick-knack desk most intrigued by my head, as I thought he would be.

He said that many thousands of heads of Nelson were cast after Trafalgar and that there are probably a dozen houses within a stone's throw of the Masonic Rooms who have got a 'Nelson' gathering dust in an attic or boxroom.

The vast majority are worth a couple of hundred quid at most. The really valuable ones are those that were cast before the battle.

'The early ones are very much sought after,' he said, 'and a good example can fetch a lot of money at auction.'

I said I thought mine definitely had an early feel to it and that, as I understood it from my mother, who was a Nelson herself and whose family had owned it for many generations, it had created considerable interest in the trade at some of the most prestigious art and antiques fairs of the twentieth century. Many tempting offers had been made for it, though none had been accepted.

He said that early nineteenth-century bronzes were not really his subject and that he wanted a second opinion before proceeding any further. Would I mind waiting for a few moments while he consulted a colleague?

I said, 'When an object of this quality has been around for nearly two hundred years, two minutes is not going to make a lot of difference.'

The man behind me in the queue said, 'When some of us have been standing here listening to you banging on for what seems like two hundred years, two more seconds make a hell of a lot of difference.'

Could have cut him down to size with sharp rejoinder, but was in no mood for confrontation. Nothing makes people feel better than someone being nice to them, and noticing that he was holding a number of cigarette-card albums, I said that I had been a keen collector in my day and would be very interested to see what he had brought along.

Needless to say, he immediately changed his tune and, before I knew what, was showing me his albums with all the pride of a man with a newborn baby.

His *pièce de resistance* was the Cycling series which Players introduced just before the war and which, by an extraordinary coincidence, I happen to own myself. It was unfortunate that he was missing a couple of the most interesting – the Coventry Rotary Tricycle and Family Tandem with Side-Car – but I said I thought that if he were to throw in Aircraft of the Royal Air Force, Uniforms of the Territorial Army, and Stars of the Silver Screen, he could expect to realize anything up to a couple of hundred pounds at auction. He could not have been more pleased.

The man standing behind him said, 'You don't happen to know anything about royal commemorative ashtrays from 1901 to 1953, I suppose?'

Said that I was not as expert as some, but would be very happy to cast an eye over his.

By the time I had given my opinion of a dozen wire-framed Victorian spectacles, a mildly pornographic collection of china Pekinese, and some quite interesting, if rather tired-looking, lead soldiers, a long queue had begun to build up at my table. I was really beginning to enjoy myself, and was quite disappointed to see my 'expert' bustling through the crowds towards me, clutching head.

He placed it on the table and said he had spoken to a colleague who had confirmed his initial suspicions.

I laughed and said, 'Thank goodness; I thought for a moment you were going to tell me it's a cheap imitation and not worth the bronze it's made from.'

He said, 'Actually, good-quality bronze can fetch surprisingly high prices these days.'

I said, 'You mean melted down?'

He said, 'I could suggest a couple of names of foundry owners who would offer you a fair price.'

I said, 'But this head has been in my family for generations.'

He said, 'So have the contents of half the junk rooms in this country. Just because something's old doesn't automatically make it valuable.'

Pointed out that Old Masters are not called 'Old' for nothing.

He said that, had my head been in the Master class, its age would certainly count in its favour. The fact that it is a modern copy – a perfectly good copy, perhaps, but a copy none the less – made its age irrelevant. Its market value is negligible. He added that he was sorry to have disappointed me, but there it was.

Was preparing a few choice ripostes when a voice in my left ear murmured, 'You heard what the man said, sunshine. You've had your turn.'

Turned to find myself face to face with bulky security guard with shaved head and face like a King Edward potato.

I said, 'Do you mind? This is being recorded.'

'Sorry to disappoint you, Eric Knowles,' he said, 'but they switched off as soon as you started talking. Now hop it.'

Rose with dignity and turned to leave, only to come face to face with Priscilla.

She said, 'Well, that obviously went well.'

I said, 'Well, what can you expect with ITV? They wouldn't know a valuable bronze if it jumped up and bit them on the leg.'

She said, 'They had no trouble identifying my egg-cup.'

'As what?' I said. 'A thing to eat boiled eggs from?'

She said, 'Apparently it's a rare example of Picasso's kitchenware period. It seems he had a thing about eggs and spent a whole week painting nothing but egg-cups, but then thought better of it and promptly destroyed the whole lot. Luckily, he forgot the ones he and his mistress had used for breakfast that morning and were still sitting in the sink waiting to be washed up. She put them away somewhere safe. One is in the hands of a private collector in Switzerland; mine is the other. I gather there are collectors in America and the Far East who would kill for it.'

I said that the way things were going, so would I. How much did they think it was worth?

She said she didn't want to tell me, it would only upset me. I said it wouldn't. She did, and it did. Was so taken aback I dropped the head which rolled under a nearby table. When I finally retrieved it, I found its left ear had broken off. Spent twenty minutes crawling round the floor looking for it, but to no avail.

Is it my imagination or did I read somewhere that Nelson may have lost part of one ear at the Battle of Copenhagen?

On the way out, caught jacket on table of antique china. Luckily, by the time anyone realized where the noise was coming from, I was halfway up Colliers Wood High Street.

Sunday, July 2nd

Am beginning to wonder if I shall ever get the break that everyone who dips a toe into the media pool needs if he or she is ever going to grow from a small fry to a big fish. However many opportunities I seize and however hard I try, nothing seems to work out quite as I hope.

Am convinced I am a born communicator. Am well educated, cultured, with a wide knowledge of the sort of subjects that interest people these days – food, wine, films, theatre, books, music etc. Am not as well travelled as some, but better than most. In Europe, mainly, but that's no bad thing.

Am as good-looking as anyone else who fronts programmes on television these days – better, in most cases – have a sophisticated sense of humour and a pleasant speaking voice and am willing to learn. All I need now is the opportunity to display my talents – on television, on radio, in newspapers, in magazines, between hard covers . . . I am happy to try anything.

Mollie Marsh-Gibbon may sneer and say I am interested in fame only for its own sake, but she couldn't be more wrong if she tried. All of us wish in some way to leave our footprints in the sands of time, and I hope that, if I do, they will match those of serious professionals like Dimbleby, Paxman and

Lynam and not the one-note amateurs whom I could list here at exhaustive length, but won't.

Monday, July 3rd

As Rilke once said 'Life is all a matter of timing.' His words have never been proved truer than they have today.

Had that road sweeper been doing his job on April Fool's Day and picked up that squashed cigarette packet, as he was supposed to, I might never have received the telephone call I did this morning from the manager of Mitcham General Hospital Radio, Colin Smoothie, asking if I would be interested in doing some broadcasting work.

It is on such tiny quirks of fate that the fortunes of all of us, great and small, so often turn.

Am to meet Smoothie at the hospital the day after tomorrow at eleven thirty for a chat, followed by a short voice test and a visit to one or two of the wards to meet some of the patients.

He said, 'As you can imagine, there's a lot of competition among would-be broadcasters to get a foot in the door at Mitcham Hospital Radio – or MHR, as it's known round the wards. However, as anyone who reads your column on a regular basis knows, you have the lively, original sort of mind we are looking for and so rarely find. It's just a question now of meeting you, seeing if you come across as well in person as you do in print and how you handle a microphone.'

Am still not entirely clear what the job entails, nor do I much care. A foot in the door is all I need at this stage, and as long as the foot is mine, the door is neither here nor there.

The BBC's loss is Mitcham General's gain.

At dinner at Paula Batty's, sat next to a woman I have never seen before in my life who, when she wasn't lighting a cigarette, was blowing her nose. Couldn't begin to remember what we talked about. Trivialities, largely.

As we were all leaving, she suddenly launched herself at me and, before I knew what, was kissing me on both cheeks as enthusiastically as if I were a lifelong friend.

Whatever happened to the good old English handshake? Is it the victim of another directive from Brussels, along with udder-fresh milk and pub opening hours? Am becoming more of a Euro-sceptic by the day.

Tuesday, July 4th

Independence Day. Were I an American, I daresay I would be feeling as high as the proverbial kite. In the event, woke to blue skies, brilliant sunshine and one of the worst sore throats I have known in years. By lunchtime I had also begun to develop a hacking cough, and by early evening had more or less lost the power of speech. Am wondering if this is a psychosomatic reaction to our tragic loss of the American colonies. Though more than two centuries have passed, it still smarts. At all events, am determined from now on never to kiss anyone I have not known for at least ten years.

It could not have come at a worse time. The last thing the powers that be at Mitcham General need is a radio host who sounds as if he should be in the TB ward. Quite apart from the possibility of introducing yet another to the long list of hospital bugs about which there has been so much publicity lately, hearing me coughing down the air waves could lower morale on the wards to the extent that some patients might actually give up the ghost before I had even spun my first disc.

Spent the day practising my audition piece for tomorrow. Have chosen the lyrics of 'Yesterday', which, more than any other song, sets the tone for the kind of easy listening I have in mind for my show, and places me slap in the mainstream of post-Elvis pop.

Unfortunately, found I could not get beyond the bit about my troubles looking as though they're here to stay without being overwhelmed by an irresistible urge to clear my throat.

Remembered that Mother always swears by hot lemon and honey, and brewed myself a large mug.

Do not imagine her larder ever boasted anything as exotic as Israeli honey, and more's the pity, since the jar I found at the back of P's jam and preserves section yielded a sweetness and a scent that spoke more of a Kentish garden in high summer than of the Golan Heights. Sir Paul McCartney's words suddenly assumed a significance that I had never recognized before.

Indeed, I might suggest to Colin Smoothie that we have a regular item in which I play a well-known pop tune and talk about some of the thoughts and memories it conjures up. It could be exactly the sort of thing that could bring untold comfort to patients as they lie there, recovering from their various operations, wondering if they are going to make it through the next few hours.

Wednesday, July 5th

It never rains but it pours. Woke this morning to find I had completely lost my voice. It wouldn't have mattered quite so much if P and Chad hadn't decided to choose today of all days to take John Julius, James and Marie-Celeste on a day trip to Brighton, of all places. As a result there was no one I could ask to telephone Smoothie and make my excuses – except poor old Mother, of course, and having found her last week trying to use the telephone in her bedroom as a hairdryer, felt it would be unwise to entrust her with a task of this importance.

Left with no alternative, therefore, but to go to the hospital in person. Remembered reading somewhere that when Laurence Olivier lost his voice, he nursed it back to life by gargling with port. It's an old actor's trick, of course, first used by David Garrick before a performance of *The Rivals* in Drury Lane.

There is no record of what type of port he used, nor whether, having finished gargling, he then drank it. It goes without saying that, had I gargled with salt water or TCP, swallowing it afterwards would have been the last thing on my mind. However, one does not go sloshing Taylor's Rich Ruby round one's tonsils, only to spit it down the plughole – vintage or no vintage. Besides, the soothing effect it has on one's inflamed larynx as it makes its way down can only be beneficial.

Disappointed to find that first gargle had no effect whatever, so tried again five minutes later to find that I could just about manage to enunciate the word 'Yesterday'. Gave it a further five and this time managed 'All my troubles seemed so far away' with barely a croak.

By ten thirty was able to recite entire song without cracking once. Was so pleased with results, I treated myself to one more dose, just to be on the safe side.

Audition could not have gone better and Colin Smoothie could not be better named. Dark hair, brushed flat against his head, thick-cut moustache, double-breasted suit, suede brogues, regimental tie, voice like Roger Moore. Not unlike mine, as it happens. Hope he didn't think I was trying to send him up.

'Welcome aboard,' he said, stuck out a large firm hand and immediately launched into a long speech about how he was my biggest fan and how he had particularly enjoyed my piece on the Royal Grill.

He said, 'I know what you mean about Indian restaurants. Maharajah's Banquet or no Maharajah's Banquet, it still looks like a dog's dinner to me. Tastes like one, too, if you ask me.'

'With added dog,' I said with a laugh.

'Steady the Buffs,' he said. 'By the way, love that voice. Warm, confidential, perfect for radio.'

I said I hoped it wasn't too fruity.

He said a microphone is to a voice what a camera is to a face: loves some, hates others. What sounds wonderful on the telephone can come across as rubbish on the mike. Why didn't we try putting a few things on tape and take it from there?

Told him I had brought along an audition piece that I thought showed my voice to its best advantage, but when I said what it was he said perhaps we ought to try something a bit more down to earth and handed me a sheet of paper headed 'Hospital Announcements'.

'Try the one that begins, "How to Fill out Your Menu Card".'

Doubt even Gielgud in his prime could have imbued words like 'mince and boiled potatoes' and 'cabinet pudding and custard' with poetry, but did my best. Unfortunately, at one point said 'mice' instead of 'rice', but don't think it was too obvious.

'Well done,' Smoothie said when I'd finished. He then asked me who my favourite artist was.

'Piero della Francesca,' I said.

'I meant musical,' he said.

'Frank Sinatra,' I said, crossing my fingers.

'Hm,' he said. It was impossible to tell from his tone whether I had made a good choice or a bad one.

He then took me down to one of the women's surgical wards to meet some of the patients.

'This is Simon Crisp,' he announced. 'He writes the Up Your Way column in the *Mitcham & Tooting Times*.'

He might have been addressing a roomful of face flannels for all the reaction he got.

'Who's your favourite singer?' he asked the nearest patient.
'Tom Jones,' she said.
'Do you like the *Mitch & Toot*?' I asked another.
'It's good for cleaning up the cat's sick,' she said.

Left in state of deep gloom. Cannot imagine any broadcaster has ever had to suffer quite such humiliation in the furtherance of his career.

Thursday, July 6th

Woke to find my voice much restored, if a little on the husky side. Chad said, 'You could make a fortune doing Henry Kissinger impersonations.'

Marie-Celeste, by contrast, rather more friendly than usual. She has taken the the cod French accent down several notches, and actually smiled at me for the first time in weeks.

Acute laryngitis is too high a price to pay for a brief moment of civility from the au pair, but from now on might seriously try lowering the voice a semitone or two on a regular basis.

Friday, July 7th

To the local library to borrow the autobiography of the late Brian Johnston. He was very much my broadcasting hero. Am only sorry he bagged the title 'It's Been a Lot of Fun' first. It sums up what I hope people will say about me when I finally hang up my headphones – not just the patients of Mitcham General, but millions of others in need of the tonic of laughter in homes up and down the land. May try incorporating the words 'laughter' and 'tonic' into programme title.

Saturday, July 8th

To Piccadilly early yesterday evening with sleeping bag, thermos and wizard's hat and cloak (metaphorically speaking, of course) to join young fans as they camped outside Waterstone's in order to be among the first to buy the new Harry Potter when the shop opened at midnight.

Must admit, have never actually read any of these stories that seem to have taken the world by storm, though am still toying with the idea of writing a children's book myself. In fact once sketched out plot for story while stuck, Rowling-like, on a train outside Basingstoke. As if that were not coincidence enough, my story was also about a boarding school, not dissimilar to the one I went to before Fenton, and the strange masters who taught there and the funny things that happened. Not that any of them were wizards, more's the pity. Am only sorry did not take it further. Who knows where it might have led?

Though a single parent myself, like JK, cannot pretend I have ever been penniless or reduced to living on benefit. However, have spent more time than I care to remember sitting alone in cafés. Am only sorry I did not put the time to more productive use. Had I done so, I might also have millions in the bank and be the proud owner of a large house with a swimming pool, with a blockbuster Hollywood movie of my book about to be made, starring Maggie Smith, Robbie Coltrane, Tim Roth, Uncle Tom Cobleigh and all.

It might also, more to the point, be *my* latest œuvre that children are queuing up in their thousands to buy all over the country. Instead of which, I am one of the ones doing the queuing – for no other reason than that it might provide a few hundred words for my next column.

Arrived at Waterstone's to find hundreds of children already there and queue stretching all down Piccadilly. Tagged on to the end and made self as comfortable as possible.

Small boy next to me said, 'Are you a pervert?'

I said, 'Do I honestly look like a pervert?'

'Yes,' he said.

I said, 'Actually, I'm a writer.'

'Gosh. Really?' he said. 'Are you famous?'

'In my own field,' I said.

A girl on the other side said, 'Do you live in a field, then?'

I said, 'Sort of. I live in a tent, actually.'

'Why?' she said. 'Are you very poor?'

I said, 'Not as poor as J. K. Rowling was when she wrote the first Harry Potter.'

'I thought she was a billionaire,' said the little boy.

'She is now,' I said. 'Thanks to people like you.'

He said, 'Actually, I think her books are pants.'

I asked him why he was there, then.

He said, 'I only came to look after my sister here. She thinks Harry Potter's great, but she's really stupid, like most girls.

She thinks Roald Dahl's great, too.'

I asked him who *he* thought was great.

'Stephen Hawking,' he said.

I said, 'You should meet my niece. She's a Stephen Hawking fan, but she thinks his black-hole theory's full of holes.'

'Great,' he said. 'What do *you* think?'

I said I hadn't really thought about it enough.

He said, 'I bet you think Harry Potter's great.'

'Not as great as Stephen Hawking,' I said.

'You're just like all grown-ups,' he said. 'You pretend to know lots of things, but when it comes to it you really only know what you've read in the Sunday papers or seen on TV.'

A small boy who had sat down next to me on the other side said, 'Do you know how to play quidditch?'

'Yes,' I said.

He said, 'Who do you think wins the Tri-Wizard Tournament?'

'Hogwarts,' I said firmly, and before anyone could say another word, got out my sleeping bag, climbed in and pretended to go to sleep.

Dozed fitfully until doors opened at midnight. It was a bit like being in school dorm again and being woken in the middle of the night for fire drill.

Became involved in ugly argy-bargy just inside door when children behind me in queue tried to push past. Had no alternative but to seize one of them bodily and deposit him in his proper place.

'Gerroff,' he shouted.

The boy in front said to his sister, 'I told you he was a pervert.'

At this point, large security man appeared from nowhere and, before I knew what, found myself being marched to very back of queue, with sounds of laughs and jeers ringing in my ears.

Thought I spotted Katie among them, but in the circumstances could easily have been mistaken.

Finally got my copy shortly after one and headed home, only to find cover torn and several of the pages badly bent.

Had been planning to go to King's Cross early to get book inscribed by the author and to join her many fans in waving her goodbye as she set off from Platform 9¾ on the Hogwarts Express on her journey to the mystical world of bookshop

signings, but have suffered enough in last few hours without exposing myself needlessly to further humiliation.

Saw Katie this evening. She gave me a funny look, but said nothing.

Neither did I.

Sunday, July 9th

Am still reeling from Anna Kournikova's surprise defeat in second round of ladies' singles at Wimbledon. Am I the only person in England who follows her because he thinks she's a great tennis player?

'The only *man*,' Chad said in a sneering tone of voice.

Alan Parker was Sue Lawley's guest on *Desert Island Discs* this morning, and very interesting he was, too. Have always been a big fan of his films and was very interested to hear that he had started off in advertising, too. It is reassuring to know I am not the only one to have changed horses in midstream. A fascinating man, and a fascinating choice of records to take to a desert island. Would not myself have chosen Pritouritze Planinata-Chant from the Thracian Plain, excellently performed though it was by Le Mystère des Voix Bulgares. But Nimrod from *Enigma Variations* has always been one of my all-time top eight.

In fact it's high time I got my own Desert Island list out and did a bit of updating. The way my career is taking off at present, one never knows when one might not be invited to spin the turntable with Sue Lawley. It pays to be prepared.

Monday, July 10th

Hugh Bryant-Fenn rang this morning to invite me to lunch at the Toad-under-the-Harrow on the 28th. He said it was just an excuse to touch base and catch up on each other's news, but have not spent twenty years in PR industry without recognizing when someone like Hugh is trying to soften up a journalist and try a few stories out on him.

I suppose this is the sort of thing one must start getting used to, now that one is on the other side of the fence. Was strongly tempted to call his bluff, but decided to go along with the subterfuge. Cannot believe he seriously thinks he is going to buy me with a pint of beer and a cheese sandwich, but shall enjoy watching him try.

Started on Harry Potter piece for this week's *Mitch & Toot*. Did not get quite as far as I had hoped.

On the plus side, James has gone to Scotland to stay with someone he met in Australia, so am able to move back on to sofa, and not before time.

John Julius brought a very pretty girl home this evening. She is called Fiona and is studying to be a clarinettist. Have always been a big fan of the clarinet. Artie Shaw is one of my big-band favourites, and of course Benny Goodman, as well as being the King of Swing, recorded several classical pieces, including the Mozart Clarinet Concerto.

Was chewing the fat with Fiona about this and other musical matters when John Julius interrupted me in mid-sentence to say, 'Actually, we've got to be somewhere.'

He came back later on his own and said, 'Look, Dad, if you want a girlfriend, find your own. Don't chat up other people's.'

Since when did a few moments of polite conversation constitute chatting up?

Tuesday, July 11th

Finished Harry Potter piece. I think Rowling would approve.

The morning post brought a cheque from Amanda's father for £100 and a note saying, 'A. tells me you might be able to find a use for this. Best, Derrick.'

How he managed to find out where I live I can't imagine.

Am strongly tempted to send it back with a firm 'Thank you, but no thank you,' but would not wish to embarrass him or his family any further.

Wednesday, July 12th

Nothing from Smoothie. I had a feeling Sinatra was a mistake as soon as the word left my lips. Why I didn't say Tom Jones I can't imagine. Even Engelbert Humperdinck might have stood me in better stead.

Thursday, July 13th

Smoothie rang at ten, shortly after *Face the Facts*. He's listened to the tape, likes my choice of music and thinks the listeners will, too. Can I start next week on a monthly trial basis?

Frankly, was rather taken aback. What exactly did the job entail, I asked him?

He said that basically I'll be hosting my own show twice a week, Tuesdays and Fridays, two till five. A lively mixture of chat, anecdote, information, requests and, of course, a good dollop of easy-listening music. Obviously he'd leave the actual ingredients up to me, though he didn't imagine I'd have any difficulty filling six hours a week.

Could hardly believe my ears. My own three-hour radio show twice a week! And at prime time, too! It's the sort of offer that would-be broadcasters dream of.

For two pins would have accepted there and then, but common sense prevailed. After half a lifetime in the communications industry, am only too aware of the importance of getting a project on to the right footing from the start and kicking off as one means to continue.

Told Smoothie am interested *en principe*, but need to check my availability before giving a definite yea or nay.

He said, 'There is a degree of urgency on this one. Frankly, I'd like to get the whole thing done and dusted within the next twenty-four hours.'

Said I'd get back to him a.s.a.p. Thought I could detect a faint undertone of anxiety in his voice, but this is no bad thing. He's obviously very keen, and it never does any harm to play hard to get.

No mention, as yet, of money, I notice. If he thinks he's going to get me for peanuts, he's got another think coming. Though perfectly capable of picking my way through the dense undergrowth of any contract anyone might care to throw at me, there comes a point in the career of any media figure when he needs strong representation by a reputable agent, and if this is not the moment, I'd like to know what is.

Who's hot in the agency world these days, though?

Drew a bow at a venture and rang my old friend Nicola Benson. Though no longer quite the top banana she once was in the world of mainstream television, the name of the company she founded ten years ago, Nicolodeon Productions, still flashes across one's screen of an afternoon, and I imagine the sort of names she manages to lure on to *Whose Pet?* adorn the client lists of some of the biggest agents in town.

Was sorry to learn that ill health has forced her to leave the company – though to judge from the fact that she now lives in Tuscany one assumes she is not exactly down to her last layer of shoe leather.

Was also sorry that the girl who gave me the information could not see her way to suggesting someone else who might help.

She said, 'We are a production company, not an agency. We book people; we don't represent them.'

Said that in that case they might like to consider me as a guest celebrity for their next series.

She said, 'Are you a celebrity?'

Had begun to explain that I am the presenter of a prime-time radio show in south-west London when suddenly realized I was talking to myself.

Am strongly tempted to get in touch with Nicola and suggest that if she wants the company that bears her name to remain at the cutting edge of television production she could do worse than suggest they hire people who are rather more open to new talent than at present. Ditto who do not put the phone down in the middle of conversations.

Unfortunately, do not know where in Tuscany she is living out her retirement, nor is there any way of finding out, short of ringing Nicolodeon again. Will almost certainly end up doing nothing about it at all. As usual.

Rang the two biggest agencies in town – ICM and William Morris – but no one has rung back, as promised. Does anyone?

Friday, July 14th

Le Quatorze Juillet. Came down to breakfast singing 'La Marseillaise' at the top of my voice and to the accompaniment of much exaggerated face-pulling by Marie-Celeste.

Mother said, 'I thought you were the milkman.'

Smoothie called just before lunch. Did I want the job or not?

Decided there was no point beating about the bush and came straight out with it. How did five hundred a programme strike him?

He said, 'Oh, we don't pay our presenters anything. The whole point about hospital radio is that it is run entirely on a voluntary basis.'

Talk about the wind being taken out of one's sails. Reminded him that I am a professional.

He said he didn't know of any professionals who were not prepared to give a proportion of their time for nothing in return for the gratitude of people less fortunate than themselves. In fact a number of celebrities have been guest presenters over the years, including Fiona Fullerton, Carol Smillie, Denise Van Outen and Christopher Biggins, and none of them asked for a penny. Either I wanted the job or I didn't. Two till five, twice a week, Tuesdays and Fridays, take it or leave it.

Finally decided to put him out of his misery and said I'd take it. I do not do enough for others, and the smile on the face of a patient in the recovery room as he or she comes round from an anaesthetic should be reward enough. It has also not escaped my notice that many of the honours given to broadcasters at New Year and on the Queen's Official Birthday are for services to charity, and it would nice to think that if – or should I say when? – I am invited to a Water Rats Dinner, I shall be able to match my OBE with my fellow guests at the top table.

I start next Tuesday.

As Smoothie was putting the phone down, thought I caught the words 'scraping' and 'barrel', but could have been mistaken. As he himself said, voices on telephones can be very deceptive.

To the Colliers Wood Playhouse with P for this production of *The Oresteia* about which there has been so much hoo-ha in the 'arts' pages of the weightier papers.

It is thirty-six years since I last enjoyed Aeschylus in the original, yet it seems only yesterday that I was regaling Dickie Dunmow's Classical VIth with my free, but I still believe faithful, translation of Agamemnon's speech to the men of Argos on his return from Troy.

Set off in good time for five o'clock curtain, my trusty old Oxford edition of *Aeschyli Tragoediae* in one hand and my Liddell and Scott lexicon in the other.

Had been looking forward to few minutes of textual limbering-up in the quiet of the Nelson Mandela Bar, but, thanks to ding-dong with female traffic warden, arrived hot and bothered seconds before curtain. Know now how Orestes must have felt being pursued by Furies.

In point of fact, verse translation curiously reminiscent of my own youthful efforts, though could not help thinking that some of the chorus work might well have rated a Beta Minus Query Minus and a 'See me afterwards' from Dickie.

Masks, on balance, earned a cautious thumbs-up from me, despite unfortunate resemblance of Argive women to Marie-Celeste at her surliest.

Suggested to P that we round off evening with a stuffed vine leaf or two and bottle of good, honest Demestika round the corner at Nikos's Akropolis Kebab and Houmus House.

Greeted waiter in typical Aeschylean fashion, but might have been addressing Elgin Marbles for all the response I got. For good measure, threw in a few key words like 'Orestes', 'Mycenae' and 'Iphigenia', but he simply shook his head and said, 'We have afelia, souvlakia, moussaka, dolmades.' So much for the glory that was Greece.

As we were leaving, discovered Nikos does a good line in takeaway. Funnily enough, was thinking of inviting a few friends round to celebrate my new career in broadcasting and cannot imagine better way of capturing festive mood than with some zesty Greek food and a bottle or two of rough red from the Peloponnese.

Monday week looks clear in my diary.

Saturday, July 15th

Am wondering if I should consider joining the Garrick Club? If so, how do I go about it?

Feel I am very much a Garrick type, but unfortunately do not know any members well enough to ask them to put me up for election. A brief encounter (no joke intended) with Sheridan Morley at the exhibition of Noel Coward's dressing gowns at the Theatre Museum last year, though cordial, hardly constitutes a firm friendship, or indeed grounds for proposal.

Stupidly mentioned my interest to Mollie Marsh-Gibbon, who cackled and said, 'You're like all the rest of them. You only want to join so you can wear that ghastly tie and swank at cocktail parties.'

This evening asked John Julius how Fiona was. 'No idea,' he said.

I said, 'I thought she was your girl-friend.'

'Was,' he said, and left the room.

Feel that in some way I am held to blame, though can't imagine why. How little one knows about one's children's private thoughts – or indeed knows one's children at all.

To bed in sombre mood with *Sunday Telegraph* Review pages and a large apple.

Sunday, July 16th

Cannot believe it. The builders are back next door and noisier than ever. Feel sure there is a law against people disturbing the peace on Sunday mornings, but have no way of finding out for certain.

Was on my out to buy mint jelly just before lunch when spotted my glamorous new neighbour standing on her door-step staring intently at her feet. She could not have looked more beautiful or been more friendly. Unfortunately, my casual enquiry as to her health resulted in a long and unnecessarily detailed account of a tummy upset in the night from which she was still suffering.

It was not quite the soil in which I had been hoping that our new-found friendship might flower, and was relieved (again, no joke intended) when the subject turned to her doorstep.

'You probably know about this sort of thing,' she said, and invited me over to have a look at the different-coloured pieces of marble which had been laid out in an intricate pattern.

I said I thought it looked very elegant.

She said, 'It would do if it had been finished.'

I asked what she meant.

She said, 'I may be very stupid, and I know I'm just a divorced woman on her own, but surely there are not meant to be those gaps between the marble pieces. Shouldn't they be filled with something? There's a word for it.'

'Grouting,' I said.

'That's it,' she said. 'Shouldn't the whole thing be grouted?'

I asked her when the marble had been laid and she said the day before yesterday.

Suggested that perhaps marble needs to bed in for a day or two before grouting can take place. She said she had mentioned it to the builders, but they had assured her the job was finished.

Had to admit I was stumped. At that moment the foreman exited through the front door with a cheery, 'Morning, Cripps!'

I said, 'We were just talking about the marble and wondering when you were thinking of grouting it.'

He said casually, 'Not necessary. This marble is self-grouting.' And he walked off down the path, got into his van and drove off up the street.

We were both staring after him when she suddenly clutched her stomach, muttered 'Must run' and disappeared indoors.

Arrived at shop to find they had just sold the last jar of mint jelly.

Monday, July 17th

Thought I had made it perfectly clear to the Hon. Sec. of the Old Fentonian Society when I wrote to him re my meeting with Charlie Ibstock that I no longer wished to receive copies of the OF Yearbook. Yet the latest edition has come winging its way from darkest Kent with yet more inconsequential news of people I have never heard of, even though several of them appear to have been my contemporaries.

My memory is pretty good for my age, though I say so myself, and when I was a Top Swine I took pride in the fact that there was not a single boy in the school whose name I did not know. Yet it would seem that Grant Flett (Rummage's, 1960–65), T. P. Widgeon (Ellis's, 1961–66) and Kenneth Tang (School House, 1961–65) completely escaped my notice.

I suppose there are some people who will be interested to learn that Tang is now head of futures at Wardle Smith Du Port in Singapore, and that Widgeon recently got married for the second time and recently met Tim Halfshaft (Hoggart's, 1959–63) at a party celebrating the fiftieth birthday of Tony Gotobed (Blunkett's, 1959–64) where the discotheque was in the capable hands of Andrew Smellie (Dyson's, 1970–75). Unfortunately, I am not one of them.

Was about to throw Yearbook, Notes and Reports, Calendar of OF Events plus invitation from a company I have never heard of to reduce my household insurance by thirty per cent, when my eye was caught by a slip of paper headed O.F. GOLFING SOCIETY.

According to someone called George Sydenham-Hill (Dumbleton's 1952–7), the society is looking for new members – the lower their handicaps the better. Membership is £250 a year, but for that one is entitled to play on a number of courses in the Home Counties, including Gosling Park and Trimbly Bottom.

Members are also entitled to half-price insurance on their golfing equipment, and fifty per cent off the price of a starter and main course at a number of selected pubs and restaurants in Kent, Surrey and Sussex.

Funnily enough, have been thinking of taking up golf again after far too long a lay-off. As a teenager I was runner-up in the Ashford and District Junior Foursomes, and in 1960 won a £2 book token when I got nearest the pin on the short eighth during the Fathers and Sons Summer Knockout, plus two golf balls in the Under-16 Long Driving Competition, so I do know my way around a golf course.

I daresay the swing that was so much admired by the professional at the time, Alan Trotter, is a little on the rusty side, but there's nothing that couldn't be sorted out by a couple of hours on a practice ground. And though I never had an official handicap, I see no reason why, with a bit of competition play, I shouldn't be playing to a respectable 18 in a very short time.

Indeed, have for some time been planning to make enquiries about membership at one of the better-known clubs near London, but will now not bother. Being able to say one is a member of Wentworth or Sunningdale may impress some, but, for those in the know, Old Fentonians has a cachet all of its own.

Have already written off to Sydenham-Hill with my application, and look forward to getting out the faithful brassie on the first at Trimbly Bottom in the very near future. Fore!

Tuesday, July 18th

Arrived at hospital shortly before one thirty, bringing several of P's Sinatra records, plus a selection of my big-band CD's – Dorsey, James, Goodman, Ellington, Basie etc. – and a couple of Mantovanis that Chad hadn't been able to sell and had chucked into the dustbin.

Was sitting outside studio waiting to be called in when Smoothie came by.

'Hello,' he said in a surprised voice. 'What are you doing here?'

I said, 'Broadcasters are like actors. They like to get in early, get a feel of the house, do some voice warm-up exercises, and generally prepare for the show.'

Smoothie said, 'Couldn't agree more. Still, twelve hours is a little on the generous side, isn't it?'

Couldn't understand what he meant, and said so.

He said, 'Well, you're not on till two.'

I said, 'Well, it's already twenty to.'

'Two in the morning,' he said, 'not two in the afternoon.'

Was dumbstruck.

He said he couldn't think how I could possibly have imagined that with my lack of experience I was going to be let loose on the patients in the middle of the afternoon. He might only be the station manager of a local hospital radio, but he hadn't been a continuity announcer with BBC Radio Ouse for five years without acquiring some standards.

I said, 'But two till five in the morning's the graveyard shift.'

He said, 'The cynics of this world may call it that, but we at MHR think of it as providing a valuable service to our listeners, not to say comfort, in the small hours before dawn.

Look on the positive side, and remember that for many people yours could be the last voice they ever hear.'

Arrived home, decidedly tight-lipped, to be met in the hall by Priscilla.

'You're home early,' she said. 'Send them all to sleep, did you?'

I said stiffly, 'If you want to know, there's been a change in the programme schedule. The man who does the night shift has moved to the West Country and I've been asked to take over at the last minute.'

She said, 'Oh, that's all right, then. They'll all be asleep before you even get there.'

Killed time watching a new Channel 4 programme called *Big Brother*. George Orwell must be turning in his grave. The idea is for a whole lot of people to share a house and be filmed twenty-four hours a day. Once a week everyone nominates two people they want to have slung out and the viewers decide who goes.

Cannot imagine anyone wanting to spend more than five minutes with any of them. The highlight of the evening was when a big black chap called Darren made a penis out of pottery and left it outside the girls' dorm. Needless to say, Chad thought that was hilarious. I'm surprised he didn't apply to take part. He'd fit in perfectly and would very likely win. P could use the £70,000 prize – especially since she has decided, for reasons best known to herself, not to sell her Picasso egg-cup.

She couldn't get over the fact that another of the contestants, Nick, had been at Gordonstoun with Prince Edward – though I would have thought that in the present political climate that would ensure his instant expulsion.

More of a worry still is that Katie seems fascinated by an Irish ex-nun called Anna. There's something not quite right about her, but can't put my finger on it.

Chad said, 'You haven't put your finger on anything for years.'

Did not rise to bait.

Can only thank goodness that there are some of us still left in this country who are prepared to maintain the high standards of broadcasting established by the likes of Richard Dimbleby, Freddie Grisewood and David Jacobs.

They did not become stars by doing rubbish, and neither will I.

Wednesday, July 19th

Up rather later than usual, feeling oddly light-headed after only a couple of hours' sleep. Would have gone to bed earlier, but, as any performer knows, when one's adrenalin has been pumping for as long as mine had, one needs time to 'come down', as the saying goes in the business.

Indeed, I seem to remember reading somewhere that after performing his famous Othello, Laurence Olivier would walk the darkened streets of Brighton for hours on end until he felt ready for sleep. On one occasion he walked to Rottingdean and back. I *think* it was Laurence Olivier.

All I can say is thank goodness I got my column done early this week. Can't remember what it was about now, and the *Mitch & Toot*'s no help, since, whatever it was, it didn't appear anyway.

Am also having some difficulty remembering everything that happened last night.

Was quite pleased with the little catchphrase I have devised to introduce my 'slot'. Have dubbed myself 'the Lad with the Lamp'. It has the twin advantages of being both witty and apposite.

The whole introduction went as follows: 'Hello, everybody. This is Mitcham General Hospital Radio broadcasting to you on 1066 AM. It's two o'clock on Wednesday, July 19th, and this is Simon Crisp, your Lad with the Lamp, helping you to make it through the night. I'll be with you from now until five, with news, views, and a little night music to soothe the fevered brow and ease the painful stitch.' Then I went into my signature tune.

Was disappointed not to get a bigger response to my call for phone-in requests, but daresay that will come in time, when my listeners have tuned into my wavelength – in every sense of the word.

Surprised to find how much of my time gets spent giving out hospital notices re events etc., delivering 'get well' messages from relatives to patients, and repeating meal times. However, managed to find time to inject some of my own brand of humour between discs. For no reason at all was reminded of a time I spent in hospital myself when I was a small boy and one of the nurses showed me how to get on and off a bedpan on my own, without disturbing the bedclothes – or, more importantly, the patients in the next-door beds!

Am sorry Smoothie does not think 'Strangers in the Night' is an appropriate signature tune for my programme. I can't think why.

He seems pleased with the Lad with the Lamp idea, though. Or at least he didn't say he wasn't.

Am supposed to go to dinner with the Varney-Birches tonight, but am wondering if I can face it. Or, more to the point, if I'll be sufficiently awake. Am wondering if Wogan finds broadcasting as exhausting as I do. But then, of course, he does have the advantage of having had a good night's sleep first.

Will doubtless bump into him at one of these radio and TV award things and we can compare notes.

Thursday, July 20th

Am beginning to have second thoughts re my next-door neighbour. Was alone in the house this evening for once and had just settled down in front of TV with a couple of breaded haddock fillets and a glass of fruity Sancerre when the whole house started vibrating.

Have put up with the inconvenience of her builders for two months now, and when they filled the whole place with the smell of boiling tar just as we were sitting down to lunch following our grouting conversation on Sunday, I thought things could not get worse. How wrong can one be?

Having completely rebuilt the whole of the top of the house, they suddenly turned their attention to the basement and have spent the last few days with drill and pickaxe demolishing the floor. Frankly, I would have thought that anyone with any sense – not to say consideration for their neighbours – would start at the bottom of the house and work their way up. But, like most builders, this lot are a law unto themselves – not least when it comes to working hours.

Have already had words with their foreman re deliveries of materials at six thirty in the morning, which they know perfectly well is in total contravention of environmental laws, but might as well have talked to a brick wall – though doubt they would recognize one if it jumped up and bit them.

Leaving aside any personal feelings I may have about the owner, the fact is I am perfectly prepared to put up with a certain amount of noise during working hours – i.e. eight till five, or even six – but enough is enough.

Put tray on floor and headed into hall. Was unable to find my own key, so grabbed spare from box on hall table and leaped for front door. Was halfway down path when suddenly remembered Woodhouse was in the house and would almost certainly have a go at my fish supper. Rushed back to find key would not go into lock. Realized I must have left my own in lock and that the only way back was via the garden.

Would normally have asked the Wisbys on the other side if I could shin over the party wall, but, as luck would have it, had words with them last Sunday re barbecuing.

The only other entry route was via the high wall at the end of the garden which runs along one side of Honeysuckle Grove. But for that I needed a long ladder, and the only people I could think of at that moment who had one readily available were the builders next door. Had no alternative, therefore, but to put a brave face on it.

Door opened by glamorous neighbour dressed in what I believe is known as a peignoir, which she had tied rather carelessly and was showing a surprising amount of cleavage.

She said, 'May I help you?' in a voice that was blatantly suggestive.

In an attempt to match her frivolous mood, I laughed and said, 'It's all right. I'm not a Jehovah's Witness.'

She said, 'Well, I am, and I don't think that's at all funny,' and slammed the door in my face.

Recced rear for second time and returned to front in time to see neighbour going out, obviously for the evening. Waited until her car was out of sight and rang bell again. This time door opened by foreman.

'Evening, Cripps,' he said.

'Actually it's Crisp,' I said.

'Cheers,' he said. 'What can I do for you? Mrs Wossname's out.'

Explained situation and said I was very sorry to be a nuisance, but could I possibly borrow a ladder? He could not have been more friendly. Unfortunately, the only one he had was in the garden, and he couldn't get out to it because he had just covered the basement floor in wet concrete. Suggested he try the garden door on the ground floor instead.

'Nice one,' he said.

It was only when we were finally in the garden that he realized he didn't have the key to the door that led out into the alley.

'Tell you what,' he said. 'Why don't you put the ladder up against the wall, I'll shin up it, pull the ladder up after me, drop down the other side and we'll get into your garden the same way.'

It was unfortunate that he landed quite so heavily in the water feature that makes the end of our garden such a delight at this time of year. Ditto that the Wisbys should have got it into their heads that we were being burgled and, without bothering to check first, had rung the police.

Arrived at front door in time to see police car drawing up outside with light flashing and siren wailing.

Whether they really will charge me for wasting police time remains to be seen. All I know for certain is that I am fifty quid down after squaring things with the foreman and at nine thirty they started drilling again. Also the dog ate my breaded haddock.

Friday, July 21st

The people on Big Brother have run out of loo paper. I know what it feels like – in every sense!

Saturday, July 22nd

An astonishing coincidence. Was on my way back to the studio just after two, following a loo break, when lift doors opened on third floor and in walked Jane Baker, of all people.

Could not believe my eyes. It is eighteen years or more since I last saw her, waitressing in a French ski resort, and a lifetime ago that we shared the flat together with Beddoes and Victoria, and I found myself having a bit of a thing with her.

She was rather plain in those days, I remember, and very spotty, and the improvement in her appearance when I ran into her in Le Ski Pub in Les Vals was quite remarkable. Had she not been involved with the owner, might well have suggested giving it another whirl.

Her hair is flecked with grey now, and there are wrinkles round her eyes, but the girl on the sun-drenched terrace has turned into a middle-aged woman of great beauty.

'Good Lord,' she said, in a voice that was deeper than I remember and oddly alluring. 'Fancy seeing you. What are you doing here at this ungodly hour?'

Explained that it was my job to ease the sick and aged into eternity with a spot of Mantovani.

She laughed and said, 'Me, too. But I use more traditional methods.'

I asked her what she meant and she said, 'Oh sorry, I'm the assistant hospital chaplain.' And she pulled open the top of her anorak to reveal a dog collar.

'Bloody hell!' I said.

She said she tried not to mention that. Had I got time for a coffee?

Unfortunately not, but have agreed to go to parish communion at the church in Shepherd's Bush where she is currently the curate, and join her for a bite afterwards.

Am more excited than I have been for years.

Had a strange phone call from a man during the programme. He said, 'How about this for a voice from the grave?' and rang off. Didn't recognize it, but then it was oddly indistinct, as if he had cotton wool in his mouth.

Tried dialling 1471 to get his number, only to discover that particular service is unavailable on switchboards.

I daresay all broadcasters get peculiar phone calls from time to time. It goes with the territory, as they say.

Have made a mental note to ask Wogan about that when we meet.

Was on my way in at five thirty when Mother appeared from nowhere in her nightie and dressing gown wanting to know where I had been. Reminded her that I am now a broadcaster with my own late-night radio show.

'You silly old fool,' she said.

Sunday, July 23rd

To St Wilfred's for parish communion at eleven. Asked John Julius if he would care to join me.

He said, 'No thanks, Dad. I'm not into all that sort of thing.'

Had never imagined that the baby, whose nappies I had once changed and with whose sick my clothes have been so often scented, would one day be almost a stranger to me.

Jane looking gorgeous in white with green stole. Vicar not so gorgeous.

Sermon on forgiveness, taking as his starting point the royal feud between the Queen Mother and the Duchess of Windsor, worthy but less than illuminating, historically and theologically. Am thinking of writing to *The Times* suggesting that all C of E churches should be equipped with electronic buttons in pews which the congregation can press when they get bored. When more than fifty per cent have been pressed, floor in pulpit opens and vicar disappears into crypt.

Is it my imagination or did Jane put extra emphasis on the words 'preserve thy body' when handing me the wafer?

Actually, she didn't say 'thy', she said 'your', which is a bit of a worry. Could she be one of these liturgical vandals who seem

to be taking over the C of E these days? As long as she doesn't expect me to go waving my arms in the air and falling over giggling. Not in church, anyway!

Afterwards we went to the Bunch of Fives and had several beers and an excellent chicken-and-leek pie with mashed potatoes.

Talking to her was like resuming a conversation one had been having only a few minutes before. We had a lot of catching up to do and did so in no uncertain terms.

Both her parents are still alive and in Oxted, though now living in sheltered accommodation. Her ex-husband – Hans, the ski instructor – married his childhood sweetheart and moved to California. Their son, Anton, is now a trainee hairdresser and lives most of the time with his father and two stepbrothers.

She also had news of our old flatmate Victoria who married Mike Pritchard. That ended in tears after five years, as one knew it would, and she is now a supply teacher in Basingstoke.

Mike's son, Tom, is apparently a very successful actor in porno films in Australia, and his sister, Gerry, is a vet on the Isle of Skye.

Jane said she was sorry to hear that Belinda and I had split up. I said that when it came to 'Sportsnight with Coleman', as we used to refer to our love-making in the old days, I could not hope to compete with a personal trainer, nor did I attempt to.

She said, 'Well, as I always tell young couples in my pre-wedding chats, it isn't sex before marriage that's a problem, it's sex *after* marriage.'

When I asked her about her own love life, she said, 'I'm currently married to God. But I'm open to offers.'

Am not sure whether she is pulling my leg or trying to send me a coded message.

Monday, July 24th

Greek party went very well. Am sorry no one took up my invitation to come masked *à la Oresteia*. Must admit my own attempt to re-create Oedipus Rex in papier mâché and tomato sauce not entirely successful, but at least I made the effort.

After dinner, pulled back carpet, put on soundtrack music from *Zorba the Greek*, and led assembled company in some typically peasant measures. Am still unable to establish for certain who threw the first plate into the middle of the floor. All I do know is that P is suddenly short of a complete Portmeirion 'Botanic Garden' tea service and not at all pleased.

Epic tragedy is certainly not confined to the Greeks.

Tuesday, July 25th

Have been reflecting on my school days and wondering whatever happened to my best friend, Waldo Harris. We arrived together in Hoggart's as New Squits in Footer Term 1961 and remained comrades in arms through thick and thin for the next five years, yet I have not see him since the moment we piled our trunks into the boots of our parents' cars after Orations on Founders' Day in July 1966 and bade one another *au revoir* and *bonne chance*.

After breakfast, rang Tommy Thompson at the OF Society, said who I was and asked if he happened to have an address for Harris.

He said, 'Are you the same Crisp that wrote to me recently about Charles Ibstock?'

I said that I was, adding that it was not a task I had enjoyed, but that I felt I owed it to Ibstock's old friends and OFs in general to alert them to his demise.

'Who knows,' I said, 'it could well be that some more fortunate OF may feel sufficiently moved by his plight to help him out of the wretched hole into which he has, perhaps not through his own making, fallen.'

Thompson said, 'I don't know who it was you met recently, but it wasn't Ibstock. Or, put it this way, it wasn't C. D. H. Ibstock OF – Cockman's 1961–65. Or, to give him his full due, Sir Charles Ibstock, CBE, JP, chairman of Manganese Conglomerates, Quantock Radio, Bulstrode Ball Bearings, the Houndsditch Tailoring Group, and Wigs-R-Us plc. Nor do I think Sir Charles, who among other things happens to be on the board of governors of Fenton, will take kindly to people putting it about that he is living in severely reduced circumstances in a cardboard box.'

Remembered that Thompson was a pompous little erk, even as a thirteen-year-old Squit, and my fingers itched to put him on Double Jankers as I did on so many occasions when I was a Top Swine. However, bit my tongue and said I was sorry if I had made a mistake, I was only trying to help, and did he have an address for Harris or didn't he?

Not only did he have an address, but, believe it or not, Waldo lives less than a mile away from me in Tooting. Am astounded that he has not been in touch. Presumably he gets his free weekly copy of the *Mitch & Toot*, like everyone else in the area, and I cannot believe he hasn't read my column once or twice and made the connection.

Rang this evening to be greeted by a BT announcement saying that the person I was calling was not available and would I please try again.

Tried again later with similar result. Felt rather flat suddenly.

Wednesday, July 26th

Programme went unusually well last night.

Had a request from a Dunkirk veteran for Vera Lynn singing 'We'll Meet Again'. Very nearly blubbed, but pulled self together in time to wish good luck to all those due to appear in theatre this morning.

Could not resist having some semantic fun with word 'theatre' and said that of course in the real theatre it's considered bad luck to say 'Good luck' and that instead actors say things like 'Break a leg', though that was perhaps not entirely appropriate in this instance.

Suggested 'Have a good one' might be more suitable and followed up my advice with the Swansea Rugby Supporters Club choir singing 'Abide With Me'.

Am wondering whether to substitute that for 'Strangers in the Night' as my sig. tune. It certainly has a little more gravitas to it.

Thursday, July 27th

Tried ringing Waldo Harris again this morning and this time got through to a woman whom I took to be his wife, but turned out to be his home help.

Joshed her and said that, if I knew Waldo, he didn't need anyone's help.

She said, 'Well, he does now.'

I can't imagine why. The voice that finally greeted me was

as strong and cheerful as any I have heard on the other end of a telephone line in years.

'Where have you been all these years, you old devil?' I cried.

'Who is this?' the voice said.

Don't know if he was having me on and, if so, what he hoped to achieve by it, but, travelling back down the corridors of memory, I seem to remember he always did seem to derive some perverse pleasure from putting me on the back foot and, if possible, keeping me there.

However, was not about to let a small character defect spoil the pleasure of hearing my old friend's voice again, and very soon we were back on familiar leg-pulling terms, the years melted away and we were in Toggers' Room again, devising yet another fiendish plot for putting the mockers on poor old Dickie Dunmow and thinking up more nasty punishments for the New Squits.

'Why don't we have lunch one of these days and take a real journey down memory lane?' I said.

He seemed rather reluctant, I thought; however, we have arranged to meet next Tuesday at this new canteen-style restaurant down by the river that's supposed to be all the rage. It'll probably cost us an arm and a leg, but we haven't been apart for three and a half decades, only to meet up again in a greasy spoon.

Friday, July 28th

To Toad-under-the-Harrow for lunch with Bryant-Fenn. Took Woodhouse along with me – unwisely, as it turned out, since he had words with a Bedlington Terrier that came strutting in just as we were getting stuck into our seared scallops with rocket salad and pecorino shavings. Can't say I blamed him. Have never seen a cockier-looking animal in my life.

Was trying, unsuccessfully, to stop him barking, when the barman called out in an unmistakably Antipodean accent, 'Either tell that dog to put a sock in it or take him out.'

Hugh said, 'Mr Crisp is a distinguished journalist, restaurant critic and broadcaster. He also happens to be my guest.'

The barman said, 'Perhaps you should take him outside, too.'

Could see Hugh was on point of flying into one of his famous rages, so rapidly defused situation by saying I ought to leave anyway and start work on my radio show.

Hugh grudgingly conceded defeat, but said that wasn't the end of the matter by any means and that someone would be feeling the rough side of his tongue in no uncertain terms.

Was wrestling with intro to 'Best of Bing' when Hugh rang to say he had spoken to the proprietor, who couldn't have been more apologetic and has invited us both to have lunch, on him, at any pub in the Toad Group whenever it suits us. Was August 14th any good for me?

Told him I'd check my diary. Rang back shortly afterwards to say I'd managed to move a few things around and now had a window at one o'clock on the 14th.

Sada got chucked out of the *Big Brother* house this evening. Can't say I'm surprised.

Saturday, July 29th

I don't believe it. I think I've got a stalker. You hear about this sort of thing happening to celebrities, but never believe it could possibly happen to you.

Presume whoever it was who left the anonymous note for me at main reception desk is the same person who rang me the other night while I was on air, but who knows?

The note, made up of words cut out of newspapers, reads: BET YOU NEVER THOUGHT YOU'D HEAR FROM ME AGAIN!

Can't decide whether to bring police in at this early stage or wait and see if he loses interest. Or should I say she?

A more immediate worry is the fact that James has come back from Scotland and I am now back in the tent. Am beginning to know what it feels like to be voted out of the *Big Brother* house.

Sunday, July 30th

To evensong at St Wilfred's. Have always enjoyed the calm of this most intimate of the Church of England's services. Am seriously considering replacing Fred Astaire singing 'Isn't This a Lovely Day?' on my *Desert Island Discs* list with 'The Day Thou Gavest, Lord, is Ended.'

In view of my return to the tent and the uncomfortable presence of my stalker, the line in the prayer about defending us from all perils and dangers of this night is suddenly filled with fresh significance.

Went round afterwards to meet Jane. Would I like to come back to her place for a light supper? she enquired.

Why not? I thought.

By an extraordinary coincidence she lives in a flat in Doxby Mansions, which is the block next door to Wentworth Mansions where we lived all those years ago. What's more, the layout is almost exactly the same.

Sitting next to her on the sofa, sipping a light Verdicchio and gossiping about old friends, I experienced a sense of déjà vu that reincarnationists would give their eye teeth for.

Dressed in simple white shirt and well-cut jeans, with dog collar and cassock consigned to the bedroom cupboard, she was suddenly not a priest any more, but a warm and beautiful woman. Do not remember her eyes being quite so blue. The more I looked at her and the more we talked, the more I cursed myself for ditching her all those years ago for the sake of a flibbertigibbet like Amanda.

Suddenly realized it was nearly midnight.

'I must go,' I said.

'Must you?' she said, and before I knew what she was in my arms and we were kissing each other with an enthusiasm that I do not remember from the somewhat perfunctory encounters of our youth.

Cannot honestly say that I have ever experienced anything approaching a religious experience, but suddenly, there on the sofa with my hair in disarray and Jane's white shirt riding up over her slim and supple trunk, had some inkling of what Jesus must have gone through in the desert with the Devil.

Not, of course, that He and Satan were exploring each other's back teeth at the time – certainly not in 14B Doxby Mansions – but the analogy is not, I believe, inappropriate.

To launch into a bout of Sportsnight with Coleman willy-nilly with one of the handmaids of the Lord could be asking for trouble – if not here and now, then very possibly in the hereafter.

Explained my moral misgivings to Jane.

She said, 'I don't know what you've got to worry about. You don't have to stand up in front of a churchful of people on Sunday morning and remind them they're all sinners and tell them to pull their socks up.'

I laughed and said that anyone who has ever read the *News of the World* knows that priests are some of the worst-behaved people of all, and that most of us take what vicars say in church these days with a large pinch of salt. Anyway, it wasn't as if she was misbehaving with one of the choirboys!

She said 'I'm not misbehaving with anyone at the moment, merely having a jolly good snog with an old boyfriend and enjoying every moment of it. I don't know about you.'

I said that I couldn't agree more.

She said, 'Well, can we please stop talking about it, then, and get on?'

Though my conversion to Christianity may be hanging in the balance, my conversion to the Rev. Jane Baker is total.

Monday, July 31st

My cup overfloweth. Who should ring up this morning but the editor of the FlemAir in-flight magazine, launched last month to coincide with their recently inaugurated service from Stansted Airport, wanting to know if I'd be interested in spending a couple of days in Antwerp next week and writing a thousand words about it.

The £250 fee is not quite as handsome as one might have hoped, but against that must be weighed the opportunity to break away from the weekly grind of local journalism, to venture into pastures new and to show that one is more than a one-note accordionist. Have told editor that I think I can see a way of squeezing it into a very busy schedule. He seemed relieved.

Passed neighbour as I was going out this afternoon. Gave her a cheery greeting, but she ignored me and walked on into the house. Is it my imagination or is she losing her looks?

August

Tuesday, August 1st

The start of what is for many the holiday season, but for me could turn out to be the busiest month of my professional and personal life.

To The Canteen at 12.30 to meet Waldo. Got slightly held up owing to bomb scare at Clapham Common, and arrived rather later than expected. Place already humming with activity. Thought I spotted Melvyn at the bar, but it could have been one of the Gallaghers.

Surprised to find no one manning desk at entrance to restaurant, so took it upon self to go on through.

Looked around to see if I could spot my old friend. Obviously realized he would have changed in three decades – which of us hasn't? On the other hand, have always prided myself on being able to recognize people I haven't seen for years and sometimes didn't even know very well at the time. It's a curious, inexplicable and totally natural talent, like Uri Geller's for bending spoons, and have often wondered if it could be put to some practical use – though have not yet managed to work out what, exactly.

Can think of many people who, faced with the elegantly suited, grey-haired figure who bore down on me from the far side of the restaurant, would have stopped in their tracks, uncertain if this was the man they had waited thirty years and more to see again. There was no such doubt in my mind, however. The face of the thirteen-year-old in his new suit and stick-up collar was as clear to me in that crowded restaurant as it had been that day in Big Hall when we exchanged our first hesitant words together – 'Shall we sit next to each other in Refec?'

'Waldemar Harris!' I cried, and though I had never once to my certain knowledge embraced a man in my life, I threw my arms round him and kissed him on both cheeks. Tears sprang unbidden to my eyes. 'My dear old friend. You haven't changed one little bit.' And I hugged him again.

He stepped back, looked me straight in the eye and said, 'Your guest is waiting for you at Table Three.'

The man sitting alone a few feet away was a complete stranger to me. For a start he looked twenty years older than me. His grey hair was thin, his cheeks were drawn and his eyes were dull and staring.

'Crisp?' he said.

'Harris?' I said. 'Is it really you?'

It really was, too. Would not have recognized him in a million years. And it was not just his appearance that had changed drastically; he just wasn't the old Waldo any more.

For a start, he drank nothing but tap water and chose the plainest dishes on the menu. Not that they were any cheaper, mind. Noticing that he seemed to leave most of his food on his plate, I said, 'You should eat more. You look as though you need feeding up.'

He said, 'I would if I had a stomach to put it in.'

Shocked to discover there is hardly a facet of his life that has not ended in tears.

When he lost his job in the City in the Nineties, he and his wife Sally moved to Devon, where they tried to make a go of organic pig farming and failed. He now lives in a basement flat in Tooting and ekes out a tiny private income with not very well-paid genealogical work for gullible Americans.

'With Sally?' I said.

'Not in fact,' he said. 'She ran off with a drummer in a Turkish pop group in 1997 and I haven't seen hair or hide of her since.'

Thinking to lighten the tone, I said, 'You should have married that cracker of a maid you had a thing with at school. You and half of Hoggart's. She was a real goer.'

'I did,' he said.

Not the jolliest lunch I have ever had, nor the cheapest. Am seriously beginning to wonder if Memory Lane is all it's cracked up to be. It certainly didn't make Proust a happy man.

I should be feeling reassured that there are people worse off than me, but for some reason am not.

Wednesday, August 2nd

Whether my lunch with Waldo – or in his case non-lunch – has had a more disturbing effect on me than I realized I do not know, but am suddenly getting rather worried about this irritating little cough I have had all summer and seem quite unable to throw off. Am no hypochondriac, but it is a well-known fact that one's fifties are the most vulnerable period of one's life, and little complaints that in one's youth one cheerfully dismissed without a second thought suddenly take on a decidedly sinister significance.

It may, of course, be nothing more than the legacy of that cough that nearly lost me the radio job. On the other hand, every life-threatening illness has its origins in the most innocent-seeming symptoms, and am fast approaching the age when 'little coughs' all too often turn out to presage something far more serious. Would pop down to the doctor's, were there not a serious risk of his suggesting I should 'have some tests', and we all know where that can lead.

Cannot believe the Queen Mother has not had a few comparable health scares in her time, yet there she is with two new hips and goodness knows what other artificial bits and pieces, beetling around the countryside like someone half her age. Which is more or less what I am.

She is an example to us all. Mother, for one, could do worse than take a leaf out her book – assuming she can remember who she is.

Thursday, August 3rd

Mother is not the only old lady who I hope will be adopting a more easy-going attitude to modern life during the Queen Mother's 100th birthday celebrations.

Was walking in the park with Woodhouse yesterday when I was astonished to see a well-dressed woman standing there watching her Pekinese struggling to do its business in the grass at the side of the path.

'Well done, darling,' I heard her say when the animal had finally deposited its load, and she walked away with her dog waddling along behind her, both looking extremely pleased with themselves.

'Excuse me,' I called after her.

At first she completely ignored me, so I repeated myself, this time a bit louder.

She finally turned and looked at me.

'Yes?' she said.

I said, 'You are going to clear that mess up, aren't you?'

'No,' she said.

I said, 'You do know that it's an offence to permit your dog to foul the public footpath?'

She pointed at the grass and said, 'That is not a footpath.'

I said that, technically speaking, she may have had a point, but it amounted to the same thing. People walked on it and, more to the point, so did children.

I said, 'Did you know that dog faeces can cause blindness in children?'

She completely ignored me, as if I had never spoken, and began to walk away.

I called after her, 'So you're perfectly happy to allow your dog to do its business wherever it feels inclined, regardless of any life-threatening diseases it may be carrying, and leave it there for people to walk in and children to put their hands in. Is that what you're saying?'

She said, 'I'm not saying anything. You're the one who's doing all the talking.'

Decided to adopt a more conciliatory tone. 'Look,' I said, 'as one dog owner to another . . .'

She said, 'As one dog owner to another, piss off,' and walked away, making a thoroughly obscene gesture.

I think I made my point.

Friday, August 4th

The 100th birthday of Her Majesty Queen Elizabeth the Queen Mother. A day that will live for ever in the memories of those of us who were fortunate enough to be alive at this time, and will surely go down in the history books as a date to be remembered by schoolchildren of succeeding generations, along with Domesday Book, the Field of the Cloth of Gold and the Great Reform Bill.

Was particularly touched by the sight of HM travelling in open landau to the Palace with Prince Charles. The more I see of him, the more I am convinced that this is a man with whom I have a lot more in common than may at first appear – not least the fact that I, too, once suffered from prominent ears.

Saturday, August 5th

Programme curiously lacklustre. Not helped by having to confess to all and sundry that my suggestion the week before last to Mrs Renshawe of Glenda Jackson Ward re getting on and off a bedpan was not a success. Can only hope her memorial service in the hospital chapel at eleven a.m. next Friday will be well attended.

Sunday, August 6th

Do people who have things with vicars – or, in this case, curates – become more religious? I wonder. Does something rub off, as it were? Not that Jane and I are over the final hurdle yet, but even so could not wait to get to matins this morning.

Looking at her rather rumpled surplice, wondered what certain members of congregation would say if they knew where that had been in the last forty-eight hours!

J's sermon on not letting oneself be deceived by appearances first-rate. Very much enjoyed her joke about hospital visitor confusing floor-polisher with life-support system and hope I did not give anything away with my somewhat over-enthusiastic laughter. Don't say I'm catching a dose of Toronto Blessing!

Is it my imagination or was she looking straight at me when she got to bit about the Lord blessing us and keeping us? Legs went quite wobbly.

Monday, August 7th

To the Pigsty Theatre in Dalston with Mollie Marsh-Gibbon to see this highly acclaimed musical version of *A la recherche du temps perdu* that everyone's talking about.

Not the most accessible of theatrical venues, and certainly not the most comfortable.

Still, there is no excuse for people to arrive just as the lights are dimming, as the two women in Row P behind us did. Had I had the faintest inkling as to the second one's bust measurement, would have taken evasive action. As it was, she caught me a heavy blow on the back of my head, jolting it forward in a reverse whiplash. Was left with such a stiff neck that I spent most of the first half staring at my knees.

An extraordinary thing happened in the second half. A man in the row in front suddenly slumped sideways into an empty seat and started making horrible croaking noises.

Man further along row said, 'I'll ring for an ambulance' and rushed up gangway and out through exit.

Mollie said, 'I do wish people wouldn't do this sort of thing in the theatre.'

The man was still making terrible sounds in back of throat, and by now half the audience was looking in his direction rather than at the stage. Not that it mattered, since the actors were also peering into the darkness to see what was happening.

Suddenly another man appeared from nowhere and said, 'It's all right. I know about these things. I'm a dentist.'

Curiously enough, have been having a bit of trouble with a filling in one of my top-left molars, and the thought did cross my mind to ask if he happened to have his card on him, when I heard him say, 'Get his tongue.'

Suddenly realized he was talking to me.

'His tongue,' he said. 'Put two fingers down his throat and grab his tongue, otherwise he might swallow it.'

'Are you sure?' I said.

'Perfectly sure,' he said.

Leaned forward, extended first two fingers of right hand in a reverse V-sign and lowered them into mouth. Fortunately it was wide open and tongue was reasonably easy to locate. Clamped fingers round it and, despite surface sliminess, was able to get good purchase.

At that moment, first man reappeared with two St John Ambulance officers, carrying stretcher.

By now everyone on stage had stopped acting and was staring at real drama in Row N.

Mollie called out, 'When I was at RADA we were taught that the show must go on.' It's the first I have heard that she was trained for the stage.

The ambulance crew were beginning to grapple with the man when he suddenly opened his eyes and looked straight up into mine. Got such a shock I sprang backwards. My fingers were halfway out of mouth when he snapped it shut, trapping them painfully between front teeth.

Have not experienced such sharp pain since Vita mistook my hand for the post when Belinda and I lived in Colliers Wood.

The man said, 'Who the hell are you and what the hell do you think you're doing in my mouth?'

Explained that I was only following orders and that we were afraid he might swallow his tongue.

He said, 'The day a chap can't go to a play and have forty winks without some complete stranger shoving his fingers down his throat is the day I give up the theatre once and for all.' And he got up, seized his coat, briefcase and copy of the *Evening Standard* and marched out.

I was not far behind. One reads stories in the paper every day about people contracting horrible diseases in unexpected ways and, in the circumstances, a check-up in the local hospital seemed very much in order.

Mollie absolutely refused to budge, so spent the next three hours sitting alone in Dickensian gloom, thumbing through torn and greasy back numbers of *Hello!* magazine.

Mind you, compared with Proust it was like a weekend in the South of France.

Tuesday, August 8th

Life is just one coincidence after another these days. What is the first thing I hear when I turn on the *Today* programme this morning? Only that Sir Alec Guinness has died.

Warm tributes in the press and on television from all and sundry, sprinkled with touching and amusing anecdotes – though not, I am sorry to say, mine.

Sat down immediately after breakfast and got out piece I had written about him following our encounter on bus in March. Topped and tailed it with appropriate sentiments and sent it off to *Mitch & Toot,* attention Barry Balls, with attached note saying URGENT. FOR TOMORROW'S PAPER.

Am only sorry Sir Alec did not live long enough to read these modest jottings of which he was the principal midwife, and to know how much I owed to that simple, ordinary-looking man I met on that spring morning on the top of the Mitcham omnibus.

I shall miss him.

Wednesday, August 9th

Was on my way out to collect Belgian francs from bank when spotty Herbert delivered *Mitch & Toot*. Could not believe my eyes. No sign of my Alec Guinness obituary, but large, unsigned piece on the late Sir Robin Day, who had the misfortune to die on the same day as Sir Alec.

I yield to no one in my respect and admiration for Sir Robin's interviewing skills, and cannot agree with his own, often expressed, belief that his work was trivial and worthless compared with the politicians he took to task with such vigour. But, as I think he himself would have been the first to agree, a warm, personal tribute to one of the greatest actors of his generation should have pride of place over a dry recital of the career highlights of a broadcaster, however distinguished.

Rang editor's office to say as much. Spoke to Sheila Hollingsworth-Palfrey who said that, as a fellow journalist, a lifelong admirer and close personal friend, the editor himself had written the piece on Sir Robin. Pointed out that there cannot be many local newspapers on the streets today that can boast a columnist who knew Sir Alec Guinness.

She said, 'Your piece certainly didn't read like that. It sounded merely as if you had spoken to him once on the top floor of a bus in Mitcham Lane. Not that that seems very likely.'

So much for the power of faith.

Thursday, August 10th

To Stansted for two-thirty flight to Antwerp. Was surprised to find myself in Tourist Class.

'No mention of an upgrade, then?' I said casually to girl at FlemAir check-in.

She looked at her computer screen. 'No,' she said.

Was wandering past Arrivals, looking for suitable place to

have snack, when man in chauffeur's uniform holding board with name on it said would I do him a favour and hold the board for a moment? He was bursting for a pee and he'd be back in two shakes. Duly obliged.

No sooner had he disappeared than a crowd came pouring through from Customs. Was praying one of them would not turn out to be the person whose name was on my board, when who should I see marching straight towards me but Derrick Trubshawe, looking very smart with a briefcase, obviously back from some business meeting.

Pretended to look the other way, but too late.

'Hello, Simon,' he said. 'Glad to see things are going better for you. Amanda will be so pleased.' And he gave my arm a little squeeze and walked away.

To cap it all, my flight was called before I had a chance to eat anything.

Could not help noticing, as stewardess was pulling curtain across, that there were several empty seats in Business Class section.

Waited until seat-belt sign switched off and made myself known to purser. He seemed genuinely pleased to have me on board and was most interested to know that I was writing a piece about my trip for in-flight magazine. He said if there was anything he could do to make my flight more comfortable, I had only to ask.

Told him an upgrade would not go amiss. He said that would not be possible, since they had only just enough Business Class lunches to go round.

I said that I would be quite happy with a complimentary glass of something.

He said he was very sorry, but it was not within his remit to upgrade passengers.

I pointed out that I was hardly a passenger, more a member of the team.

He finally relented and said I could sit in one of stewardesses' seats for a while if it would make me any happier.

Did not say so, but anything would have been preferable to sitting next to the red-faced man in the window seat who looked, and smelt, like a pig farmer.

'I'm being upgraded,' I told him as I collected my bits and pieces.

'Good,' he said.

Had I realized stewardess's seat was next to lavatory, might have thought twice about taking up purser's offer. Had no idea Business Class passengers went quite so often. I know businessmen lead busy lives, but surely they can spare a few minutes to do their other sort of business after breakfast like everyone else.

Also slightly regretted not having had something to eat before boarding. The smoked salmon and prawns, the fillet steak and the fresh fruit salad, which the purser was at great pains to show me, looked really delicious, and the glass of complimentary Chardonnay, though perfectly acceptable in it's own simple way, did little to fill an increasingly empty stomach.

Finally told purser my research had been concluded and returned to pig-pen, only to find lunch service at an end.

Finally arrived in Antwerp – the City of Rubens, as we art lovers know it – at half past five to find there had been a mix-up with the hotels and had to move to another, so did not get unpacked until nearly six. Not quite the four-star luxury I had been expecting, but perfectly adequate for one night.

At least it was very well situated, so was able to spend remaining hours of daylight on walking tour of city centre. My guidebook said, 'Antwerp is a pedestrian-friendly city.' It certainly is.

Very impressed by guild houses in Grote Markt, Town Hall and Commodity Exchange. Just missed famous carillon playing in Vlaeykensgang, but much enjoyed Hendrik Conscienceplein, where, in words of guidebook, 'The city takes you in its protective arms.' Could not have put it better myself.

Strolled down the Meir, Antwerp's most famous shopping area (remembering to keep an eye open for what remains of the nineteenth century eclectic façades) and thought about buying a small diamond for Jane, but, seeing prices, felt she might not approve of such ostentation. Instead had delicious snack in street café in Keyserlei, dropped in at Central Station to see famous domed ticket hall and went back to hotel to relax and take stock of everything I had experienced in a long and often confusing day.

In side street on way back, bought beer and packet of crisps from street trader and ate them in bed while watching *Inspector Morse* in Flemish.

Got up for last widdle, threw sheet back and had the shock

P. P. RUBENS

of my life. Lying in the middle of the bed was a small plastic bag filled with white powder. It must have fallen out of the bag the beer and crisps were in.

One hears all too often about innocent people being caught at Customs carrying drugs which a dealer in some foreign city, posing as a tout or another tourist, has planted on them, but have always associated this trade with India and Thailand. Did not realize it had reached Europe.

Wondered about ringing police, but would they believe my story? I would look very silly being thrown into a Belgian jail, having turned myself in.

In the end, tore bag open, poured contents down lavatory, flushed it several times, burnt bag in waste-paper bin and went to bed with windows wide open to get rid of smell.

Am writing all this down now so that, in the event of any trouble, will be able to quote chapter and verse.

Friday, August 11th

Woke after best night's sleep in months, still worrying slightly about packet, but convinced I did the only thing possible in the circumstances.

Beautiful morning. Strolled to river and breakfasted in Jean-Claude van Damme Café and Internet Chat Lounge down by docks with Belgian papers. Good croissants, though probably not a place to be recommended to those of nervous disposition.

Morning spent on 'Footsteps of Van Dyck' tour. Was specially fascinated to see site in Grote Markt of the house where he was born, since had always thought of him as Dutch. One learns something every day.

Returned to hotel via street where I had bought beer and crisps. Street trader still there, looking shifty, as well he might. Could have walked on, and most people probably would have, but my journalistic instincts held me back. The smell of a juicy news story was too good to resist.

Casually bought a can of lager and a packet of plain crisps, and was on my way when voice called out, 'Hello!'

Stopped and turned to see him holding up small packet identical to last night's.

'Don't you want your packet of salt?' he said.

In normal circumstances would have taken the matter further. Unfortunately, was booked on noon flight and had other, more pressing, fish to fry. Pity, but that's journalism for you.

Plane surprisingly full. Cannot imagine who would wish to fly from Belgium to East Anglia in the middle of the day. Said as much to stolid-looking girl at FlemAir check-in desk.

She said, 'Well, *you* do.'

Took opportunity to do some in-depth testing on in-flight catering, and when the catering trolley hove into view, told steward with shaved head and big moustache that I wanted the kosher meal.

Am no fan of the latke and the bagel, but that is not the point. Airline regulations stipulate that anyone of any persuasion is entitled to ask for kosher food, and, let's face it, anything is preferable to rubber chicken and cardboard vegetables. Even chopped liver.

Steward said was I quite sure? The chicken was very popular.

I replied that I was positive.

He said, 'It could pose a problem.'

I said that, problem or not, according to airline regulations I was perfectly within my rights to order the kosher alternative.

He said if I could bear with him he'd make some enquiries.

I said I could bear with him all the way back to Stansted, if necessary. His smile smacked of artificiality.

Male passenger in seat next to me said, 'You don't look very Jewish.'

Asked him if he was questioning my religious faith.

'Not at all,' he said. 'It's merely an observation. If someone were to ask me what religion you were, the last thing I'd say was Jewish.'

I asked him if, as a matter of interest, anyone had engaged him on this highly implausible topic.

He said he was merely hypothesizing.

'All right, then,' I said. 'Hypothesize about this. Supposing someone were to ask you what religion Michael Douglas is.'

'I'd say Episcopalian,' he said.

At this point, middle-aged woman on the other side of the aisle chipped in.

'He's of Viking stock, isn't he? Danish, Norwegian, something of the sort. His father is anyway. Kirk.'

The man said, 'I always thought Kirk was Italian. He was in *Spartacus*. Roman, anyway.'

I said that just goes to show how deceptive appearances can be. In fact Kirk Douglas is Jewish.

The woman said, 'Kirk Douglas Jewish? Don't be ridiculous.'

I said, 'To prove how Jewish he is, he recently celebrated his bar mitzvah.'

The man said, 'His bar mitzvah? Kirk Douglas? I thought he was dead.'

Suddenly the steward appeared from nowhere and said, 'You're thinking of Burt Lancaster.'

The male passenger said, 'How do you know what I'm thinking? We've never met before.'

'Oh,' said the steward. 'Pardon me for breathing.'

I said to the man next to me that he couldn't possibly have been a Roman in *Spartacus*. He was a slave. Greek, probably.

'Or Scythian,' the steward said. 'He had Scythian thighs.'

'He's eighty-three, if you must know,' I said. 'Possibly eighty-four.'

'Spartacus?' said the woman.

I said since when did they have geriatric gladiators in Rome?

The man said, 'Since when did eighty-three-year-olds have bar mitzvahs?'

I pointed out that, according to the Jewish faith, once you have achieved your biblical span of threescore years and ten, you start all over again – from scratch, as it were – and that, in the eyes of God, Kirk is actually only thirteen.

The man said that couldn't possibly be right, because, if it were, it would mean that Michael Douglas hasn't actually been born yet.

'Doesn't *know* he's been born, more likely,' said the woman.

'Neither would you if you were married to that Catherine Zeta whatsername woman.'

'Jones,' I said. 'Catherine Zeta Jones. She's Welsh.'

'Excuse me,' the steward interrupted.

I said, 'She certainly is. Born in the Welsh valleys. Land of my fathers and all that.'

The man said, 'Why? Are you Welsh, then?'

'No,' I said.

'It's not possible,' the steward said.

I said I was very sorry if he thought otherwise, but the fact is I am not Welsh. I am a Man of Kent, born and bred.

The woman said, 'Oh, perhaps you can tell me. What is the difference between a Man of Kent and a Kentish Man? I've always wondered.'

The steward said, 'What I mean is, it's not possible to serve you a kosher meal on this flight.'

Was reminding him, yet again, of airline regulations, when he interrupted me in a decidedly snippy tone of voice to say that he had just looked them up. He then read out the appropriate paragraph. 'On flights of less than one hour's duration, a cold snack is served with a choice of tea, coffee or fruit juice from the trolley.'

He said to his way of thinking a chicken sandwich is a chicken sandwich in any religion, as he felt sure Jehovah would be the first to agree. And he flounced off down the aisle.

When I next saw him, behind the duty-free trolley, I said that, as a guest of FlemAir, I had expected a certain degree of preferential treatment.

He said, 'Perhaps sir would care to try this free VIP sample.' And he gave me a complimentary squirt of Schwarzenegger Eau de Toilette for Real Men.

Unfortunately, happened to move my head slightly at crucial moment and took the full brunt in my left ear.

Shall be very interested to hear how the powers that be at FlemAir head office react when I hint that I may, after all, not be able to give them quite the whole-hearted plug they had been anticipating.

Obviously cannot hold them responsible for the fact that my visit coincided with a nasty dose of catarrh following my recent cough and cold. On the other hand, the speed with which Captain Rukkers depressurized the cabin on our descent over the Essex marshes was at best cavalier and, at worst, smacked of collusion with certain members of the cabin crew.

At all events, cannot believe I was the only passenger who descended the airline steps that afternoon with his hearing seriously diminished, his sinuses severely blocked and his balance dangerously disturbed.

It was sheer bad luck that I happened to catch my foot on the bottom step and went head first on to the tarmac. There was no call whatever for the man who had been sitting next to me to shout out, 'I never realized we had the Pope on board.'

More trouble in Baggage Reclaim when the trolley I picked

seemed to have a will of its own and, despite my efforts to steer it towards Green channel at Customs, found myself heading willy-nilly into Red.

Was walking nonchalantly through when I heard a voice saying, 'Excuse me!' Turned to see customs officer gesturing in my direction.

I asked him if he was speaking to me.

He said, 'No, sir. The Invisible Man. If you wouldn't mind stepping over here and placing your luggage on the counter.'

Told him that, actually, I should really have been in Green channel.

'Oh really?' he said. 'Why aren't you, then?'

Explained about faulty wheels, adding that, as a guest of FlemAir, a travel correspondent and a columnist for a London newspaper, I would be dropping a sharp note to the press office at the British Airports Authority the moment I got back to my office.

He seemed very sympathetic. 'You say that you tried to go through the Green channel, but in some mysterious way found your way here?'

I said that I realized it sounded implausible, but that was exactly what happened.

He said, 'Do you know what that sounds like to me, sir?'

'No,' I said.

'That sounds like a guilty conscience to me, sir,' he said. 'Now then, if you wouldn't mind unzipping your bag.'

How I came to find myself in the Examination Room with my trousers round my ankles and a customs officer pulling on a pair of rubber gloves I shall never know. Just because he had never heard of Schwarzenegger Eau de Toilette for Real Men and his wretched sniffer dog took such a shine to it, that was no reason to adopt the zero-tolerance attitude he did. Nor am I entirely convinced that he was telling the truth when he said that it was no more fun for him than it was for me. The relish with which he snapped the gloves open was all too obvious.

As for his assurance to the effect that 'This will not hurt', was strongly tempted to tell him where he could put his finger, but was not ideally placed to do so.

Am not a vengeful man, but if today's events do not lend themselves to a few trenchant words of complaint to *Holiday Watchdog*, I don't know what do.

Saturday, August 12th

Hardly the Glorious Twelfth for me, or for my bottom.

By an extraordinary coincidence, happened to read in newspaper on way back from airport that prostate examinations for men over fifty are more popular than at any time since the Second World War. Not with me. However, it made an appropriately medical intro to my Antwerp experiences and afterwards, which formed the highlight of my radio show last night.

Should perhaps have thought twice about segueing from thoughts on rubber gloves to Dickie Valentine singing 'The Finger of Suspicion'. Put it down to stress. Not, unfortunately, that Mr Diggle in Ann Widdecombe Ward saw it that way. He rang through to the studio shortly before four o'clock to say that he was recovering from an extremely painful haemorrhoid operation and that he did not consider it an area to be gone into lightly. He hoped for my sake that I would never have to suffer to the extent that he had. I hope so, too.

All in all, not the happiest night of my broadcasting career.

As if I didn't have enough to worry about, Loretta Young has died.

Sunday, August 13th

Came down to breakfast to find Chad's Sunday rag open at page 11 with story ringed in red Pentel about a Spaniard with the improbable name of José Tango who is claiming a world record after cracking forty-seven walnuts in an hour between his buttocks. Just thinking about it makes me feel even more uncomfortable than I do already. But then I presume that's exactly what Chad was hoping for. More to the point, how did José discover this bizarre talent in the first place?

To evensong at St Wilfred's. Jane's choice of text for sermon – 'And Adam and Eve were naked and they were not ashamed' – rather apt in the light of our activities later at Doxby Mansions!

Jane was always a robust soul, and just because she has taken holy orders does not mean that she is not also a healthy middle-aged woman with healthy appetites to match. And nor am I.

At the same time, sense that she has not cleared things with the Almighty to her total satisfaction – or to His. God is not easily mocked, any more than are his servants, and feel I was right to suggest that we should not try and clear the final hurdle until we are both ready and happy to stretch the leg and take the leap of faith that I believe we both crave and deserve.

Have a shrewd suspicion that it is only a matter of time before we are under starter's orders. Was bemoaning my unsatisfactory sleeping arrangements at Bermuda Avenue when Jane suddenly said why didn't I move in with her? There is plenty of room.

Am not entirely clear whether by 'room' she meant in her bed or in the flat generally. Time alone will tell. God, too, I hope. In the meantime, have decided to play it very much by ear.

I move in next Sunday. The week cannot go fast enough for me.

Monday, August 14th

To lunch with Hugh at Toad-in-the-Hole in Parson's Green. Found him established at outside table with jug of Pimms and two glasses.

Had barely sat down when a large man with bow tie and dark-red face emerged from saloon bar holding a fat cigar and stood there looking thoroughly pleased with himself. Talk about 'the purple-headed mountain'!

Hugh called out, 'Hello, Tarquin. How's it hanging?'

'Hugh!' the man called back. 'Very nicely, thanks for asking. Mind if I join you?' And he came across and sat on the bench next to me, taking up so much room that I had to squeeze up against the wall.

'Tarquin Nethercliff,' he said, seizing my hand. 'I own the joint. Well, all the Toad pubs, actually. Always had a thing about Toad in *Wind in the Willows*. One of the great characters of English fiction. Parp parp.'

Was on point of telling him my name when Hugh said, 'Pimms?' and, before I knew what, he had grabbed my glass, filled it to the brim and he and Tarquin were toasting each other's health and carelessly knocking it back as if it were as innocuous as Orange Barley Water.

Went indoors to get another glass and cast eye over menu. Very much liked the sound of the seared sea bass with summer leaves.

Asked the pretty girl who was serving the food what the *soupe du jour* was. 'I'll just enquire,' she said, and disappeared through swing door beside bar. She was away for ages and was on point of giving up when she reappeared.

'I've found out what it is,' she said. 'It's the soup of the day.'

Returned to table to find Hugh emptying last of Pimms into Tarquin's glass.

'Oh, while you're up,' he said, handing me the jug.

A tenner seemed rather steep for a drink consisting largely of lemonade, some assorted fruit and a few sprigs of mint, but in the circumstances didn't like to say anything.

The two of them chatted on for a further hour about this and that, customers at the next table came and went, as did two more jugs of Pimms and another large cigar.

Finally, at about two fifteen, Tarquin looked at his watch and said, 'Is that the time? I must be on my way. You two lunching?'

'Hope so,' I said with a laugh.

'Great,' he said. 'The sea bass is particularly good. If there's any left.'

He stood up and shook my hand and said, 'Nice to have met you.' Then he turned to Hugh. 'Oh by the way,' he said, 'Next time you come, bring that journalist chappie with you. Lunch on me. Toodle-oo.' And he strode off down the road in a cloud of cigar smoke.

When I asked Hugh why he hadn't said anything, he replied, 'One of the cardinal rules of PR: Never embarrass your client.'

Tuesday, August 15th

Was gathering a few odds and ends in a black plastic bag when an enormous bird landed on chimney pot of the house opposite.

Am no David Attenborough, but I know a Golden Eagle when I see one – though what a bird like this was doing flying around Mitcham landing on people's chimney pots is anybody's guess.

Ran out into the street for a closer look. Several people had already gathered and were taking photographs and peering up at it through binoculars. Couldn't help noticing that the only people who were not among them were the owners of the house, so went and rang their front doorbell. After a while the door opened and a man stood there, with a copy of the *Daily Mail* in one hand and a cup of tea in the other.

I said that I was sorry to disturb him, but did he realize there was a Golden Eagle sitting on his chimney pot?

He said, 'I'm not a birdwatcher,' and closed the door on me.

The sooner I leave Bermuda Avenue the better.

Wednesday, August 16th

Can behaviour in the country get any worse? Was walking down Honeysuckle Grove this morning, pondering Liz Hurley's less than loyal comments re Hugh Grant's sexual performance, when a cyclist suddenly shot by me at high speed, brushing against my bag full of Sainsbury's shopping and giving me the fright of my life.

Had I chanced to move an inch to my left at that moment I could have suffered serious physical injury, if not worse.

What *is* the point of the council putting signs up at either end of this attractive, peaceful, almost rural pedestrian path if people don't take a blind bit of notice?

'Excuse me,' I called after him. 'Cycling's not allowed.'

'I couldn't give a toss, mate,' he shouted back, and cycled on faster than ever.

Mentioned the incident to P who said, 'I have always believed in the principle of live and let live.'

Said I was very sorry, but I had been brought up to believe that it is the duty of the older generation to set an example to the young and to pull them up short when they overstep the mark. If we do not tell them how to behave, who will?

P said, 'You were also brought up to believe that everyone under the age of fifteen should be in bed by nine o'clock at night, that it's a policeman's job to give a child a sharp clip round the ear every time he sees one, and that you aren't allowed to have any cake until you've eaten all your bread and butter.'

'Meaning?' I said.

'Meaning,' she said, 'that you're a stupid old fart.'

I sometimes wonder if we are even remotely related, let alone the fruit of our parents' loins.

Thursday, August 17th

Quel drame! Nasty Nick has been thrown out of the *Big Brother* house. The man who was the most popular member in the eyes of the entire nation has been unmasked as a compulsive liar who all this time has been trying to rig the eviction nominations.

Apparently we are to witness the showdown on tomorrow night's programme. Not only is he now the most famous person in England, but it wouldn't surprise me to hear shortly that he has been given a column in one of the tabloids.

Expressed my views in very forcible tones indeed.

'Whatever became of talent?' I asked. 'Dr Bronowski must be turning in his grave.'

Mother said, 'And to think he went to Gordonstoun.'

Said I didn't realize Bronowski was at Gordonstoun.

She said, 'Don't be dafter than you need be.'

Chad said, 'Only a public schoolboy would have done what he did. Everyone for himself. That's what they teach you at places like that. It's what you pay for.'

Mother said, 'Some people I know seem to have learned it for nothing.'

Chad said, 'Meaning what, exactly?'

Mother said, 'You know very well what I mean.'

Chad said he didn't, otherwise he wouldn't have asked. P told him not to be rude and said to Mother that if she had something to say about Chad she should come out with it.

Mother said it was none of her business; why didn't she ask Marie-Celeste?

John Julius was sent to fetch Marie-Celeste, but before he could get out of the room Chad told him not to bother. He said there was no need to involve her; he was the one to blame. He then confessed that he and Marie-Celeste had been having an affair for the last two months.

Then everybody started shouting and screaming, and P hit him and told him to get out, and Katie was crying, and John Julius was trying to comfort her, and Mother was asking if anyone was going to put the kettle on, and Woodhouse was running round in circles barking because he heard the word 'out' and thought he was being taken for a walk.

The upshot is that P has asked Marie-Celeste to pack her *valise* and be out of the house first thing tomorrow morning.

Where that leaves her and Chad I do not know, nor does it greatly concern me, since soon I, too, shall be folding my tent and stealing away like the thief in the night.

Can't wait.

Friday, August 18th

Marie-Celeste left soon after breakfast. Surprised to find I was quite sorry to see her go, and, to judge by the way she lingered over her farewell kiss, so was she.

'*Soyez bonne*,' I murmured.

'*Sage*,' she said. '"*Bonne*" means "nursery maid" and I do not wish to be that.'

Why is it that the French always manage to make one look foolish whenever one tries to speak their language?

After we had all waved her goodbye, took John Julius aside and broke news about my plans re Jane. Must confess, felt quite nervous.

He said, 'Does that mean you're going to become a religious nutter?'

'No chance,' I said.

'In that case,' he said, 'go for it, Dad.' And he gave me a reassuring pat on the shoulder.

Pleasure at having achieved a small breakthrough with JJ dampened by feelings of guilt towards Mother. Attempted to assuage them by keeping her company while she watched an animal hospital programme from Australia. At one point a turtle was brought in, completely covered with barnacles. They were everywhere. On his shell, on his eyes, even on his mouth. I say his, but it could have been hers; you can't always tell with turtles.

Apparently they get blown up with some sort of gas and, instead of sinking below the surface, float on the top of the water and the barnacles gather.

Presumably there are thousands more like him in ponds and streams all over Australia and, happy and relieved though I was to know that one, at least, had been found and was being treated, I couldn't help wondering about the less lucky ones.

As if one doesn't have enough to worry about.

Saturday, August 19th

Had just come to the end of my regular 'What's on the Menu?' spot in my programme and was singing praises of hospital's macaroni cheese when call came through from Reception to say a man was asking to see me. He wouldn't give his name, but said he was a fan, and that if he said it was a voice from the grave I'd know who he was.

Quickly put on recording of Frankie Vaughan singing 'The Food of Love', told Reception I'd be down as soon as possible and rang police.

Duty sergeant could not have been more understanding. Said he was a big fan of mine, and if it hadn't been for me did not know how he could have got through the first night following his ingrowing-toenail operation.

He said that, seeing it was me, he'd get someone down there immediately.

Was chatting with Mrs Holbrook in Barbara Windsor Ward and commiserating with her re her varicose veins when Reception rang again to say would I come down straight away, there was a bit of a problem.

Told Mrs H not to go away, put on *The Best of Max Bygraves*, and took lift to ground floor. Stepped out to be confronted by my old friend, erstwhile flatmate and general thorn-in-the-side Ralph Beddoes, wearing an inappropriate moustache and a silly, smug expression. Standing nearby were a couple of policeman looking less than happy.

Beddoes advanced on me with his arms outstretched, and

before I had a chance to take evasive action, he had seized me in a bear-hug.

'I'm back,' he said.

Looking over his shoulder, suddenly recognized one of the policemen as the officer who had arrested me the night of the unfortunate misunderstanding over John Julius.

He gave me a look, but said nothing.

Beddoes said, 'Sorry about all this, officer,' and he went across and the two of them exchanged a few quiet words.

'Quite understand, sir,' the policeman said, and gave Beddoes a little salute. 'We all make silly mistakes from time to time.' And the two of them walked off towards the main entrance.

Felt sure something had changed hands, but couldn't swear to it.

'Must dash,' said Beddoes. 'Got to see a woman about a dog. How about lunch tomorrow? Say one o'clock at the Carlton Tower?'

And before I had a chance to say another word, he, too, disappeared into the night.

Got back to studio as Bygraves was coming to last track of LP.

Had just finished back-announcing Max when Mrs Holbrook rang to say she could just about put up with varicose veins and she could just about put up with Max Bygraves singing about a mouse in a windmill in Old Amsterdam, but the combination was more than even a woman with a MBE for services to the community could tolerate.

Sunday, August 20th

To Carlton Tower at one to meet Beddoes for lunch. By one fifteen was on point of calling it a day when in he rolled with a beautiful girl in tow. She looked half his age, at least. He introduced her as Miss Poppitt.

'My friends call me Dolly,' she said.

Beddoes said, 'Traditional roast beef and all the trimmings do you, laddie?'

Lunch an enjoyable enough affair, if somewhat marred by Beddoes's irritating habit of shoving his nose into his wine glass and sniffing loudly before each mouthful.

'Ralph's a connoisseur,' said Dolly.

'And not just of wine,' Beddoes said with a terrible stage wink.

When I asked Dolly what she did for a living, Beddoes said, 'She's a Page Three scorcher, aren't you, darling?'

Dolly frowned and said that actually she was a model and TV quiz hostess. I asked her what that entailed exactly and she said, 'I bring the contestants on, hand them their prizes and take them off again.'

Beddoes said, 'She's particularly good at taking them off.'

Dolly didn't say much after that and I can't say I blamed her. Neither did I, but then I didn't get much of a chance once Beddoes got going.

He has certainly had a very interesting time in Washington, most recently as Special Adviser to President Clinton. When I asked him what he advised him on, he tapped the side of his nose and said, 'This and that, but mainly the other.'

He refused to elaborate beyond saying, 'Does the name "Lewinsky" mean anything to you?'

I said, 'Do you know Monica Lewinsky?'

'Not as well as some, but better than most,' he said. 'Cigar?'

From what I can gather, he has left America for good (under a cloud, I shouldn't wonder) and is now back in England, living in a service apartment near Sloane Square with Miss Poppitt and, as he put it, 'Moving into the next phase of my life.'

When I asked him whether he had anything specific in view, he said, 'Just let's say I'm considering various options.'

I said, 'Does that include professional harassment and wasting police time?'

He said, 'Thought you might enjoy a spot of intrigue. The police took it all in good part. I think I made it worth their while.'

When I asked him how, exactly, he tapped the side of his nose and said, 'Wheels within wheels, laddie.'

Have no idea what he was talking about. But then I never really did. Indeed, I had never imagined he would ever re-appear in my life, let alone in the guise of a stalker. I asked him how on earth he had managed to track me down.

He said, 'I didn't spent fifteen years in the White House without knowing how to find people when I want to.'

I said, 'Were you really ever in the White House, Beddoes?'

He said, 'Does the Pope ever crap in the wood?'

More to the point, did I really once share a flat with this man and call him my friend?

Delighted though I always am to wander down Memory Lane and tread a measure or two to the Music of Time, there are those with whom one feels that once is more than enough. And when Beddoes said, 'We must do this again,' I played my cards very close to my chest and said, 'Let's be in touch.'

Realized as the two of them disappeared down Sloane Street in taxi that he had not asked me a single thing about myself. Remembering some of the things he has said in the past about Jane, am not sorry.

To Doxby Mansions plus luggage after evensong. Don't *think* anyone saw me.

Felt immediately at home. The room layout is slightly different from our old flat next door in Wentworth Mansions, but atmosphere eerily similar. Even the sofa looks like the one on which Jane, Victoria and I sat and watched so many editions of *Dr Finlay's Casebook* and Beddoes romped with women of every nationality, creed and colour.

I said, 'This is all very familiar.'

'Isn't it just?' she said.

'Quite like old times,' I said.

'I do hope so,' she said.

'Except, of course, that in those days God didn't come into it.'

She said, 'I'm sure He did. It's just that we didn't notice Him.'

I said I couldn't help wondering how big a part He played in the proceedings now.

She said that her dialogue with God was an ongoing thing and this was no exception.

I laughed and said, 'Just as long as He's not up there tutting and wagging His finger at us. One wouldn't want to get on the wrong side of Him. You remember what happened to Lot's wife.'

She said, 'I hope you're not having second thoughts?'

I said, more to the point, was she?

'Oh dear,' she said, 'I am beginning to think this might all be a big mistake.'

I can think of many people who would have lost their nerve at this juncture and when invited, as I was, to sleep in the spare bedroom felt decidedly crushed. In point of fact her suggestion could not have been more welcome, since, as fate would have it, I suddenly felt my cough coming on again. This was hardly the ideal moment in which to consummate our passion for the second – and possibly crucial – time in our lives and, besides, one doesn't want to rush these things.

At the same time, very much hope it clears up soon. Spare-room bed even more uncomfortable than the one in Bermuda Avenue. When I commented on this fact, Jane pointed out – rather sharply, I thought – that only through suffering can we find true happiness.

Hope to goodness she knows what she's talking about.

Monday, August 21st

Great news. P rang this morning to say that a messenger on a motorbike had just hand-delivered a letter from Itchy Feet Television Productions. It was obviously urgent. Did I want her to open it and see what it said?

Told her to go ahead.

There was a sound of tearing paper, followed by a long pause, then she said, 'Did you apply to be on some sort of quiz show?'

Suddenly remembered. Hugh Bryant-Fenn had put me up to it back in the spring. He had been asked to do some pre-publicity work for a travel quiz show on ITV called *Winton's World*, starring Dale Winton. At Hugh's urging, had agreed to allow him to put my name forward as one of the contestants in the pilot show to be made later in the year and shown as a one-off in the early part of the new autumn schedule.

Only agreed because I thought it might make an interesting subject my column and, frankly, had never imagined for a moment it would come to anything. Indeed, had not given it a second thought.

Explained all this to P who said, 'Well, you're not going to do it, are you?'

Replied that I might as well. Who knew where it might not lead?

She said, 'Well, certainly not to any of the exotic destinations listed among the prizes. What's the first prize, anyway? A round-the-world trip on a supermarket trolley?'

I said that prizes were neither here nor there. It was the spin-offs that interested me. Reminded her that it wasn't for the £350,000 prize money that Tiger Woods was so desperate to win the British Open. It's the millions of dollars' worth of endorsement deals that are the victor's real spoils.

P said that if I honestly imagined I would one day be modelling swimwear for Marks & Spencer, I must be even barmier than she thought.

Told her she was being ridiculous. The freelance life is a series of stepping stones across a fast-flowing river. It's only in midstream that the offers start coming in in any serious numbers.

She said the only offer I was likely to get was my tube fare home.

If there is one thing I can't bear it's getting involved in long discussions with people who don't know what they're talking about.

Cut to the chase by asking her when I am needed for the recording.

'Sunday, September 3rd,' she said.

By a happy coincidence, that happens to be the anniversary of the start of the Second World War. Have a feeling I shall be a good deal better prepared for battle than the nation was sixty-one years ago.

Have rung to accept and will be receiving detailed instructions re time, place, transport etc. within the next week.

In the meantime, must get down to some serious revision work with atlas, guidebook and gazetteer.

Tuesday, August 22nd

Was in Mitcham Public Library this morning, doing some initial work on capital cities of the world, when found myself drawn instinctively towards latest edition of *Who's Who*.

Have often wondered what qualifies a person for inclusion, and glancing through some of the names can see no reason why mine should not one day be among them. My CV is as good as most, though am woefully light on clubs. The sooner my Old Fentonian Golf Club membership comes through the better. Does the National Trust count as a club? I wonder.

Have been jotting down a few ideas to put in 'Hobbies' section. How, though, to make oneself sound interesting, but not pretentious? 'Collecting edible fungi' is one thing, but 'Reading Homer in the original' might risk suggest pretentiousness.

Not that I have ever done either. Unfortunately, the things I do enjoy in the little spare time I have – walking the dog on Mitcham Common, doing the *Daily Telegraph* crossword, watching American TV sitcoms – would make me sound dreadfully suburban.

Am seriously considering ditching the whole lot in favour of something rather more intriguing, like 'People', or 'Life'.

Rang P to ask what she thought. She said, 'Why don't you just put "Faffing about" and be done with it? It's what you spend most of your spare time doing. Most of your time, in fact.'

Am sorry now I involved her. I usually am.

Wednesday, August 23rd

Tried out a small-scale travel quiz of my own devising on my MHR listeners last night. First prize, a ticket to be a member of the audience for the recording of *Winton's World* on the 3rd. The questions could not have been easier – What is the capital of Outer Mongolia? Name one of the chateaux of the Loire. What is Old Faithful? – but not a single person took part.

Why do I bother?

To dinner at the Varney-Birches' with Jane. It was just like old times, except that in the old days, of course, Jane was not invited to say grace before we tucked in.

Sat next to Theresa de Grande-Hauteville. Haven't seen her or Philippe for weeks. Frankly, she is not ageing well. Am no great advocate of artificial colourants, but grey hair does put the years on a woman, especially when worn long and pulled back in a rough pony tail.

Could not help noticing that one hair had fallen across her chin. Its presence became ever more irritating as the evening wore on and the urge to remove it increasingly stronger. Waited until she turned to talk to Roland Batty on her left and went to pull it away. Had barely got fingers on it and given first tentative tug when noticed skin puckering on her cheek and realized it must be attached.

Was faced with two options: to abort operation or continue and face consequences. For reasons that I cannot explain, plumped for latter.

Have never heard anyone make such a fuss in all my life. It couldn't have hurt that much. Tried to make light of it, but for once my famous persiflage failed to work its charms and had no alternative but to apologize to all concerned and retire with as much dignity as possible.

Can't say I was entirely sorry. Verena's bavarois has never been her forte. Remarked to Jane on way home (as I now like to think of Doxby Mansions) that this was one occasion when turning the other cheek would not have been advisable. She was less amused than I had expected. Hope I have not over-estimated her capacity for putting the temporal before the spiritual.

Thursday, August 24th

Talk about good timing. George Sydenham-Hill rang this morning to say would I like to play for the Old Fentonians in their annual golf match against Dewberry?

'It's all very informal,' he said. 'Foursomes in the morning, bite of lunch, singles in the afternoon. Do say yes.'

Pointed out that I am not, as yet, a member. Had applied for membership some weeks ago, but have still not heard anything.

George said, 'Well, you're a fully paid-up member as far as I'm concerned – or you certainly will be if you say yes.'

Said in that case I'd be delighted to represent the Alma Mater. Where was the match and when?

'Trimbly Bottom, this Saturday,' he said. 'Rather short notice, I know, but we do need you. You're top of my list.'

Made pretence of havering, but finally accepted. Am wondering who else will be playing. Waldo Harris was always a useful player and wondered if by chance he might have been recruited. If so, we could drive down together.

Rang him to discover he wasn't feeling at all well. He was supposed to have been playing, but had had to scratch.

He said, 'Sydenham-Hill asked me if I could think of anybody who might fill in at the last moment and I suggested you.'

No comment.

Friday, August 25th

Beddoes rang this morning. Did I want to join him and Dolly on Monday evening at a special showing of a film called *Time*

Code? Thought I was pretty *au courant* with London arts scene, but have to admit have never even heard of this one.

He said, 'I think that, as one who is at the cutting edge of twenty-first-century culture, you'll find it rather interesting.'

Having spent so many years at the receiving end of his barbed tongue, had been planning to keep quiet about my relationship with Jane. However, it's bound to come out sooner or later and decided this could be the moment to reveal all.

I said, 'You'll never guess who I ran into the other day. Jane Baker. As it happens, we were planning to do something on Monday. I'm sure she'd love to see you again. Any chance of another ticket?'

Beddoes could not have been more enthusiastic. 'No problemo,' he said. 'I was very fond of Jane. In fact I always thought you and she would have been perfect for each other. But then along came that gorgeous nymphet Amanda and that was you done for.'

Said he was hardly in a position to talk about nymphets.

He said, 'Dolly is not only a highly paid professional television performer, but she also happens to have a Ph.D. in media studies.'

And I'm the Duke of Westminster.

I said I did not doubt her intelligence, it was the difference in their ages I was referring to.

Beddoes said, 'Nothing like a workout with a fit twenty-four-year-old to keep you young and healthy.'

Reminded him that he was not as young as he used to be and that too much sex could prove fatal.

He said, 'If she dies, she dies.'

Saturday, August 26th

Snatched a couple of hours' sleep after radio show, then up at eight, packed faithful old clubs into Polo and set off in high spirits for Trimbly Bottom.

Could not have picked a more perfect day to make my debut for the old school. Driving through the dappled Surrey woods, could not resist a snatch or two of the Bing Crosby golf classic, 'It Went Straight Down the Middle'. Am only sorry I don't know any more of the words.

No sign of any OF ties, so decided to get in some much-needed practice on putting green before everyone arrived.

Was lacing up golf shoes in changing room when man with bright-red face and white hair like a baby's came in and said, 'Are you quite sure you're meant to be here?'

I said, 'I *am* a member.'

'Really?' he said. 'I don't recognize your face.'

'Crisp,' I said. 'Simon Crisp. Writer and broadcaster.'

'Roger Taffrail,' he said. 'Captain.'

'Naval man?' I said.

'Not in fact,' he said. 'Why do you ask?'

'The rank,' I said.

He said, 'I am captain of this golf club and I don't believe you're a member.'

I said, 'As an Old Fentonian, I understand I have rights here.'

He said, 'Sorry, old boy. You understand wrong. Visitors' dressing room next door.'

Did not feel like arguing the toss, but will certainly be taking the matter up with Sydenham-Hill at the earliest opportunity.

Surprised to find my putting was well up to standard of yore. Was not the only one who was impressed. Large man with fair curly hair and bulging golf bag with word 'MacGregor' in large letters down the side came across and said, 'I gather we're partners today. Charles Ibstock,' and he swallowed my hand in a huge paw.

'Simon Crisp,' I said.

'That name sounds familiar,' he said. 'Do I know you?'

'I don't believe so,' I said.

As we were waiting to drive from the first tee, he said, 'You wouldn't believe it, but some bastard wrote in to Tommy Thompson the other day and said I was living in a cardboard box behind the Savoy. Bloody cheek! I have never been *behind* the Savoy in my life. Just wait till I get my hands on him. I'll give him cardboard box.'

Did not realize a man could drive a golf ball quite so far as he did. It hit the middle of the fairway, bounced slightly left, and ended up in the light rough.

'Bugger,' he said. 'Came off it.'

Our opponents were at least a hundred yards shorter and among the trees on the right. They finally managed to squirt ball out on to fairway.

'Just swing slowly, keep your head down and don't try and do anything clever,' Ibstock murmured as we headed for our ball.

Don't know quite what happened, but end result was that ball shot out at right angles and into thick rough on far side.

'Thank you very much,' he said through gritted teeth.

He chopped it on to fairway, leaving me an easy chip to the green. Pulled out trusty eight-iron and was addressing ball when one of our opponents said, 'Excuse me, but may I see your club?'

Felt he could have chosen a more convenient moment, but, being in relaxed mood, acceded to his request. Have always been very proud of my matching set of Frank Hobson Specials. They did my father proud in his golfing heyday in the Thirties and have stood me in equally good stead since I inherited them nearly thirty years ago.

The man said, 'Thought so. This club is illegal.'

I said, 'What do you mean illegal? They're hand-made. You won't find a better example of the club-maker's craft anywhere in the country.'

'Except in a golf museum,' the man said. 'Dimpled club faces like those were banned by the R & A years ago.'

Asked him what on earth I was supposed to do. They were the only clubs I had.

The man said, 'The penalty for using illegal equipment is disqualification. So that's a win for Dewberry, I'm afraid. Thank you very much, gentlemen.' And before I knew what we were shaking hands and walking back to the clubhouse.

Don't think I have ever seen anyone quite as angry as Ibstock. Decided not to stay for lunch. As I was heading for the car, he came across and said, 'Are you quite sure we haven't met before?'

'Quite sure,' I said, got in the car and drove off down the long avenue of silver birches towards the A3 and London.

Jane was writing her sermon when I came in. 'How did that go?' she said.

'Pushover,' I said.

Wish I could say the same thing about my love life. The spare-room bed really is extremely lumpy.

Sunday, August 27th

No sooner got home after Holy Communion than P rang in a panic-stricken voice to say could I come over straight away: it was Mother.

Drove to Mitcham at high speed, praying I would get there in time, and walked in to find whole family in sitting room and Mother in an upright chair dressed in her hat and coat, surrounded by luggage and bulging plastic shopping bags.

P said, 'Kitchen.'

Followed her out to discover that Mother had come across a pile of girlie magazines that Chad had been unable to sell and had pushed under her bed and forgotten about.

'She could have had a stroke,' P said. 'She didn't know such things existed.'

I said, 'She must do. She had two children.'

P said, 'I meant the magazines.'

The upshot is that Mother has said that she will not spend another night in the house and is going to stay with her old school friend Madge Humphries near Colchester. Would I be an angel and run her down?

Pointed out that struggling sixty miles through the East End of London and up the A12 on a hot Sunday in August could hardly be described as a 'run'.

P said, 'Can you take her? Yes or no.'

Was in no mood to argue. Bundled her into car, amid a lot of grizzling from P, assurances that they'd see her soon from John Julius and James, and undisguised glee from Chad.

Mother did not utter a word until we were halfway through the Rotherhithe Tunnel, when she suddenly turned to me and said, 'You're taking me to a home, aren't you?'

I said no, we were going to Madge's.

She said, 'It's no good trying to pull the wool over my eyes. I wasn't born yesterday. You're taking me to a home.'

I sighed and said, 'Have it your own way.'

There was a long pause. 'You bugger,' she said.

Got rather lost near Tolleshunt D'Arcy and finally arrived at Marsh House just before two.

As Mother got out of the car, she looked up at the house and said, 'I've been to this one before. I didn't like it the first time. It's a house of ill repute.'

As I was leaving after a snack lunch, Madge said, 'Anything else I need to know?'

I said, 'There's just one little thing. If she says anything about Dad having an affair with a black woman in Streatham, take no notice. She lives in a dream world a lot of the time these days.'

Madge said, 'Oh I knew he had a thing with a black woman, but I never realized she lived in Streatham. What a hoot!'

In my opinion, those two are made for each other.

Monday, August 28th

With Jane to the Empire, Leicester Square, to meet Beddoes and Miss Poppitt. It was a rather more starry occasion than I had expected, and was glad I had slipped tie in jacket pocket, in case. Jane looking sensational in turquoise. It brought her eyes out a treat. Beddoes rather taken with her, I thought. Gave me several looks and wiggled his eyebrows up and down suggestively. Did not respond.

Dolly pointed out several TV and pop celebrities. Pretended to be more excited than I was. Jane smiled serenely throughout.

On the way into auditorium, a pudgy girl with a mass of dark hair and shiny eyes called out, 'Hi, Ralphie.'

Beddoes said, 'Oh hi, Monica,' and gave her a huge kiss on both cheeks.

I said, 'That wasn't . . . ?'

Beddoes shrugged and walked on in, wearing that silly smug smile he knows I can't abide.

Might have enjoyed the film more (a) if the director hadn't decided to go all arty-farty and split the screen into four sections which showed separate single takes of ninety-seven minutes – each played simultaneously with the rest, as a result of which I ended up with a splitting headache – and (b) we hadn't been asked to put our hands in our pockets and give generously to an organization in the Midlands I had never heard of.

'You never told us this was a charity do,' I said to Beddoes.

'I must have forgotten,' he said.

As we debouched into the street, Beddoes said, 'How about a bite to eat? I don't know about you, but I'm starving.'

Was casting round in my mind for a cheap Italian when he said, 'Let's try the Ivy.'

Pointed out that it is impossible to get a table at the Ivy these days unless one books up weeks ahead and, even then, one's name has to be on a special list approved by the owner. Only A-list celebrities can walk in off the street unannounced without being laughed out again.

Beddoes said, 'Let's give it a go, anyway. You never know your luck.'

Entered famous doors to be confronted by long queue of hopefuls. Beddoes said, 'Wait there' and went to front of queue. Came back a moment or two later and said, 'OK. We're in.'

The next thing I knew, we were being ushered through tables full of famous faces, all looking up to see who we were.

While we were taking our seats, Beddoes went to the loo.

I said to Jane, 'Only Beddoes could walk into the Ivy and get a table just like that.'

Dolly said, 'Oh, he booked this weeks ago. Shall we have a drink?'

Tuesday, August 29th

Am not, in the words of The Kinks' famous song, 'a dedicated follower of fashion', but have decided to buy myself one of these scooters that are all the go these days.

Basically, of course, they're a children's craze, but that is no reason why grown-ups should not put them to some useful purpose. It is not as if I had suddenly started wearing a pair of huge trainers with spirit levels in the heels or buying Robbie Williams records.

With traffic in London getting heavier every day and a busy schedule to keep, what could be more sensible and practical than gliding along the pavement between appointments on two wheels? They are noiseless, give out no exhaust emissions to add to global warming and present no danger to pedestrians.

They also fold up into something that can be carried under the arm when not being used.

Can't for the life of me think why I never thought of getting one before.

For two pins would have hauled out my faithful old wooden Triang with its large wobbly wheels and its plain but sturdy handlebars, dusted it down, squirted a drop or two of 3-in-One oil between the spindles, and shown the children of Mitcham what scootering is really all about.

Unfortunately, my ex-wife, with typical lack of imagination, sensitivity and foresight, threw it out one day with 'the gubbins' – as she will insist on calling anything that doesn't match up to her high standards of usefulness.

Could not believe my ears when she told me. Pointed out that it was not only an integral part of my childhood, but an interesting artefact in itself – the sort of thing that people who put on exhibitions cry out for and which adds colour and texture to some of the most important museum collections in the country.

She said, 'I don't know what you're complaining about. Horseface Gossage's father came back from the war to find *his* father burning Chippendale chairs on a bonfire at the bottom of the garden.'

Said there is no comparison between Chippendale chairs and my old scooter.

'Exactly,' she said.

Is it any wonder our marriage foundered?

Wednesday, August 30th

To Peter Jones to buy a scooter. They sell three makes: the 'Micro', the 'Evolution' and the 'Snakeboard'. Am not entirely clear why the Micro costs so much more than the other two, beyond the fact that it is very slightly larger and has its own carrying strap.

Frankly, am perfectly capable of carrying a small piece of folded-up metal, with or without a strap, and though, as a man with a marketing background, have never been taken in by product names, must admit that the word 'Snakeboard' has a bite to it which 'Micro' can never hope to muster.

Practised up and down pavement for an hour after lunch. Feeling the roughness of the flagstones and the bump of the lines beneath my feet, I was once again that small boy in his grey shorts and sunburst-patterned sandals, his long woollen socks concertinaed round his ankles, on his way to meet his best friend Robin and make a plan for a long summer's day.

The next thing I knew, an elderly man had stepped out from nowhere and I felt the wheels of my scooter going over his foot.

Heard him yelling at the top of his voice something about pavements not being racetracks, but, quite honestly, if someone is stupid enough to step out from their front gate without warning, they deserve everything that's coming to them.

Thursday, August 31st

After supper, got down to some serious revision work with Jane for Sunday's quiz with a question-and-answer session designed to test my general travel knowledge.

Regret I had to pull her up over her pronunciation of 'Accademia' in very first question – 'Where is the Accademia Bridge?' Fortunately, my answer ('The most famous bridge in Venice after the Rialto; it crosses the Grand Canal from the church of San Vitale to the Accademia Art Museum') correct in every particular.

Felt the question 'What do Omsk, Tomsk, Krasnoyarsk and Novosibirsk have in common?' too easy for words, and said so.

Quite why I said that the 'rose-red city half as old as time' was Palmyra in Syria I can't for the life of me imagine.

Jane curiously unsympathetic when I cursed my foolish error.

'It's a TV travel quiz, Simon,' she said, ' not an interview for a prize fellowship at All Souls.'

Perhaps not, but that is no reason not to take it as seriously as if it were.

September

Friday, September 1st

To the West End to find something suitable to wear for Sunday night. Serious but not pompous, light-hearted but not frivolous – that is the keynote to my personality, and my clothes should shout that out in no uncertain terms.

Assistant at Aquascutum slightly nonplussed by my brief at first, but at the mention of the word 'television' he soon entered into the spirit of the proceedings and I came away with a jacket in a lively check that evokes the spirit of Kenneth Clark with just a dash of Roy Strong.

Decided to wear it straight away, so that, when the time comes, I will look as though I actually own the thing and not like one of those middle-aged male models one sees in mail-order catalogues, trying to look casual and failing.

Tried to re-create first impression viewers will have of me by catching sight of myself unawares in shop windows as I walked along.

Unfortunately, lost concentration outside British Home Stores and went hard into lamp-post. Don't think anyone noticed and, if they did and happen to be watching the show, can't imagine they will make the connection. However, may have to have quiet word with make-up girl if bump on fore-head shows no sign of subsiding.

Saturday, September 2nd

Infuriated to see that, as I predicted, Nasty Nick from *Big Brother* has been signed up as a columnist by the *Sun*. Not only that, but he was photographed at the premiere of this new

British gangster film that everyone's talking about, hobnob-bing with Brad Pitt.

What *is* the point in trying to do a proper, professional job when amateurs with no training, talent or charm can be snatched from obscurity and given highly paid jobs in national newspapers merely for behaving badly? Any day now we'll read that he's been given his own TV show.

Sunday, September 3rd

To studios after lunch in minicab sent by TV company. The heating was full on, and even though I opened both windows I still could not get rid of the smell of stale cigarettes and air-freshener.

Bored-looking receptionist said, 'May I help you?'

'Simon Crisp for *Winton's World*,' I said.

'Bear with me,' she said and dialled a number.

'Hi, Sue,' she said. 'Reception here. I've got Mr . . . Sorry, what was your name again?'

'Crisp,' I said.

'Mr Crisp,' she said. 'Right . . . I'll tell him.'

At that moment her face broke into a beaming smile.

'Hi! How are you?' she said.

Turned to find Mariella Frostrup standing next to me. Could not have been more delighted. She is very much my kind of TV presenter. In fact I think I'm right in saying she started on a local newspaper, too.

'You're here to see Jackie, right?' said the receptionist.

'Yes,' she said, in a voice that is as smoky in real life as it is on the screen.

The receptionist dialled a number.

'Oh hi, Jackie,' she said. 'Mary's here.'

Have always suspected Mariella is a *nom de guerre*. There's probably another Mary Frostrup working in the business somewhere.

'She'll be right down,' the receptionist said, giving her a huge smile. She looked at me. 'Sorry, you are, again . . . ?'

Told her for the third time. She glanced down at a list of names.

'Oh yes,' she said. 'You're one of the contestants on *Winton's World*. Take a seat. Someone will be down shortly.'

Went and sat next to Mariella, who was leafing through the latest copy of *OK!*

I said, 'Are you in there?'

'I don't think so,' she said.

'Ah well,' I said. 'You can't win them all.'

'I suppose not,' she said.

What a joy it is to be working in a business where one has such an instant and easy rapport with one's fellow performers.

'By the way,' I said, *sotto voce*, 'I'm not a contestant per se.'

'Oh?' she said.

'I'm really here in a professional capacity.'

'Really?' she said.

'I'm writing a piece, actually,' I said. 'It's all rather hush-hush.'

'Good for you,' she said.

'One has a crust to earn,' I said.

'Absolutely,' she said. 'Oh good. Here's Jackie.'

As the two of them headed towards the lift I called out, 'See you again soon,' but I don't think she could have heard me.

Finally scooped up by harassed-looking young woman with clipboard. As we were going up in the lift she said, 'Is that your only jacket?'

The only one I'd brought, I said.

She said, 'We may get away with it.'

I said, 'What do you mean "get away with it"? It's Aquascutum.'

She said, 'The quality is not in dispute. It's the pattern that worries me.'

I said that Richard Whiteley never seems to have any problems with his brightly coloured jackets.

She said, 'Richard Whiteley wouldn't have a problem if he came on dressed as Coco the Clown.'

As we entered rear of studio, stupidly caught my foot on a cable.

'Mind the cables,' she said.

Looking around at the cameras, the lights and the huge bank of audience seats, was transported back to that moment eighteen years ago when I first realized that the TV studio is my natural home. Had fate – and badly designed furniture – not conspired against me, my television career might now be at its zenith.

Make-up girl very interested to hear about my conversation with Mariella.

'She seems very well,' I said.

'Good,' she said.

My amusing anecdote about the time Belinda and I hired an entertainer for John Julius's tenth birthday party who painted the children's faces and I ended up with a cow on mine, less well received.

Was tackling cold chicken leg in Hospitality and making polite conversation to fellow contestants when Dale burst into room and rushed round greeting everyone in the flamboyant style for which he is so well known – and, I have no doubt, well paid.

Suddenly felt tap on shoulder and turned to find myself face to face with Dolly Poppitt. Assumed at first she was another contestant, but then realized she was one of show's 'hostesses'.

She said, 'You'll be in good hands with me,' and gave me a lovely smile. She really is very beautiful. Cannot think what Beddoes has done to deserve her.

At long last, after hours of sitting around twiddling our thumbs, the floor manager gestured 'Roll VTR!' and we were up and running.

Contestants arrived on set seated in a series of model vehicles – ships, trains, cars, aeroplanes etc. – which travelled round a huge revolving globe, like a merry-go-round. Each vehicle was accompanied by a hostess dressed in a different national costume. Delighted to see Miss Poppitt standing next to my sleigh, dressed in Eskimo outfit – though doubt many Inuit would dare reveal as much as she did in sub-zero temperatures.

Found myself sandwiched in with Peter Lightfoot from Bishop's Stortford, Debbie Brewer from Newport, Julie Underwood from Norwich and Derek Nicholson from the Wirral in Cheshire.

As each name was called out, we had to jump out of our vehicle, assisted by our hostess, who led us across to a row of lecterns in the shape of tall glasses of exotic drinks, with a sunshade over each one and a tall stool behind. There was a small screen in front for registering scores.

The announcer said, 'You're all here to have a whale of a time in *Winton's World*. And here is your tour leader, Da-a-a-ale WINTON!'

At that moment the globe broke open into quarters, like a Terry's chocolate orange, and out of it came Dale, seated in a gondola with a gondolier in the stern in traditional dress, leaning on an oar and miming to 'Just One Cornetto'. Dale himself dressed like an entertainments officer on a cruise ship, licking an ice cream and waving. As the gondola came to a halt in mid-set, he bounded out and rushed along the line of contestants, shaking the men's hands and kissing the women.

He turned to the camera and said, 'Hello, hello, *bonsoir, guten abend, buona sera*. Thank you. Thank you. *Merci, gracias, danke schön*. And welcome to *Winton's World.*'

There was then a certain amount of unnecessary ribbing at our expense. Did not join in general hilarity. This was a mistake, since I promptly became the whipping boy for his humorous asides – e.g. 'Ooh, I do love that jacket, Simon. Where can I get one like that? Sandown Park Racecourse?' etc.

He then announced to the camera that one of us would be winning the grand prize of a luxury three-month round-the-world cruise for two aboard the famous *Sea Princess*, and went into a comic routine about grass skirts in Tahiti and rubbing noses with Maoris in New Zealand, before explaining that the more questions we got right, the more travel miles we earned.

The traveller with the most miles would go on to the next round, and the runners-up would go away with as many miles of free travel as they had accumulated during the show.

Show started with a quick general knowledge round. Each correct answer was worth ten miles, and a picture of it was flashed up on a giant screen.

It was absurdly easy. Peter was asked whether the capital of Hungary was Budapest, Bucharest or Bratislava and got that right, to wild applause. Unfortunately, Debbie thought the Pyramids of Giza were in Japan.

When it came to my turn, I was asked if the Prado Museum is in Rome, Madrid or Barcelona. Just to say Madrid seemed dreadfully jejune, so added that it is the home of Velázquez and Goya. *The Sunshade* is there, and *The Naked Maja* of course – one of the few surviving female nudes in Spanish painting, apart from *The Rokeby Venus* by Velázquez. Could not resist mentioning that there are one or two El Grecos and that, although he was Greek-born, as his name suggests, spiritually he was Spanish.

Dale said, 'Ooh! Eat your heart out, *University Challenge*!'

Did not rise to the bait.

The next round was on 'Famous Places and Their Products'. Peter made a mess of the Napa Valley, and Debbie thought that Strasbourg was a kind of wine, so could not have been more relieved when my question was about the island of Burano.

By way of making up for the disappointing failures of my two co-contestants, I filled in with a few germane facts.

I said that not only is Burano one of the great traditional lace-making centres of the world, and, of course, the second largest island in the Venetian lagoon, but, interestingly enough, it was where they made Mary Tudor's bridal gown for her wedding to Philip of Spain.

Stupidly put the date at 1565, but quickly apologized and said that of course I meant '66.

Astounded to hear Dale say, 'I'm sorry, Simon. The answer is glass. Murano is where all that lovely Venetian glass comes from,' and a shot of a rather hideous mauve-and-green vase came up on the screen.

The next thing I knew he was asking Julie what Kimberley is famous for.

I said, 'Sorry, Dale, did you say Murano or Burano?'

Dale said, 'Murano. With an M.'

I said, 'I'm so sorry. I misheard you. I thought you said Burano. Can you give me another one?'

Dale said, rather sharply, 'I'm afraid not. Julie . . . Kimberley . . .'

Am not one of nature's pedants, but was not prepared to be fobbed off in this cavalier fashion. I had distinctly heard the word 'Burano' and felt sure everyone else had, too.

Enquired as much of Peter and Debbie, but attention by now very much on Julie and my question fell on deaf ears – Dale's among them.

'Kimberley . . . ' he was saying to her. 'What's a girl's best friend?'

'Her mother?' said Julie.

'Oh, for goodness' sake,' I said. 'Doesn't anyone know anything? It's diamonds.'

Took the opportunity of a sudden silence to ask Dale once again if he was *quite* sure he hadn't said Burano? Perhaps it had been a slip of the tongue?

Again he tried to ignore me, but I was in no mood for games.

'I don't want to make a scene over this,' I said. 'Everyone knows that glass has been made on Murano ever since furnaces were banned from Venice as a precaution against fire back in the thirteenth century, but the fact is you asked about Burano, which is different kettle of fish altogether.'

Dale said, 'Would you please sit down, Mr Crisp?'

I said, 'Why don't we ask the audience?'

Dale repeated his request for me to take a seat.

I said, 'This is a farce,' and was on point of calling for the producer when events began to take a rather ugly turn. Have no idea where the cameras were pointing, but was suddenly aware that I was very much the centre of attention – something that could not have been further from my mind when I first agreed to take part in this absurd charade.

The audience appeared to be enjoying every minute of it, and were beginning to call out things like, 'You tell 'im, mate,' and '*I* heard Burano,' and 'Tell 'im where he can put his vase' etc.

Heard Dolly hissing in my ear, 'Sit down, you silly prat,' but, before I had a chance to do so, found myself being frogmarched from studio by two large security men, to the accompaniment of loud cheers and wolf whistles from the audience.

Suddenly knew how Nasty Nick must have felt when he was being led out of the *Big Brother* house.

For many people this would have been one of the most humiliating moments of their lives. However, am nothing if not a man of principle, and if people like me are not prepared to point a finger at these icons of popular culture when they fall short of the high standards we expect of them, who is?

Jane not quite as supportive as I had expected. She said, 'It might make a good piece in the *Mitch & Toot*, if they can be bothered to print it, but I presume that's your television career down the pan.'

Am secretly wondering if this is God's way of testing my moral fibre. Unless, of course, it's a slap over the wrist for misbehaving with one of His chosen ones. You never can tell with God.

Monday, September 4th

Beddoes rang to say he has had to give up his service apartment for some reason and would I ask Jane if he can avail himself of her spare room for a few days until he gets himself sorted out.

'We won't be any trouble,' he added.

'We?' I said.

'You know me, laddie,' he said. 'Bag and baggage.'

Have said I'll ask, but did not imagine for a second that Jane would entertain the thought of sleeping under the same roof as Beddoes and a Page Three scorcher after all we had to put up with all those years ago in Wentworth Mansions. I know that charity suffereth long and is kind. Ditto that it beareth all things, believeth all things, hopeth all things, endureth all things etc., but surely there's a limit?

Not in Jane's book, evidently. They move in tomorrow.

Tuesday, September 5th

Was in the middle of *Winton's World* piece for *Mitch & Toot* when Beddoes rang from the street to say they had arrived and could I give them a hand. They had rather more luggage than they had anticipated.

Went downstairs and opened front door to be confronted

by Beddoes with enough suitcases for a year-long cruise on the *QE2* and a stunningly beautiful black girl whom he introduced as Naomi.

She said, 'Don't look so surprised.'

I said that I was sorry, I was expecting someone else.

She said, 'Yeah, well that's life in the fast lane for you.'

As we were going up in the lift with the last of the luggage, I asked her what she did.

'Don't be silly,' Beddoes said.

Finally got him on my own. 'What happened to Miss Poppitt?' I said.

'Don't ask,' he said. So I didn't.

Wednesday, September 6th

What a relief to get back to my little cubicle at MHR last night after the razzmatazz of the television studio. Like Wogan, I am essentially a radio man at heart. Give me a small room, a few discs, some heart-warming stories, a microphone and just one happy listener and I am content.

Only wish I could say the same about my new sleeping arrangements. Still can't quite work out why Beddoes and his latest doxy are now happily ensconced in the spare room and I have finished up on the sofa.

Will I ever rest my bones on a comfortable piece of furniture again, I wonder?

One would think that Jane, of all people, would realize that if anyone needs any Good Samaritan treatment round here it's me.

Thursday, September 7th

Thought my sister was on the noisy side re her Sportsnight activities, but she's like a member of a silent order of nuns compared with the Creature from the Black Lagoon in the next room. Would not have minded quite so much if she had confined her moans and shrieks and groans to the hours before midnight, but they seemed to go on all night. Hardly slept a wink.

Goodness knows how she's up bright and early and ready for the catwalk every morning. *I* certainly couldn't manage it.

Have decided to recharge my batteries with a weekend

break in Melvyn Bragg country. Alone.

Shan't bother to book anywhere. Will journey as men did in the old days, wandering the countryside, eating when I'm hungry, sleeping when I'm tired, living life at my own pace, far from the hurly-burly of ambition and the false gods of fame.

Will also do so without my diary. Like London, it can wait.

Rang Colin Smoothie mid-morning to say I thought I was going down with flu and could he possibly find a replacement for me on Friday as I didn't think I'd be up to it.

He said, 'You will be sadly missed.' Hope he means just for the night.

Monday, September 11th

Back from Cumbria with actual flu. Fortunately, the worst is over now and I am definitely on the mend, but I doubt the landlady to whom I gave it in Buttermere is as lucky.

Not the happiest holiday I have known. Wandering lonely as a cloud is one thing: wandering lonely in the pouring rain at ten o'clock at night when your car has broken down five miles

from the nearest habitation is an experience that would have caused even Wordsworth to have second thoughts about the spirit of nature.

To compound my woes, realized with a shock that I have missed Clarissa Dickson Wright on *Desert Island Discs*.

Jane was full of it. Clarissa's choice of *'Cumha Dhomhnuill Bhain Mhiccruimein'* – the famous lament for Donald Ban Maccimon – sounded particularly interesting. Glad to know that, like me, she is a fan of Saki. Am seriously beginning to wonder if I, too, might plump for his short stories as my Desert Island reading alongside the Bible and Shakespeare, but in the end will probably stick with *Right Ho, Jeeves*, as planned.

Tuesday, September 12th

Have experienced many flashes of déjà vu in the course of a busy and varied life, but nothing rocked me back on my heels quite so forcibly as the sight that greeted me when I came into the flat late this afternoon.

Thought at first there was no one there and that the TV had been left on by mistake. Went to switch it off when man's voice said, 'Do you mind? We're watching that.' Turned to see Beddoes and Naomi spreadeagled across sofa in a state of considerable disarray.

It was as if I had stepped into H. G. Wells's time machine and been carried back in time to those days in Wentworth Mansions when the sofa was permanently occupied by that man and yet another in his inexhaustible supply of well-endowed and apparently insatiable women.

Had barely recovered from one psychological blow than I was reeling from a second when Jane entered room, followed by tall woman in glasses with mad-looking grey hair, dressed in a shapeless, dun-coloured shift. Her face seemed oddly familiar.

'You remember Victoria,' Jane said.

Could not believe my eyes. Was this the same woman for whom I had harboured such passionate longings when the four of us had shared a flat together all those years ago? How could I possibly have preferred her to Jane and been so *boule-versé* when she took up with the oafish Mike Pritchard? Went to greet her with the usual double kiss, to which she responded by dropping her head slightly so that my lips went hard into her bony cheek on one side and her ear on the other.

'How lovely to see you,' I said, without great conviction. 'Sorry about you and Mike.'

'I'm not,' she said.

Jane said, 'Victoria's got a teaching job in London. She's coming to stay for a few days while she looks for a flat. Hope you don't mind.'

Said it was nothing to do with me, it was entirely up to her, but couldn't help wondering where she would be sleeping.

Victoria said, 'Jane's very kindly said I can put up on a mattress in her room.'

Beddoes said, 'Talk about *A la recherche du temps* thingy.'

'*Perdu,*' I said.

'Whatever,' he said. 'Makes you wonder, though, doesn't it? Here we all are, exactly where we were twenty-four years ago, almost to the day. *Où sont les neiges . . . ?*'

'*D'antan,*' I said.

'If you say so, laddie,' he said. 'Point is, we're all a bit longer in the tooth, but are we any wiser? What's it all about? I often ask myself, but I still haven't got a bloody clue. I know no more now than I did when I was a teenager. Except that the older you get, the better your sex life.'

'I'll drink to that,' Naomi said.

'I'll put the kettle on,' said Victoria.

'I'll just go and take something for this cough,' I said.

Jane said nothing. As well she might.

Wednesday, September 13th

Had barely slept for a couple of hours after a particularly gruelling three hours in the studio, when was woken by Jane to say Ted Chapman, the producer of *Winton's World*, was on the phone.

Assumed he'd rung to complain about the unfortunate incident the other night, so was speechless when he announced that Itchy Feet were planning a new quiz show called *Whose Ex?* and would I be interested?

The idea is along the lines of *Blind Date*. Each contestant has to try and guess, with the help of the studio audience, which of the three people behind the screen is his, or her, ex-wife or husband. Whoever gets it right wins either an all-expenses weekend with a marriage counsellor, who will help them to reconcile their differences and get back together again, or a lump sum to put towards the alimony.

Evidently it has been tried out with great success in Holland and they are pretty sure it'll be a hit here, too.

I said it was very kind of him to ask, but I did not think that my ex-wife would be interested in taking part in that sort of thing.

Ted said, 'Oh, we don't want you to be a contestant. We want you to host the show.'

Was completely taken aback and said was he sure I was the right man for the job? Had always seen myself more as an arts presenter.

He said that there is obviously a certain degree of risk involved – there always is when an unknown is put in charge of a prime-time TV show – but he is convinced that abrasiveness is the keynote to personality television. He believes viewers are crying out for a fresh new cantankerous presenter who can lift the family quiz show out of its present rut of mild mediocrity and into the realms of gladiatorial cut and thrust, blood and guts. A male version of Anne Robinson. Looking again at my performance the other night on tape, he and his colleagues at Itchy Feet are convinced that I have exactly the qualities they are looking for.

He said, 'Natural television presenters are few and far between, but when they come leaping out of the screen like you did, you know you've struck gold. Carry on the way you were going the other night and you could be the new Gilbert Harding.'

Cannot imagine how anyone could possibly see me in this light, nor am I entirely convinced that this is the direction in which I wish my career to proceed. On the other hand, everyone needs some sort of quirky character trait if they wish to make it on television these days, and not being afraid to let interviewees and smart-alec students feel the rough side of one's tongue when the need arises has certainly not done Paxman's career any harm. *Au contraire.* And, unlike all too many who get plucked from obscurity and pushed into the limelight these days, I am nothing if not a professional.

Am meeting Ted early next week to talk further.

Sorry to see that the *Mitch & Toot* has not run my column about being on the show. Perhaps just as well in the circumstances.

Evening spent practising my autograph.

Thursday, September 14th

By a curious coincidence, opened my *Daily Telegraph* to see that members of the public are being invited to apply for membership of the new House of Lords. Not entirely clear what qualifications are required, but am strongly tempted to throw hat in ring.

On the other hand, it can surely be only a matter of time before more figures from the media are invited to join Melvyn in donning the scarlet and ermine and adding their wisdom to the mighty debates that will decide the future of this great nation of ours. If and when the call comes, I shall not be wanting.

In the meantime, can only hope that the nostalgic glow in Doxby Mansions, in which at least two of my ex-flatmates are currently basking, will end in a similar blaze of irritation, recrimination, alienation and outright warfare as it did twenty odd years ago. The sooner Jane and I can have the place to ourselves, and begin to enjoy the pre- (and, who knows, possibly full?) marital relations I know that deep down in her heart she wants, the better. If there is one thing more irritating than not knowing where one stands in a relationship – or in my case sleeps – it is Beddoes reminding one of that uncomfortable fact on a daily, if not hourly, basis.

Talking of irritation, must make an appointment to see the doctor about this wretched cough of mine. I *think* that's all it is.